# LOVE
# 3000

# LOVE
# 3000

## Edited by CHARLES WAUGH
## and MARTIN H. GREENBERG

ELSEVIER/NELSON BOOKS
*New York*

Copyright © 1980 by Charles Waugh and Martin H.
Greenberg

Library of Congress Cataloging in Publication Data

Main entry under title.
Love, 3000.
    1.   Science fiction, American.   2.   Love stories,
American.   I.   Greenberg, Martin Harry.   II.   Waugh,
Charles.
PZ1.L944   1980     [PS648.S3]     813'.0876'08
ISBN 0-525-66691-5             80-36790

Published in the United States by Elsevier/Nelson
Books, a division of Elsevier-Dutton Publishing Com-
pany, Inc., New York. Published simultaneously in Don
Mills, Ontario, by Nelson/Canada.

Printed in the U.S.A.      First Edition

10  9  8  7  6  5  4  3  2  1

# ACKNOWLEDGMENTS

*Child by Chronos* by Charles L. Harness, copyright 1953 by Fantasy House, Inc. From *The Magazine of Fantasy and Science Fiction*. Reprinted by permission of the author and his agents, the Scott Meredith Literary Agency, Inc., 845 Third Ave., New York, New York 10022.

*A Message from Charity* by William Lee, copyright © 1967 by Mercury Press, Inc. From *The Magazine of Fantasy and Science Fiction*. Reprinted by permission of the author and his agents, the Scott Meredith Literary Agency, Inc., 845 Third Ave., New York, New York 10022.

*When You Hear the Tone* by Thomas N. Scortia, copyright © 1971 by UPD Publishing Corporation. Reprinted by permission of the author's agents, Curtis Brown, Ltd.

*Share Alike* by Daniel F. Galouye, copyright © 1957 by Galaxy Publishing Corporation, Inc. Reprinted by permission of the agents for the author's estate, Blassingame, McCauley, and Wood.

*The Littlest People* by Raymond E. Banks, copyright 1954 by Galaxy Publishing Corporation, Inc. Reprinted by permission of the author and his agents, the Scott Meredith Literary Agency, Inc., 845 Third Ave., New York, New York 10022.

*Ring Around the Redhead* by John D. MacDonald, copyright 1948, copyright renewed © 1975 by John D. MacDonald. Reprinted by permission of the author.

*Human Man's Burden* by Robert Sheckley, copyright © 1956 by Robert Sheckley. Reprinted by permission of The Sterling Lord Agency, Inc.

*Home the Hard Way* by Richard McKenna, copyright © 1967 by Mercury Press, Inc. From *The Magazine of Fantasy and Science Fiction*. Reprinted by permission of the author's estate.

*Tin Soldier* by Joan D. Vinge, copyright © 1974 by Joan D. Vinge. Reprinted by permission of the author.

# CONTENTS

# INTRODUCTION

Most of us stumble through life, picking up what little we know about love from experience and the advice of friends. But there are two sources of written information that can provide us with assistance.

One is the findings of social scientists. Though they have only seriously been studying love and romance for about twenty-five years, they have already made a number of interesting findings, addressing such questions as: Is liking the same as loving? Are women more romantic than men? Are people who are single happier than people who are married? Does having children increase marital happiness? And, when it comes to romance, do birds of a feather flock together more than opposites attract?

Unfortunately, much of what social scientists write is not widely read, partly because some of it is conjecture, but mostly because it is usually presented in such a dull, technical fashion.

On the other hand, literature, the second written source of information, might lack the consistency and precision of research, but it is much more dramatic and provides the implicit assurance that it is possible to be happy, needed, and loved.

In particular, science fiction has always provided very fertile ground for love and romance. A part of science fiction's mainstream is not only optimistic about the possibility that we will have a future, but also views that future as an exciting place to live. Time travel, technological breakthroughs and exotic worlds offer larger than life backdrops for romance and give plenty of opportunities for fresh twists on old themes. For example, in this anthology, you will read about a young man falling in love with an eighteenth-century Puritan girl, a society that figures out how members of the opposite sex can share an apartment without being able to see or touch each other, and a world in which a cyborg falls in love with a woman he sees only once every quarter century.

Nevertheless, romance has always been secondary to plot, action, and ideas in science fiction, and the number of quality stories in which romance played a major role were few. Recently, however, the situation has been changing, as increasing numbers of mature, skilled writers (both men and women) enter the field, and as earlier taboos against sex disappear from science fiction publishing.

Here, then, is a way to be entertained while gaining a little bit of painless knowledge about love and life. So, don't wait, turn the page!

# LOVE
# AND TIME

# CHARLES L. HARNESS

# CHILD BY CHRONOS

*Charles Harness' total output in the science fiction field has been relatively small, but his stories and novels are treasured by knowledgeable readers because of their imaginative ideas and powerful emotive content.*

*In 1984, Winston Smith's job was to rewrite history each time the ruling party changed its line. Although this seems appalling on the national level, it is really quite natural and necessary on the personal level. For example, if we once thought our parents' rules too strict, we may now recognize that they were quite fair. As we grow older and gain more knowledge, we see the world from other points of view, and that often forces us, like this story's nameless heroine, to reevaluate our past experiences.*

You just lie there and listen. The sunshine will do you good, and anyhow the doctor said you weren't to do much talking.

I'll get to the point.

I have loved three men. The first was my mother's lover. The second was my husband. The third . . .

I'm going to tell you all about these three men—and me. I'm going to tell you some things that might send you back to the hospital.

Don't interrupt.

As a child I never knew my father. He was declared legally dead several months before I was born. They said he had gone hunting and had never returned. Theoretically you can't miss what you never had. Whoever said that didn't know me. I missed my lost father when I was a brat and when I was a gawky youngster in pigtails and when I was a young lady in a finishing school in Switzerland.

Mother made it worse. There was never any shortage of males when Mother was around, but they wouldn't have anything to do with me. And that was her fault. Mother was gorgeous. Men couldn't stay away from her. By the time I was ten, I could tell what they were thinking when they looked at her. When I was twenty they were still looking at her in the same way. That was when she finally took a lover, and when I fled from her in hate and horror.

There's nothing remarkable about a daughter's hating her mother. It's just that I did more of it than usual. All the hate that I ever commanded, ever since I was in diapers, I saved, preserved, and vented on her. When I was an infant, so they said, I wouldn't nurse at her breast. Strictly a bottle baby. It was as though I had declared to the world that I hadn't been born in the way mortals are born and that this woman who professed to be my mother wasn't really. As you shall see, I wasn't entirely wrong.

I always had the insane feeling that everything she had really belonged to me and that she was keeping me from claiming my own.

Naturally, our tastes were identical. This identity of desire became more and more acute as I grew older. Whatever she had, I regarded as really mine, and generally tried to confiscate it. Particularly men. The irritating thing was that, even though Mother never became serious about any of them (except the last one), they still couldn't see me. Except the last one.

Mother's willingness to turn over to me any and all of her

gentlemen friends seemed to carry with it the unrelated but inevitable corollary, that none of them (with that one exception) had any desire to *be* turned over.

You're probably thinking that it was all a consequence of not having a father around, that I subconsciously substituted her current male for my missing father, and hence put claims on him equal to hers. You can explain it any way you want to. Anyway, except at the last, it always turned out the same. The more willing she was to get rid of him, the less willing he was to have anything to do with me.

But I never got mad at *them*; only at *her*. Sometimes, if the brush-off was particularly brusque, I wouldn't speak to her for days. Even the sight of her would make me sick to my stomach.

When I was seventeen, on the advice of her psychiatrist, she sent me to school in Switzerland. This psychiatrist said I had the worst Electra complex with the least grounds for it of any woman in medical history. He said he hoped that my father was really dead, because if he should ever turn up alive . . . Well, you could just see him rubbing the folds of his cerebrum in brisk anticipation.

However, the superficial reason they gave for sending me to Switzerland was to get an education, There I was, seventeen, and didn't even know the multiplication table. All I knew was what Mother called "headline history." She had yanked me out of public school when I was in the second grade and had hired a flock of tutors to teach me about current events. Nothing but current events. Considering that she made her living by predicting current events before they became current, I suppose her approach was excusable. It was her method of execution that made the subject unutterably dull—then. Mother wouldn't stand for any of the modern methods of history teaching. No analysis of trends and integration of international developments for Mother. My apologetic tutors were paid to see that I memorized every headline and caption in every New York *Times* printed since Bold Ruler won the Preakness in 1957—which was even several months before I was born. That and nothing more. There were even a couple of memory experts thrown in, to wrap up each daily pill in a sugar-coated mnemonic.

So, even if the real reason for sending me to Switzerland was not to get an education, I didn't care. I was glad to stop memorizing headlines.

But I'm getting ahead of my story.

One of the earliest memories of my childhood was a big party Mother held at Skyridge, our country lodge. I was six years old. It was the night after James Roosevelt's re-election. Of all the public opinion diagnosticians, only Mother had guessed right, and she and the top executives of the dozen odd firms that retained her prophetic services congregated at Skyridge. I was supposed to be upstairs asleep, but the laughter and singing woke me up, and I came down and joined in. Nobody cared. Every time a man put his arm around Mother and kissed her, I was there clutching at his coat pockets, howling, "He's *mine!*"

My technique altered as the years passed; my premise didn't.

Do you think it bothered her?

Ha!

The more I tried to take from her, the more amused she became. It wasn't a wry amusement. It gave her real belly laughs. How can you fight *that*? It just made me madder.

You might think I hadn't a shred of justice on my side. Actually, I did.

There was *one* thing that justified my hatred: she didn't really love me. I was her flesh and blood, but she didn't love me. Perhaps she was fond of me, in a lukewarm way, but her heart had no real love in it for me. And I knew it and hated her, and tried to take everything that was hers.

We must have seemed a strange pair. She never addressed me by my name, or even by a personal pronoun. She never even said such things as, "Dear, will you pass the toast?" Instead it was

"May I have the toast?" It was as though she considered me a mere extension of herself, like another arm, which had no independent identity. It was galling.

Other girls could keep secrets from their mothers. I couldn't hide anything important from mine. The more I wanted to conceal something, the more certain she was to know it. That was another reason why I didn't mind being shipped off to Switzerland.

I'm sure she wasn't reading my mind. It wasn't telepathy. She couldn't guess phone numbers I had memorized, nor the names of the twenty-five boys on the county high school football team. Routine things like that generally didn't "get through." And telepathy wouldn't explain what happened the night my car turned over on the Sylvania Turnpike. The hands that helped pull me through the car window were hers. She had been parked by the roadside, waiting. No ambulance; just Mother in her car. She had known where and when it would happen, and that I wouldn't be hurt.

After that night I was able to figure out all by myself that Mother's business firm, Tomorrow, Inc., was based on something more than a knowledge of up-to-the-minute trends in economics, science, and politics.

But *what*?

I never asked her. I didn't think she would tell me, and I didn't want to give her the satisfaction of refusing an explanation. But perhaps that wasn't the only reason I didn't ask. I was also afraid to ask. Toward the end it was almost as though we had arrived at a tacit understanding that I was not to ask, because in good time I was going to find out without asking.

Tomorrow, Inc., made a great deal of money. Mother's success in predicting crucial public developments was uncanny. And she never guessed wrong. Naturally, her clients made even more money than she did, because they had more to invest initially. On her advice they plunged in the deeply depressed market two weeks before the Hague Conference arrived at the historic Concord of 1970. And it was Mother who predicted the success of Bartell's neutronic-cerium experiments, in time for Cameron Associates to corner the world supply of monazite sand. And she was equally good at predicting Derby winners, Supreme Court decisions, elections, and that the fourth rocket to the moon would be the first successful one.

She was intelligent, but hardly in the genius class. Her knowledge of the business world was surprisingly limited. She never studied economics or extrapolated stock market curves. Tomorrow, Inc., didn't even have a news ticker in its swank New York office. And she was the highest paid woman in the United States in 1975.

In 1976, during the Christmas holidays, which I was spending with Mother at Skyridge during my junior year at college, Mother turned down a three-year contract with Lloyds of London. I know this because I dug the papers out of the wastebasket after she tore them up. There were eight digits in the proposed annual salary. I knew she was making money, but not that kind. I called her to task.

"I can't take a three-year contract," she explained. "I can't even take a year's contract. Because I'm going to retire next month." She was looking away from me, out over the lodge balcony, into the wood. She couldn't see my expression. She murmured, "Did you know your mouth was open rather wide?"

"But you *can't* retire!" I clipped. And then I could have bitten my tongue off. My protest was an admission that I envied her and that I shone in her reflected fame. Well, she had probably known it anyhow. "All right," I continued sullenly. "You're going to retire. Where'll you go? What'll you do?"

"Why, I think I'll stay right here at Skyridge," she said blithely. "Just fixing up the place will keep me busy for a good many months. Take those rapids under the balcony, for instance. I think I'll just do away with them. Divert the stream, perhaps. I've grown a little tired of the sound of running water. And then there's all that dogwood out front. I've been considering cutting them all down and maybe putting in a landing field. You never know when a copter might come in handy. And then there's the matter of haystacks. I think we ought to have at least one somewhere on the place. Hay has such a nice smell, and they say it's so stimulating.''

"Mother!''

Her brow knitted. "But where could I put a haystack?''

Just why she was using such a puerile method of baiting me I couldn't understand. "Why not in the ravine?'' I said acidly. "It'll be dry after you divert the rapids. You'd be famous as the owner of the only ground-level haystack in New England.''

She brightened immediately. "That's *it*! What a clever girl!''

"And what happens after you get him in the haystack?''

"Why, I guess I'll just keep him there.''

"You *guess*!'' I cried. (I'd finally trapped her!) "Don't you *know*?''

"I know only the things that are going to happen during the next six months—up until the stroke of midnight, June 3, 1977. As to what happens after that, I can't make any predictions.''

"You mean you *won't*.''

"*Can't*. My retirement is not arbitrary.''

I looked at her incredulously. "I don't understand. You mean—this ability—it's going to leave you—like *that*?'' I snapped my fingers.

"Precisely.''

"But can't you stop it? Can't your psychiatrist do something?''

"Nobody could do anything for me even if I wanted him to. And I don't want to know what is going to happen after midnight, June 3.''

With troubled eyes I studied her face.

At that moment, just as though she'd planned it, the clock

began to chime, as if to remind me of our unwritten agreement not to probe into her strange gift.

The answer was only six months away. For the time being I was willing to let it ride.

The epilog to our little conversation was this:

A couple of months later, after I was back at school in Zurich, a friend of mine wrote me that (1) the rapids had been diverted from the stream bed; (2) that just below the balcony the now dry ravine contained ten feet of fresh hay; (3) that the hay was rigged with electronic circuits to sound an alarm in the lodge if anyone went near it; (4) that the dogwood trees had been cut down; (5) that in their place stood a small landing field; (6) and that on the field there stood an ambulance copter, hired from a New York hospital, complete with pilot and interne.

"Anility," wrote my friend, "is supposed to develop early in some cases. You ought to come home."

I was having fun at school. I didn't want to come home. Anyway, if Mother was losing her mind, there was nothing anybody could do. Furthermore, I didn't want to give up my plans for summering in Italy.

A month later, early in May, my friend wrote again.

It seems that the haystack alarm had gone off one night, two weeks previous, and Mother and the servants had hurried down to find a bloody-faced one-eyed man crawling up the gravelly ravine bank. In one hand he was clutching an old pistol. According to reports, Mother had the copter whisk him in to a New York hospital, where he still was. He was due to be discharged May 6. The next day, by my calculations.

There were details about how Mother had redecorated two bedrooms at the lodge. I knew the bedrooms. They adjoined each other.

Even before I finished the letter I realized there was nothing the matter with Mother's mind and never had been. That witch had foreseen all this.

The thing that *was* the matter, and which had apparently escaped everyone but me and Mother, was that mother had finally fallen in love.

This was serious.

I canceled the remainder of the semester and the Italian tour and caught the first jet home. I didn't tell anyone I was coming. So, when I paid off the taxi at the gatehouse, I was able to walk unannounced and unseen around the edge of the estate, and then cut in through the woods toward the ravine and lodge just beyond it.

The first thing I saw on emerging from the trees along the ravine bank was the famous bargain basement haystack. It was occupied.

The sun was shining, but it was early in May, and not particularly warm. Still, Mother was wearing one of those new sun briefs that—well, you get the idea. I guess haystacks generate a lot of heat. Spontaneous combustion.

Mother was facing away from me, obstructing *his* one good eye. I hadn't made a sound, but I was suddenly aware of the fact that she had been expecting me and knew I was there.

She turned around, sat up, and smiled at me. "Hi there! Welcome home! Oh, excuse me, this is our good friend Doctor . . . ah . . . Brown. John Brown. Just call him Johnny." She picked a sliver of hay from her hair and flashed a grin at "Johnny."

I stared at them both in turn. Doctor Brown raised up on one elbow and returned my stare as amiably as the glaring black patch over his right eye would permit. "Hello, honey," he said gravely.

Then he and Mother burst out laughing.

It was the queerest sound I'd ever heard. Just as though nothing on earth could ever again be important to either of them.

That summer I saw a lot of Johnny. Things got on an interesting basis very quickly. It wasn't long before he was giving me

the kind of look that said, "I'd like to get involved—but. . ."
And there he'd stop. Still, I figured that I was making more
headway with him than I ever had with any of Mother's previous
friends.

Finally, though, his "thus far and no farther" response grew
irritating. Then challenging. Then. . .

I guess it was being around him constantly, knowing that he
and Mother were the way they were, that made things turn out
the way they did. In the process of trying to reel him in for closer
inspection, I got pulled in myself. Eventually I became quite
shameless about it. I began trying to get him off to myself at
every opportunity.

We talked. But not about *him*. If he knew how he'd had his
accident, and how he'd got here, he apparently never told
anybody. At least he would never tell me.

We talked about magnetrons.

Don't look so surprised.

Like yourself, he was an expert on magnetrons. I think he
knew even more than you about magnetrons. And you thought
you were the world's only expert, didn't you?

I pretended to listen to him, but I never understood more than
the basic concepts—namely, that magnetrons were little entities
sort of like electrons, sort of like gravitons, and sort of like I
don't know what. But at least I grasped the idea that a magnetronic field could warp the flow of time, and that if you put an
object in such a field, the results could be rather odd.

We talked a lot about magnetrons.

I planned our encounters hours, sometimes days, ahead.
Quite early, I started borrowing Mother's sun briefs. Later, at
times when he *theoretically* wasn't around, I sunbathed *au
naturel*. With no visible results except sunburn.

Toward the last I started sneaking out at night into the pines
with my sleeping bag. I couldn't stand it, knowing where he
probably was.

Not that I gave up.

He was building a magnetronic generator. The first in the world. I'd been helping him all one day to wire up some of his equipment.

He had torn down the balcony railing and was building his machine out on the balcony, right over the ravine. He could focus it, he said. I mean, there was a sort of "lens" effect in the magnetronic field, and he was supposed to be able to focus this field.

The queer thing was, that when he finally got the lens aligned, the focus was out in thin air, just beyond the edge of the balcony. Directly over the ravine. He didn't want anyone stumbling through the focus by accident.

And through this lens you could hear sounds.

The ravine had been dry for months, ever since Mother had diverted the rapids. But now, coming through the lens, was this endless crash of water.

You could hear it all over the house.

The noise made me nervous. It seemed to subdue even them.

I didn't like that noise. I hauled my sleeping bag still farther into the pines. I could still hear it.

One night, a quarter of a mile from the house, I crawled out of my sleeping bag and started back toward the house. I was going to wake him up and ask him to turn the thing off.

At least, that was my excuse for returning. And it was perfectly true that I couldn't sleep.

I had it all figured out. Just how quietly I'd open his door, just how I'd tiptoe over to his bed. How I'd bend over him. How I'd put my hand on his chest and shake him, ever so gently.

Everything went as planned, up to a point.

There I was, leaning over his bed, peering through the dark at the blurry outlines of a prone figure.

I stretched out my hand.

It was not a male chest that I touched.

"What do you want?" Mother whispered.

In the length of time it took me to get my breath back I decided that if *I* couldn't have him, *she* couldn't either. There comes a limit to all things. We were racing toward the showdown.

He always kept his old pistol on the table ledge, the one he'd brought with him. Soundlessly I reached for it and found it. I knew it was too dark for Mother to see what I was now pointing toward her.

I had a clairvoyant awareness of my intent and its consequences. I even knew the place and the time. Murder was building up in Doctor John Brown's bedroom at Skyridge, and the time was five minutes of midnight, June 3, 1977.

"If that goes off," whispered Mother calmly, "it'll probably awaken your father."

"My—*who*?" I gasped. The gun butt landed on my toe; I hardly knew I'd dropped it.

I heard what she'd said. But I suddenly realized it didn't make sense. They'd have told me long before, if it had been true. And he wouldn't have looked at me the way he did, day after day. She was lying.

She continued quietly: "Do you really want him?"

When one woman asks this question of another, it is ordinarily intended as an announcement of a property right, not a query, and the tone of voice ranges from subtle sardonicism to savage gloating.

But Mother's voice was quiet and even.

"Yes!" I said harshly.

"Badly enough to have a child by him?"

I couldn't stop now. "Yes."

"Can you swim?"

"Yes," I parrotted stupidly. It was obviously not a time for logic or coherence. There we were, two witches bargaining in life and death, while the bone of our contention slumbered soundly just beyond us.

She whispered: "Do you know when he is from?"

"You mean *where*?"

"*When*. He's from 1957. In 1957 he fell into a magnetronic field—into my 1977 haystack. The lens—out there—is focused—"

"—on 1957?" I breathed numbly.

"*Early* 1957," she corrected. "It's focused on a day a couple of months prior to the moment he fell into the lens. If you really want him, all you've got to do is jump through the lens, find him in 1957, and hang on to him. Don't let him fall into the magnetronic field."

I locked my lips. "And suppose he does, anyway?"

"I'll be waiting for him."

"But you already have him. If I should go back, how could I stop something that has already happened?"

"If you hold on to him in 1957, this particular stereochronic alternate of 1977 must collapse, just as though it never happened."

My head was whirling. "But, if I go back to 1957, how can I be sure of finding him in time? Suppose he's on safari in South Africa?"

"You'll find him, right here. He spent the spring and summer of 1957 here at Skyridge. The lodge has always been his property."

I couldn't see her eyes, but I knew they were laughing at me.

"The matter of a child," I said curtly. "What's that got to do with him?"

"Your only chance of holding him permanently," she said coolly, "is the child."

"*The* child?"

"There will be only one. I *think* . . ."

I couldn't make any sense out of it. I stopped trying.

For a full minute there was silence, backgrounded by the gentle rasp of Johnny's breathing and the singing water twenty years away.

I blinked my eyes rapidly.

I was going to have Johnny. I was going back to 1957. Suddenly I felt jaunty, exhilarated.

The hall clock began to chime midnight.

Within a few seconds June 3, 1977 would pass into history. Mother would be washed up, a has-been, unable to predict even the weather.

I kicked off my slippers and pajamas. I gauged the distance across the balcony. My voice got away from me. "Mother!" I shrieked. "Give us one last prediction!"

Johnny snorted violently and struggled to sit up.

I launched my soaring dive into time. Mother's reply floated after me, through the lens, and I heard it in 1957.

"You didn't stop him."

His real name was James McCarren. He *was* a genuine Ph.D., though, a physics professor. Age, about forty. Had I expected him to be younger? He seemed older than "Johnny." And he had two good eyes. No patch.

He owned Skyridge, all right. Spent his summers there. Liked to hunt and fish between semesters.

And now, my friend, if you'll just relax a bit, I'll tell you what happened on the night of August 5, 1957.

I was leaning over the balcony, staring down at the red-lit tumult of the rapids, when I became aware that Jim was standing in the doorway behind me. I could feel his eyes sliding along my body.

I had been breathing deeply a moment before, trying to slow down the abnormal surging of my lungs, while simultaneously attempting to push Jim's pistol a little higher under my armpit. The cold steel made me shiver.

It was too bad. For during the past two months I had begun to love him in a most interesting way, though, of course, not in the much more interesting way I had loved Johnny. (A few weeks with Mother can really change a man!) In 1957 Johnny—or Jim—was quaintly solicitous, oddly virginal. Almost fatherly. It was too bad that I was beginning to love him as Jim.

Still, there was Mother's last prediction. I had thought about it a long time. So far as I could see, there was only one way to make sure he didn't "go through" to her.

"Come on out," I said, turning my face up to be kissed.

After he had released me, I said, "Do you realize it's been exactly two months since you fished me out of there?"

"The happiest months of my life," he said.

"And you still haven't asked me how I happened to be there—who I am—anything. You're certainly under no illusion that I gave that justice of the peace my right name?"

He grinned. "If I got too curious, you might vanish back into the whirlpool, like a water nymph."

It was really sad. I shrugged bitterly. "You and your magnetrons."

He started. "*What*? Where did you ever hear about magnetrons? I've never discussed them with anyone!"

"Right here. From you."

His mouth opened and closed slowly. "You're out of your mind!"

"I wish I were. That would make everything seem all right. For, after all, it's only after you get to thinking about it logically that you can understand how impossible it is. It's got to stop, though, and now is the time to stop it."

"Stop *what*?" he demanded.

"The way you and I keep jumping around in time. Especially you. If I don't stop you, you'll go through the lens, and Mother will get you. It was her last prediction."

"Lens?" he gurgled.

"The machine. You know, the one with the magnetrons."
"Huh?"

"None of that exists yet, of course," I said, talking mostly to myself. "At least, not outside of your head. You won't build the generator until 1977."

"I can't get the parts now." His voice was numb.

"They'll be available in 1977, though."

"In 1977 . . .?"

"Yes. After you build it in 1977, you'll focus it back to 1957, so that you *could* jump through, now, into 1977, right back into Mother's arms, where you already are, in 1977, that is. Only I'm not going to let you. When Mother made her last prediction she couldn't have known to what lengths I'd go to stop you."

He passed his hand plaintively over his face. "But . . . but . . . even assuming you're from 1977, and even assuming I'll build a magnetronic generator in 1977, I can't just jump into 1977 and build it. I certainly can't move forward in time to 1977 through a magnetronic field that won't be generated and beamed backwards to 1957 until I arrive in 1977 and generate it. That's as silly as saying that the pilgrims built the *Mayflower* at Plymouth Rock. And anyway, I'm a husband who'll soon be a father. I haven't the faintest intention of running out on my responsibilities."

"And yet," I said, "if the sequence proceeds normally, you *will* leave me . . . for *her*. Tonight you're my lawful husband, the father of our child to be. Then—bing! You're suddenly in 1977—wife-deserter, philanderer, and Mother's lover. I won't let that happen. After all I've been through, I *won't* let her get you. My blood goes into a slow boil, just thinking about her, smiling way up there in 1977, thinking how she got rid of me so she could eventually have you all to herself. And me in my condition." My voice broke in an artistic tremulo.

"I *could* age normally," he said. "I could simply wait until 1977 and *then* build the generator."

"You didn't, though—that is, I mean you *won't*. When I last saw you in 1977 you looked even younger than you do now. Maybe it was the patch."

He shrugged his shoulders. "If your presence *here* is a direct consequence of my presence *there*, then there's nothing either of us can do to change the sequence. I don't want to go through. And what could happen to force me through I can't even guess. But we've got to proceed on the assumption that I'll go, and you'll be left stranded. We've got to make plans. You'll need money. You'll probably have to sell Skyridge. Get a job, after the baby comes. How's your shorthand?"

"They'll use vodeographs in 1977," I muttered. "But don't you worry, you cheap two-timer. Even if you succeeded in running off to Mother, the baby and I'll get along. As a starter, I'm going to put the rest of your bank account on Bold Ruler to win the Preakness next Saturday. After that—"

But he had already switched to something else. "When you knew me in 1977, were we—ah—intimate?"

I snorted. "Depends on who 'we' includes."

"What? You mean . . . *I* . . . and your *mother* . . . *really* . . .?"

He coughed and ran his finger around his collar. "There must be some simple explanation."

I just sneered at him.

He giggled. "Your mother—ah—in 1977—a good-looking woman, I gather?"

"A wrinkled, painted harridan," I said coldly. "Forty, if she's a day."

"Hmph! *I'm* forty, you know. Contrary to the adolescent view, it's the best time of life. You'll feel the same way about it in another twenty years."

"I suppose so," I said. "They'll be letting me out of the penitentiary about then."

He snapped his fingers suddenly. "I've got it! Fantastic!" He turned away and looked out over the balcony, like Cortez on his peak. "Fantastic, but it hangs together. Completely logical. Me. Your mother. You. The child. The magnetrons. The eternal cycle."

"This isn't making it easier for me," I said reproachfully. "The least you could do would be to remain sane until the end." He whirled on me. "Do you know where *she* is—now—tonight?"

"No, and I spent two-thirds of our joint bank account trying to locate her. It's just as though she never existed."

His eyes got bigger and bigger. "No wonder you couldn't find her. You couldn't know."

"Know what?"

"Who your mother is."

I wanted to scream at him. "Oh," I said.

But he was off on another tangent. "But it's not entirely without precedent. When a cell divides, which of the resultant two cells is the mother? Which the daughter? The answer is, that the question itself is nonsense. And so with you. The cell divides in space; you divide in time. It's nonsense to ask which of you is mother, which is daughter."

I just stood there, blinking.

He rambled on. "Even so, why should I want to 'go through'? That's the only part that's not clear. Why should I deliberately skip twenty years of life with you? Who'd take care of you? How could you earn a living? But you must have. Because you didn't have to sell Skyridge. You stayed here. You educated *her*. But of course!" He smacked his fist into his palm.

"Simplest thing in the world," he howled happily. "Bold Ruler at the Preakness. You'll become a professional predictor. Sports. Presidential elections. Supreme Court decisions. All in advance. You've got to *remember*. Train your ability to recall. Big money in it!"

My mouth was hanging open.

"Isn't that what happens?" he shouted.

"I know all the headlines already," I stammered. "Only that's the business *Mother* started . . . predicting for a living . . ."

"Mother . . . Mother . . . *Mother*!" he mimicked. "By the

great Chronos, child! Can't you face it? Does your mind refuse to accept the fact that you and your 'mother' and your unborn daughter are iden—''

I screamed. "No!"

I pulled out the pistol.

I raised it slowly, as though I had all the time in the world, and shot him through the head.

Even before he hit the floor I had grabbed his right hand and was flexing his fingers around the handle.

A moment later I was out the door and racing toward the garage.

I thought it would be best to "find" his body on returning from a shopping expedition in the village, where I had happened to pick up a couple of friends. The only thing wrong with this plan was that he wasn't there when I returned with my witnesses.

It was generally agreed that James McCarren had become lost in the woods while hunting. Poor fellow must have starved to death, they supposed. Neither he nor the pistol were ever found. A few months later he was declared legally dead, and I collected his insurance.

The coroner and the D.A. did give me a bad moment when they discovered some thin smudges of dried blood leading toward the edge of the balcony. But nothing turned up, of course, when they dragged the whirlpool. And when I informed them of my condition, their unvoiced suspicions turned to sympathy.

From then on, I had plenty of time to think. Particularly during the first lean months of Tomorrow, Inc., before I landed my first retainer.

And what I thought was this: what other woman ever had a man who loved her so much, even after she had shot him through the eye, that he would willingly drag himself after her, through twenty years, to claim her again, sight unseen?

The very least I could do was to drain the ravine and break your fall with this haystack.

Do you honestly like my new sun brief? The red and green checks go nicely with the yellow hay, don't they? Do you really want me to come over and sit by you? Oh, don't worry about interruptions. The servants are down in the village, and she won't come sneaking around through the woods for an hour yet . . . Oooh, *Johnny*!

# WILLIAM LEE

# A MESSAGE FROM CHARITY

*In a popular song of the early sixties, Chubby Checker claimed he walked eighteen miles a day to see his "baby." For most of us, however, space is a barrier to romance. Dating someone near us is easier and undoubtably why geographical proximity exerts such an important influence on marriage.*

*But time is an even more formidable barrier, as Peter Wood discovers. For what can be done when you fall in love with a person who died in the eighteenth century?*

That summer of the year 1700 was the hottest in the memory of the very oldest inhabitants. Because the year ushered in a new century, some held that the events were related and that for a whole hundred years Bay Colony would be as torrid and steamy as the Indies themselves.

There was a good deal of illness in Annes Towne, and a score had died before the weather broke at last in late September. For the great part they were oldsters who succumbed, but some of the young were sick too, and Charity Payne as sick as any.

Charity had turned eleven in the spring and had still the figure and many of the ways of thinking of a child, but she was tall and strong and tanned by the New England sun, for she spent many hours helping her father in the fields and trying to keep some sort of order in the dooryard and garden.

During the weeks when she lay bedridden and, for a time, burning up with fever, Thomas Carter and his good wife Beulah came as neighbors should to lend a hand, for Charity's mother had died abirthing and Obie Payne could not cope all alone.

Charity lay on a pallet covered by a straw-filled mattress which her father, frantic to be doing something for her and finding little enough to do beyond the saying of short fervent prayers, refilled with fresh straw as often as Beulah would allow. A few miles down Harmon Brook was a famous beaver pond where in winter the Annes Towne people cut ice to be stored under layers of bark and chips. It had been used heavily early in the summer, and there was not very much ice left, but those families with sickness in the home might draw upon it for the patient's comfort. So Charity had bits of ice folded into a woolen cloth to lay on her forehead when the fever was bad.

William Trowbridge, who had apprenticed in medicine down in Philadelphia, attended the girl, and pronounced her illness a sort of summer cholera which was claiming victims all up and down the brook. Trowbridge was only moderately esteemed in Annes Towne, being better, it was said, at delivering lambs and foals than at treating human maladies. He was a gruff and notional man, and he was prone to state his views on a subject and then walk away instead of waiting to argue and perhaps be refuted. Not easy to get along with.

For Charity he prescribed a diet of beef tea with barley and another tea, very unpleasant to the taste, made from pounded willow bark. What was more, all her drinking water was to be boiled. Since there was no other advice to be had, they followed it and in due course Charity got well.

She ran a great fever for five days, and it was midway in this period when the strange dreams began. Not dreams really, for she was awake though often out of her senses, knowing her father now and then, other times seeing him as a gaunt and frightening stranger. When she was better, still weak but wholly rational, she tried to tell her visitors about these dreams.

"Some person was talking and talking," she recalled. "A man or perchance a lad. He talked not to me, but I could hear or understand all that he said. 'Twas strange talk indeed, a porridge of the King's English and other words of no sense at all. And with the talk I did see some fearful sights."

"La, now, don't even think of it," said Dame Beulah.

"But I would fen both think and talk of it, for I am no longer afeared. Such things I saw in bits and flashes, as 'twere seen by a strike of lightning."

"Talk and ye be so minded, then. There's naught impious in y'r conceits. Tell me again about the carriages which traneled along with nary horse."

Annes Towne survived the Revolution and the War of 1812, and for a time seemed likely to become a larger, if not an important community. But when its farms became less productive and the last virgin timber disappeared from the area, Annes Towne began to disappear too, dwindling from two score of homes to a handful, then to none; and the last foundation had crumbled to rubble and been scattered a hundred years before it could have been nominated a historic site.

In time dirt tracks became stone roads, which gave way to black meanderings of macadam, and these in their turn were displaced by never ending bands of concrete. The cross-roads site of Annes Towne was presently cleared of brambles, sumac and red cedar, and overnight it was a shopping center. Now, for mile on spreading mile the New England hills were dotted with ranch houses, salt boxes and split-level colonial homes.

During four decades Harmon Brook had been fouled and poisoned by a textile bleach and dye works. Rising labor costs had at last driven the small company to extinction. With that event and increasingly rigorous legislation, the stream had come back to the extent that it could now be bordered by some of these prosperous homes and by the golf course of the Anniston Country Club.

With aquatic plants and bull frogs and a few fish inhabiting its waters, it was not obvious to implicate the Harmon for the small outbreak of typhoid which occurred in the hot dry summer of 1965. No one was dependent on it for drinking water. To the discomfort of a local milk distributor, who was entirely blameless, indictment of the stream was delayed and obscured by the fact that the organisms involved were not a typical strain of *Salmonella typhosa*. Indeed they ultimately found a place in the American Type Culture Collection, under a new number.

Young Peter Wood, whose home was one of those pleasantly situated along the stream, was the most seriously ill of all the cases, partly because he was the first, mostly because his symptoms went unremarked for a time. Peter was sixteen and not highly communicative to either parents or friends. The Wood Seniors both taught, at Harvard and Wellesley respectively. They were intelligent and well-intentioned parents, but sometimes a little off-hand, and like many of their friends, they raised their son to be a miniature adult in as many ways as possible. His sports, tennis and golf, were adult sports. His reading tastes were catholic, ranging from Camus to Al Capp to science fiction. He had been carefully held back in his progress through the lower grades so that he would not enter college more than a year or so ahead of his age. He had an adequate number of friends and sufficient areas of congeniality with them. He had gotten a driver's license shortly after his sixteenth birthday and drove seriously and well enough to be allowed nearly unrestricted use of the second car.

So Peter Wood was not the sort of boy to complain to his family about headache, mild nausea and other symptoms. Instead, after they had persisted for forty-eight hours, he telephoned for an appointment on his own initiative and visited the family doctor. Suddenly, in the waiting room, he became much worse, and was given a cot in an examining room until Dr. Maxwell was free to drive him home. The doctor did not seriously suspect typhoid, though it was among several possibilities which he counted as less likely.

Peter's temperature rose from 104 degrees to over 105 degrees that night. No nurse was to be had until morning, and his parents alternated in attendance in his bedroom. There was no cause for alarm, since the patient was full of wide-spectrum antibiotic. But he slept only fitfully with intervals of waking delirium. He slapped at the sheet, tossed around on the bed and muttered or spoke now and then. Some of the talk was understandable.

"There's a forest," he said.

"What?" asked his father.

"There's a forest the other side of the stream."

"Oh."

"Can you see it?"

"No, I'm sitting inside here with you. Take it easy, son."

"Some deer are coming down to drink, along the edge of Weller's pasture."

"Is that so?"

"Last year a mountain lion killed two of them, right where they drank. Is it raining?"

"No, it isn't. It would be fine if we could have some."

"It's raining. I can hear it on the roof." A pause. "It drips down the chimney."

Peter turned his head to look at his father, momentarily clear eyed.

"How long since there's been a forest across the stream?"

Dr. Wood reflected on the usual difficulty of answering explicit questions and on his own ignorance of history.

"A long time. I expect this valley has been farm land since colonial days."

"Funny." Peter said. "I shut my eyes and I can see a forest. Really big trees. On our side of the stream there's a kind of a garden and an apple tree and a path goes down to the water."

"It sounds pleasant."

"Yeah."

"Why don't you try going to sleep?"

"Okay."

The antibiotic accomplished much less than it should have done in Peter's case, and he stayed very sick for several days. Even after diagnosis, there appeared no good reason to move him from home. A trained nurse was on duty after that first night, and tranquilizers and sedatives reduced her job to no more than keeping a watch. There were only a few sleepy communications from her young patient. It was on the fourth night, the last one when he had any significant fever, that he asked.

"Were you ever a girl?"

"Well, thanks a lot. I'm not as old as all that."

"I mean, were you ever inside a girl?"

"I think you'd better go back to sleep, young man."

He uttered no oddities thereafter, at least when there was anyone within hearing. During the days of his recovery and convalescence, abed and later stretched out on a chaise longue on the terrace looking down toward Harmon Brook, he took to whispering. He moved his lips hardly at all, but vocalized each word, or if he fell short of this, at least put each thought into carefully chosen words and sentences.

The idea that he might be in mental communication with another person was not, to him, very startling. Steeped in the lore of science fiction whose heroes were, as like as not, adepts at telepathy, the event seemed almost an expected outcome of his wishes. Many nights he had lain awake sending out (he hoped) a mental probe, trying and trying to find the trick, for surely there must be one, of making a contact.

Now that such a contact was established he sought, just as vainly, for some means to prove it. How do you know you're not dreaming, he asked himself. How do you know you're not still delirious?

The difficulty was that his communication with Charity Payne could be by mental route only. Had there been any possibility for Peter to reach the girl by mail, by telephone, by travel and a personal visit, their rapport on a mental level might have been confirmed, and their messages cross-checked.

During their respective periods of illness, Peter and Charity achieved a communion of a sort which consisted at first of brief glimpses, each of the other's environment. They were not—then—seeing through one another's eyes, so much as tapping one another's visual recollections. While Peter stared at a smoothly plastered ceiling, Charity looked at rough hewn beams. He, when his aching head permitted, could turn on one side and watch a television program. She, by the same movement, could see a small smoky fire in the monstrous stone fireplace, where water was heated and her beef and barley broth kept steaming.

Instead of these current images, current for each of them in their different times, they saw stored-up pictures, not perfect, for neither of them was remembering perfectly; rather like pictures viewed through a badly ground lens, with only the objects of principal interest in clear detail.

Charity saw her fearful sights with no basis for comprehension—a section of dual highway animated by hurtling cars and trucks and not a person, recognizable as a person, in sight; a tennis court, and what on earth could it be; a jet plane crossing the sky; a vast and many storied building which glinted with glass and the silvery tracings of untarnished steel.

At the start she was terrified nearly out of her wits. It's all very well to dream, and a nightmare is only a bad dream after you waken, but a nightmare is assembled from familiar props. You could reasonably by chased by a dragon (like the one in the picture that St. George had to fight) or be lost in a cave (like the one on Parish Hill, only bigger and darker). To dream of things which have no meaning at all is worse.

She was spared prolongation of her terror by Peter's comprehension of their situation and his intuitive realization of what the experience, assuming a two way channel might be doing to her. The vignettes of her life which he was seeing were in no way disturbing. Everything he saw through her mind was within his framework of reference. Horses and cattle, fields and forest, rutted lanes and narrow wooden bridges were things he knew, even if he did not live among them. He recognized Harmon Brook because, directly below their home, there was an immense granite boulder parting the flow, shaped like a great bear-like animal with its head down, drinking. It was strange that the stream, in all those years, had neither silted up nor eroded away to hide or change the seeming of the rock, but so it was. He saw it through Charity's eyes and knew the place in spite of the forest on the far hill.

When he first saw this partly familiar, partly strange scene, he heard from somewhere within his mind the frightened cry of a little girl. His thinking at that time was fever distorted and incoherent. It was two days later after a period of several hours of normal temperature when he conceived the idea—with sudden virtual certainty—these pastoral scenes he had been dreaming were truly something seen with other eyes. There were subtle perceptual differences between those pictures and his own seeing.

To his mother, writing at a table near the windows, he said, "I think I'm feeling better. How about a glass of orange juice?"

She considered. "The doctor should be here in an hour or so. In the meantime you can make do with a little more ice water. I'll get it. Drink it slowly, remember."

Two hundred and sixty-five years away, Charity Payne thought suddenly, "How about a glass of orange juice?" She had been drowsing, but her eyes popped wide open. "Mercy," she said aloud. Dame Beulah bent over the pallet.

"What is it, child?"

"How about a glass of orange juice?" Charity repeated.

"La, 'tis gibberish." A cool hand was laid on her forehead. "Would ye like a bit of ice to bite on?"

Orange juice, whatever that might be, was forgotten.

Over the next several days Peter Wood tried time and again to address the stranger directly, and repeatedly failed. Some of what he said to others reached her in fragments and further confused her state of mind. What she had to say, on the other hand, was coming through to him with increasing frequency. Often it was only a word or a phrase with a quaint twist like a historical novel, and he would lie puzzling over it, trying to place the person on the other end of their erratic line of communication. His recognition of Bear Rock, which he had seen once again through her eyes, was disturbing. His science fiction conditioning led him naturally to speculate about the parallel worlds concept, but that seemed not to fit the facts as he saw them.

Peter reached the stage of convalescence when he could spend all day on the terrace and look down, when he wished, at the actual rock. There for the hundredth time he formed the syllables, "Hello, who are you?" and for the first time received a response. It was a silence, but a silence reverberating with shock, totally different in quality from the blankness which had met him before.

"My name is Peter Wood."

There was a long pause before the answer came, softly and timidly.

"My name is Charity Payne. Where are you? What is happening to me?"

The following days of enforced physical idleness were filled with exploration and discovery. Peter found out almost at once that, while they were probably no more than a few feet apart in their respective worlds, a gulf of more than a quarter of a thousand years stretched between them. Such a contact through time was a greater departure from known physical laws, certainly, than the mere fact of telepathic communication. Peter reveled in his growing ability.

In another way the situation was heartbreaking. No matter how well they came to know one another, he realized, they could never meet, and after no more than a few hours of acquaintance he found that he was regarding this naïve child of another time with esteem and a sort of affection.

They arrived shortly at a set of rules which seemed to govern and limit their communications. Each came to be able to hear the other speak, whether aloud or subvocally. Each learned to perceive through the other's senses, up to a point. Visual perception became better and better especially for direct seeing while, as they grew more skillful, the remembered scene became less clear. Tastes and odors could be transmitted, if not accurately, at least with the expected response. Tactile sensations could not be perceived in the slightest degree.

There was little that Peter Wood could learn from Charity. He came to recognize her immediate associates and liked them, particularly her gaunt, weather-beaten father. He formed a picture of Puritanism which, as an ethic, he had to respect, while the supporting dogma evoked nothing but impatience. At first he exposed her to the somewhat scholarly agnosticism which prevailed in his own home, but soon found that it distressed her deeply and he left off. There was so much he could report from the vantage of 1965, so many things he would show her which did not conflict with her tenets and faith.

He discovered that Charity's ability to read was remarkable, though what she had read was naturally limited—the Bible from cover to cover, *Pilgrim's Progress*, several essays and two of Shakespeare's plays. Encouraged by a schoolmaster who must have been an able and dedicated man, she had read and reread everything permitted to her. Her quite respectable vocabulary was gleaned from these sources and may have equaled Peter's own in size. In addition she possessed an uncanny word sense which helped her greatly in understanding Peter's jargon.

She learned the taste of bananas and frankfurters, chocolate ice cream and Coke, and displayed such an addiction to these delicacies that Peter rapidly put on some of the pounds he had lost. One day she asked him what he looked like.

"Well, I told you I am sixteen, and I'm sort of thin."

"Does thee possess a mirror?" she asked.

"Yes, of course."

At her urging and with some embarrassment he went and stood before a mirrored door in his mother's bedroom.

"Marry," she said after a dubious pause, "I doubt not thee is comely. But folk have changed."

"Now let me look at you," he demanded.

"Nay, we have no mirror."

"Then go and look in the brook. There's a quiet spot below the rock where the water is dark."

He was delighted with her appearance, having remembered Hogarth's unkind representations of a not much later period and being prepared for disappointment. She was in fact very much prettier by Peter's standards than by those of her own time, which favored plumpness and smaller mouths. He told her she was a beauty, and her tentative fondness for him turned instantly to adulation.

Previously Peter had had fleeting glimpses of her slim, smoothly muscled body, as she had bathed or dressed. Now, having seen each other face to face, they were overcome by embarrassment and both of them, when not fully clothed, stared resolutely into the corners of the room.

For a time Charity believed that Peter was a dreadful liar. The sight and sound of planes in the sky were not enough to convince her of the fact of flying, so he persuaded his father to take him along on a business flight to Washington. After she had recovered from the marvels of airplane travel, he took her on a walking tour of the Capitol. Now she would believe anything, even that the American Revolution had been a success. They joined his father for lunch at an elegant French restaurant and she experienced, vicariously, the pleasures of half of a half bottle of white wine and a chocolate eclair. Charity was by way of getting spoiled.

Fully recovered and with school only a week away, Peter decided to brush up his tennis. When reading or doing nothing in particular, he was always dimly aware of Charity and her immediate surroundings, and by sharpening his attention he could bring her clearly to the forefront of his mind. Tennis displaced her completely and for an hour or two each day he was unaware of her doings.

Had he been a few years older and a little more knowledge-able and realistic about the world, he might have guessed the peril into which he was leading her. Fictional villainy abounded, of course, and many items in the news didn't bear thinking about, but by his own firsthand experience, people were well intentioned and kindly, and for the most part they reacted to events with reasonable intelligence. It was what he expected instinctively.

A first hint of possible consequences reached him as he walked home from one of his tennis sessions.

"Ursula Miller said an ill thing to me today."

"Oh?" His answer was abstracted since, in all truth, he was beginning to run out of interest in the village gossip which was all the news she had to offer.

"Yesterday she said it was an untruth about the thirteen states. Today she avowed that I was devil ridden. And Ursula has been my best friend."

"I warned you that people wouldn't believe you and you might get yourself laughed at," he said. Then suddenly he caught up in his thinking. "Good Lord—Salem."

"Please, Peter, thee must stop taking thy Maker's name."

"I'll try to remember. Listen, Charity, how many people have you been talking to about our—about what's been happening?"

"As I have said. At first to Father and Aunt Beulah. They did believe I was still addled from the fever."

"And to Ursula."

"Aye, but she vowed to keep it secret."

"Do you believe she will, now that she's started name calling?"

A lengthy pause.

"I fear she may have told the lad who keeps her company."

"I should have warned you. Damn it, I should have laid it on the line."

"Peter!"

"Sorry. Charity, not another word to anybody. Tell Ursula you've been fooling—telling stories to amuse her."

"'Twould not be right."

"So what. Charity, don't be scared, but listen. People might get to thinking you're a witch."

"Oh, they couldn't."

"Why not?"

"Because I am not one. Witches are—oh, no, Peter."

He could sense her growing alarm.

"Go tell Ursula it was a pack of lies. Do it now."

"I must milk the cow."

"Do it now."

"Nay, the cow must be milked."

"Then milk her faster than she's ever been milked before."

On the Sabbath, three little boys threw stones at Charity as she and her father left the church. Obadiah Payne caught one of them and caned him, and then would have had to fight the lad's father save that the pastor intervened.

It was on the Wednesday that calamity befell. Two tight-lipped men approached Obadiah in the fields.

"Squire wants to see thy daughter Charity."

"Squire?"

"Aye. Squire Hacker. He would talk with her at once."

"Squire can talk to me if so be he would have her reprimanded. What has she been up to?"

"Witchcraft, that's what," said the second man, sounding as if he were savoring the dread news. "Croft's old ewe delivered a monstrous lamb. Pointy pinched-up face and an extra eye." He crossed himself.

"Great God!"

" 'Twill do ye no good to blaspheme, Obadiah. She's to come with us now."

"I'll not have it. Charity's no witch, as ye well know, and I'll not have her converse with Squire. Ye mind the Squire's lecherous ways."

"That's not here nor there. Witchcraft is afoot again and all are saying 'tis your Charity at bottom of it."

"She shall not go."

First one, then the other displayed the stout truncheons they had held concealed behind their backs.

" 'Twas of our own good will we told thee first. Come now and instruct thy daughter to go with us featly. Else take a clout on the head and sleep tonight in the gaol house."

They left Obie Payne gripping a broken wrist and staring in numbed bewilderment from his door stoop, and escorted Charity, not touching her, walking at a cautious distance to either side, to Squire Hacker's big house on the hill. In the village proper, little groups of people watched from doorways and, though some had always been her good friends, none had the courage now to speak a word of comfort.

Peter went with her each reluctant step of the way, counting himself responsible for her plight and helpless to do the least thing about it. He sat alone in the living room of his home, eyes closed to sharpen his reading of her surroundings. She offered no response to his whispered reassurances and perhaps did not hear them.

At the door her guards halted and stood aside, leaving her face to face with the grim-visaged squire. He moved backward step by step, and she followed him, as if hypnotized, into the shadowed room.

The squire lowered himself into a high-backed chair. "Look at me."

Unwillingly she raised her head and stared into his face.

Squire Hacker was a man of medium height, very broad in the shoulder and heavily muscled. His face was disfigured by deep pock marks and the scar of a knife cut across the jaw, souvenirs of his earlier years in the Carib Islands. From the Islands he had also brought some wealth which he had since increased many-fold by the buying of land, share cropping and money lending.

"Charity Payne," he said sternly, "take off thy frock."

"No. No, please."

"I command it. Take off thy garments for I must search thee for witch marks."

He leaned forward, seized her arm and pulled her to him. "If thee would avoid public trial and condemnation, thee will do as I say." His hands began to explore her body.

Even by the standards of the time, Charity regularly spent extraordinary hours at hard physical labor and she possessed a strength which would have done credit to many young men. Squire Hacker should have been more cautious.

"Nay," she shouted and drawing back her arm, hit him in the nose with all the force she could muster. He released her with a roar of rage, then, while he was mopping away blood and tears with the sleeve of his ruffled shirt and shouting imprecations, she turned and shot out the door. The guards, converging, nearly grabbed her as she passed but, once away, they stood no chance of catching her and for a wonder none of the villagers took up the chase.

She was well on the way home and covering the empty road at a fast trot before Peter was able to gain her attention.

"Charity," he said. "Charity, you mustn't go home. If that

s.o.b. of a squire has any influence with the court, you just fixed yourself.''

She was beginning to think again and could even translate Peter's strange language.

"Influence!" she said. "Marry, he is the court. He is the judge.''

"Ouch!''

"I wot well I must not be found at home. I am trying to think where to hide. I might have had trial by water. Now they will burn me for surety. I do remember what folk said about the last witch trials.''

"Could you make your way to Boston and then maybe to New York-New Amsterdam?''

"Leave my home forever! Nay. And I would not dare the trip.''

"Then take to the woods. Where can you go?''

"Take to—? Oh. To the cave, mayhap.''

"Don't too many people know about it?''

"Aye. But there is another across the brook and beyond Tom Carter's freehold. I do believe none know of it but me. 'Tis very small. We must ford the brook just yonder, then walk that fallen tree. There is a trail which at sundown will be tromped by a herd of deer.''

"You're thinking about dogs?''

"Aye, on the morrow. There is no good pack in Annes Towne.''

"You live in a savage age, Charity.''

"Aye,'' she said wryly. "'Tis fortunate we have not invented the bomb.''

"Damn it,'' Peter said, "I wish we'd never met. I wish I hadn't taken you on the plane trip. I wish I'd warned you to keep quiet about it.''

"Ye could not guess I would be so foolish.''

"What can you do out here without food?''

"I'd liefer starve than be in the stocks, but there is food to be had in the forest, some sorts of roots and toadstools and autumn berries. I shall hide myself for three days, I think, then seek out my father by night and do as he tells me."

When she was safely hidden in the cave, which was small indeed but well concealed by a thicket of young sassafras, she said:

"Now we can think. First, I would have an answer from thy superior wisdom. Can one be truly a witch and have no knowledge of it?"

"Don't be foolish. There's no such thing as a witch."

"Ah well, 'tis a matter for debate by scholars. I do feel in my heart that I am not a witch, if there be such creatures. That book, Peter, of which ye told me, which recounts the history of these colonies."

"Yes?"

"Will ye look in it and learn if I came to trial and what befell me?"

"There'd be nothing about it. It's just a small book. But—"

To his parents' puzzlement, Peter spent the following morning at the Boston Public Library. In the afternoon he shifted his operations to the Historical Society. He found at last a listing of the names of women known to have been tried for witchcraft between the years 1692 and 1697. Thereafter he could locate only an occasional individual name. There was no record of any Charity Payne in 1700 or later.

He started again when the reading room opened next day, interrupting the task only momentarily for brief exchanges with Charity. His lack of success was cheering to her, for she overestimated the completeness of the records.

At close to noon he was scanning the pages of a photostated doctoral thesis when his eye caught a familiar name.

Jonas Hacker born Liverpool, England, date uncertain,

perhaps 1659, was the principal figure in a curious action of law which has not become a recognized legal precedent in English courts.

Squire Hacker, a resident of Annes Towne (cf. Anniston), was tried and convicted of willful murder and larceny. The trial was posthumous, several months after his decease from natural causes in 1704. The sentence pronounced was death by hanging which, since it could not be imposed, was commuted to forfeiture of his considerable estate. His land and other possessions reverted to the Crown and were henceforward administered by the Governor of Bay Colony.

While the motivation and procedure of the court may have been open to question, evidence of Hacker's guilt was clear cut. The details are these . . .

"Hey, Charity," Peter rumbled in his throat.

"Aye?"

"Look at this page. Let me flatten it out."

"Read it please, Peter. Is it bad news?"

"No. Good, I think." He read the paragraphs on Jonas Hacker.

"Oh, Peter, can it be true?"

"It has to be. Can you remember any details?"

"Marry, I remember well when they disappeared, the ship's captain and a common sailor. They were said to have a great sack of gold for some matter of business with Squire. But it could not be, for they never reached his house."

"That's what Hacker said, but the evidence showed that they got there—got there and never got away. Now here's what you must do. Late tonight, go home."

"I would fen do so, for I am terrible athirst."

"No, wait. What's your parson's name?"

"John Hix."

"Can you reach his house tonight without being seen?"

"Aye. It backs on a glen."

"Go there. He can protect you better than your father can until your trial."

"Must I be tried?"

"Of course. We want to clear your name. Now let's do some planning."

The town hall could seat no more than a score of people, and the day was fair; so it was decided that the trial should be held on the common, in discomforting proximity to the stocks.

Visitors came from as far as twenty miles away, afoot or in carts, and nearly filled the common itself. Squire Hacker's own armchair was the only seat provided. Others stood or sat on the patchy grass.

The squire came out of the inn presently, fortified with rum, and took his place. He wore a brocaded coat and a wide-brimmed hat and would have been more impressive if it had not been for his still swollen nose, now permanently askew.

A way was made through the crowd then, and Charity, flanked on one side by John Hix, on the other by his tall son, walked to the place where she was to stand. Voices were suddenly stilled. Squire Hacker did not condescend to look directly at the prisoner, but fixed a cold stare on the minister: a warning that his protection of the girl would not be forgiven. He cleared his throat.

"Charity Payne, is thee willing to swear upon the Book?"

"Aye."

"No mind. We may forego the swearing. All can see that ye are fearful."

"Nay," John Hix interrupted. "She shall have the opportunity to swear to her word. 'Twould not be legal otherwise." He extended a Bible to Charity, who placed her fingers on it and said, "I do swear to speak naught but the truth."

Squire Hacker glowered and lost no time coming to the attack. "Charity Payne, do ye deny being a witch?"

"I do."

"Ye do be one?"

"Nay, I do deny it."

"Speak what ye mean. What have ye to say of the monstrous lamb born of Master Croft's ewe?"

"I know naught of it."

"Was't the work of Satan?"

"I know not."

"Was't then the work of God?"

"I know not."

"Thee holds then that He might create such a monster?"

"I know naught about it."

"In thy own behalf will thee deny saying that this colony and its neighbors will in due course make wars against our King?"

"Nay, I do not deny that."

There was a stir in the crowd and some angry muttering.

"Did ye tell Mistress Ursula Miller that ye had flown a great journey through the air?"

"Nay."

"Mistress Ursula will confound thee in that lie."

"I did tell Ursula that someday folk would travel in that wise. I did tell her that I had seen such travel through eyes other than my own."

Squire Hacker leaned forward. He could not have hoped for a more damning statement. John Hix's head bowed in prayer.

"Continue."

"Aye. I am blessed with a sort of second sight."

"Blessed or cursed?"

"God permits it. It cannot be accursed."

"Continue. What evil things do ye see by this second sight?"

"Most oftentimes I see the world as it will one day be. Thee said evil. Such sights are no more and no less evil than we see around us."

Hacker pondered. There was an uncomfortable wrongness about this child's testimony. She should have been gibbering with fear, when in fact she seemed self-possessed. He wondered if by some strange chance she really had assistance from the devil's minions.

"Charity Payne, thee has confessed to owning second sight. Does thee use this devilish power to spy on thy neighbors?"

It was a telling point. Some among the spectators exchanged discomfited glances.

"Nay, 'tis not devilish, and I cannot see into the doings of my neighbors—except—"

"Speak up, girl. Except what?"

"Once I did perceive by my seeing a most foul murder."

"Murder!" The squire's voice was harsh. A few in the crowd made the sign of the cross.

"Aye. To tell true, two murders. Men who corpses do now lie buried unshriven in a dark cellar close onto this spot. 'Tween them lies a satchel of golden guineas."

It took a minute for the squire to find his voice.

"A cellar?" he croaked.

"Aye, a root cellar, belike the place one would keep winter apples." She lifted her head and stared straight into the squire's eyes, challenging him to inquire further.

The silence was ponderous as he strove to straighten out his thoughts. To this moment he was safe, for her words described every cellar in and about the village. But she knew. Beyond any question, she knew. Her gaze, seeming to penetrate the darkest corners of his mind, told him that, even more clearly than her words.

Squire Hacker believed in witches and considered them evil and deserving of being destroyed. He had seen and shuddered at the horrible travesty of a lamb in farmer Croft's stable yard, but he had seen like deformities in the Caribbee and did not hold the event an evidence of witchcraft. Not for a minute had he thought Charity a witch, for she showed none of the signs. Her wild talk and the growing rumors had simply seemed to provide the opportunity for some dalliance with a pretty young girl and possibly, in exchange for an acquittal, a lien upon her father's land.

Now he was unsure. She must indeed have second sight to have penetrated his secret, for it had been stormy that night five years ago, and none had seen the missing sailors near to his house. Of that he was confident. Further, shockingly, she knew how and where they lay buried. Another question and answer could not be risked.

He moved his head slowly and looked right and left at the silent throng.

"Charity Payne," he said, picking his words with greatest care, "has put her hand on the Book and sworn to tell true, an act, I opine, she could scarce perform, were she a witch. Does any person differ with me?"

John Hix looked up in startled hopefulness.

"Very well. The lambing at Master Croft's did have the taint of witchcraft, but Master Trowbridge has stated his belief that some noxious plant is growing in Croft's pasture, and 'tis at the least possible. Besides, the ewe is old and she has thrown runty lambs before.

"To quote Master Trowbridge again, he holds that the cholera which has afflicted us so sorely comes from naught but the drinking of bad water. He advises boiling it. I prefer adding a little rum."

He got the laughter he sought. There was a lessening of tension.

"As to second sight." Again he swept the crowd with his gaze. "Charity had laid claim to it, and I called it a devilish gift to test her, but second sight is not witchcraft, as ye well know. My own grandmother had it, and a better women ne'er lived. I hold it to be a gift of God. Would any challenge me?

"Very well. I would warn Charity to be cautious in what she sees and tells, for second sight can lead to grievous disputations.

I do not hold with her story of two murdered men although I think that in her own sight she is telling true. If any have aught of knowledge of so dire a crime, I adjure him to step forth and speak.''

He waited. ''Nobody? Then, by the authority conferred on me by his Excellency the Governor, I declare that CharityPayne is innocent of the charges brought. She may be released.''

This was not at all the eventuality which a few of Squire Hacker's cronies had foretold. The crowd had clearly expected a day long inquisition climaxed by a prisoner to bedevil in the stocks. The Squire's aboutface and his abrupt ending of the trial surprised them and angered a few. They stood uncertain.

Then someone shouted hurrah and someone else called for three cheers for Squire Hacker, and all in a minute the gathering had lost its hate and was taking on the look of a picnic. Men headed for the tavern. Parson Hix said a long prayer to which few listened, and everybody gathered around to wring Obie Payne's good hand and to give his daughter a squeeze.

At intervals through the afternoon and evening Peter touched lightly on Charity's mind, finding her carefree and happily occupied with visitors. He chose not to obtrude himself until she called.

Late that night she lay on her mattress and stared into the dark.

''Peter,'' she whispered.

''Yes, Charity.''

''Oh, thank you again.''

''Forget it. I got you into the mess. Now you're out of it. Anyway, I didn't really help. It all had to work out the way it did, because that's the way it had happened. You see?''

''No, not truly. How do we know that Squire won't dig up those old bones and burn them?''

''Because he didn't. Four years from now somebody will find them.''

''No, Peter, I do not understand, and I am afeared again.''

"Why, Charity?"

"It must be wrong, thee and me talking together like this and knowing what is to be and what is not."

"But what could be wrong about it?"

"That I do not know, but I think 'twere better you should stay in your time and me in mine. Goodbye, Peter."

"Charity!"

"And God bless you."

Abruptly she was gone and in Peter's mind there was an emptiness and a knowledge of being alone. He had not known that she could close him out like this.

With the passing of days he became skeptical and in time he might have disbelieved entirely. But Charity visited him again. It was October. He was alone and studying, without much interest.

"Peter."

"Charity, it's you."

"Yes. For a minute, please, Peter, for only a minute, but I had to tell you. I—" She seemed somehow embarrassed. "There is a message."

"A what?"

"Look at Bear Rock, Peter, under the bear's jaw on the left side."

With that, she was gone.

The cold water swirled around his legs as he traced with one finger the painstakingly chiseled message she had left; a little-girl message in a symbol far older than either of them.

# THOMAS N. SCORTIA

# WHEN YOU HEAR THE TONE

*The will to live is extremely important. Indeed, scientists have found that the more famous people are, the more likely it is that when final illness strikes them, they will delay death until after their next birthday, so that they can enjoy, for one last time, the encomiums that will be heaped upon them.*

*Among the old, particularly, survival is strongly related to a sense of worth, and, as Mr. Mark Fleiker discovers, one way to promote such self-esteem is through a bit of romance.*

*Thomas N. Scortia was a prolific science fiction writer during the second half of the 1950's who later turned his attention to what has been called "the near future novel," especially those involving various forms of disasters. He is best known as the coauthor (with Frank M. Robinson) of the novel that formed the basis of the film* The Towering Inferno.

"Hello," he said loudly in the way old people have. "Hello, hello, this is Fleiker. Hello."

"When you hear the tone—"

"Damn," he said, wheezing. "I didn't dial the—"

"—the time will be—"

"Hello," a voice said, a woman's voice, age indeterminate, certainly not young.

"Hello," he said. "Hello—Walter, why don't you answer?"

"Oh, how nice of you to call," the voice said. "It was awfully nice of you to call."

"Who is this?" he demanded. "Who are you?"

"Yes, yes, happy New Year to you, Michael. Yes, it has been a nice year."

"What kind of nonsense is this?" he snapped.

"A good year. Yes, a very good year—the best since I've retired. I went to the class reunion in Denver last month, just before Christmas."

"Is this some kind of joke?" he said. "New Year? Christmas last month? It's the middle of summer."

"Hello. Yes, yes, happy New Year, dear. Happy nineteen-sixty-three."

"Shut up, damn you. What kind of trick are you pulling? It's nineteen-seventy. It's mid-August, and hot as hell, and if you don't—"

"That's sweet of you, awfully sweet of you. Thank you, thank you."

"Hello," he shouted, losing patience. "Hello, hello, hello, hello, damn it, hello—"

"Good night. Merry Christmas—thank you, good night."

"Stop it," he yelled. "Don't go away. Don't try that—"

"When you hear the tone, the time will be—"

"Hello, hello," he shouted.

*Click* . . .

" . . .the time will be exactly—"

He slammed the phone into its cradle and stood, shaking, his eyes misty with sweat. The pulse in his neck throbbed with anger. Cold played across the liver-spotted tissue of his scalp, rousing the few remaining wisps of crepe hair that grew there.

Damn pranksters, he raged. Who the hell did they think they were trying to kid? He stopped, wondering who would want to try such a banal trick.

His nephew's boy? The one with the yellowed teeth, white-flecked mouth opening in the start of a braying laugh?

Or Schulz or Carpenter or Wilkenson? He snorted at the thought. Ineffectual weaklings. The thought of one of them getting the better of him after all these years... They still remembered their hatred of him, though, even at well past eighty, when all hatred and lust and sorrow should be dead. Or the vultures downstairs—the endless relatives, whispering, *How is he today? That's good, that's very good.* Meaning, *If he dies it will be just great because of all that money, and he's too old to need it or care about what life can bring . . .*

Alone, embattled. His withered lips twisted in contempt. He had built, had cut throats, and wrecked better than they in the process. Let them go out and grub for it the way he had done, with no one to help. Not even his wife, the pretty tinsel thing he had bought after no one else would touch him.

He sat for a long moment, looking at the phone. Then, gently, he lifted it from its cradle and, after consulting his phone index (there had been a time when his memory was sharp and unfailing), he carefully dialed his brother's number again.

*Click . . . click . . . click . . .*

" . . . hear the tone, the time will be exactly—"

"No," he said, and stabbed at the cradle button with his finger. He dialed the number once again.

*Click . . .*

"When you hear the tone—"

His hand darted forward.

"Wait, don't hang up. Who are you?"

He pressed the phone tightly to his ear, his breath hissing in the perforations of the mouthpiece.

"I said, who are you? I can hear you breathing—"

"Hello, hello, why are you bothering me? It's two o'clock in the morning," the voice said.

"Liar," he said. "It's six in the afternoon, daylight saving

time, in the middle of August, and the sun is so bright you can
look at the asphalt without glasses and you—''

''No, don't shout, Jimmy. It doesn't do to get excited—''

''My name is not Jimmy,'' he said, trying to control his
voice.

''No, it's board policy, and if they want me to retire—''

The same voice, he realized. Female—probably middle-
aged. A very pleasant voice, he thought, and then shook off the
thought with annoyance. There wasn't any point in thinking that
way at his age.

''Hello, who are you?''

''I know, just to June . . . Well, it's been a year . . . Ever since
the end of the war, ever since you came back from Korea.''

''The war?'' he shouted. ''The Korean war? Damn, the war's
ended over seventeen years ago. Nineteen-fifty-three to nineteen-seventy is seventeen years. Can't you count?''

''Thank you, thank you,'' the voice said. Middle-aged, but
with young overtones. Whom did he know who sounded like
that? Someone, someone, someone—who?

''Wait,'' he pleaded. ''Don't go.''

'' . . . the time will be exactly six-fourteen, daylight sav—''
*Click . . .*

''Damn,'' he said, his voice shrill and cracking. His eyes
filled with tears. Ridiculous. He hadn't cried in twenty years,
not since his wife had died, and then for pure formality. He
would have cried at the death of a favorite hunting dog or of a
stranger into whose cortege he had blundered. Tears were easy
then because you had strength and were unassailable.

He was too old for crying. Eighty-two, and only the vague
warmth of life animating him with the memory of endless dead
years, when life might have had some meaning, had he sought
for it. Now there was only the leaden silence of his room
secreted among many rooms, with whispering servants moving
like phantoms through the dusk, and beefy young nephews and

glassy-eyed nieces waiting for his last gasp, their thoughts clawing over bonds and cash and other empty symbols of eighty-two years.

*How terrible*, he thought. *How terrible, how terrible, how terrible . . .*

Terrible? What was terrible?

Growing old. Withering and cracking like ancient celluloid movie film. The images on it broken and dusty. Thrown on a fire, curling and shriveling an instant before extinction, and then gone with a single puff of sooty flame.

But age was not that dramatic—not even that significant. He would simply run down, cease to move, become quiescent, and the dark men who hovered at hand would come and do secret things with his body so that his face became a mask of wax and talc and scented rouge and his body shrank in withered majesty secretly within the shroud.

And the young ones, drunk with the negotiable fragments of his life, would scarcely remember that he had been.

"Oh, no," he said softly. "Oh, no, no, no, no, no, there is somebody. There is somebody. Or there was somebody. There must have been somebody."

But he could not think of one—not even his brother Walter, whom he had fed and clothed and looked after and whose sprawling, middle-aged brood hovered on the edge of his existence like circling condors. Walter did not even answer his phone.

If he could have had someone, somewhere. If in the midst of all his life he had found someone who cared and worried and cheered and wept. But he had not, and now not even the possibility existed that . . .

He paused. The possibility? Vaguely, dimly, the possibility. Only it was late, and life had a way of losing detail in the amorphous mass of years that spilled out and vanished, leaving your body older and more tired and wrinkled and crackling and your mind vague and many-chambered and without cohesive form.

Walter, he thought. He had been trying to talk to Walter, who was his one link with life, the only person of his blood remaining. (Forget those creatures downstairs who had been generated out of some ferment that was not a part of him.)

His fingers, stiff with pain and calcification, dialed the number and he waited, hearing the burr of the bell at the other end.

"When you hear the tone—"

"Damn," he shouted. "Damn, damn, damn—"

*Click* . . .

Again, carefully, patiently, noting each digit, with deliberate precision, all seven carefully dialed digits.

At the sixth digit the sound of ringing . . . not the soft burr, but a shriller sound, tinny, as though the signal were in a hollow metal-lined room.

"Hello, hello," the voice said.

"Hello," he said, "Who—"

"Oh, it's you, I wanted so much for it to be you again," the woman's voice said.

"Yes, it's me. It's me," he said savagely. "It's me, Mark Fleiker, and who the hell are you?"

"Yes, I know it's you, Mark. How could I forget the voice?"

"Forget what voice?" he demanded.

"After all these years, how could I forget the voice?"

"I've never talked with you before," he shouted into the mouthpiece.

"All those times," she whispered. "So few without ever seeing you or touching you and knowing that you were somewhere out there. I wondered where you were during the war—"

"Woman," he said plaintively. "Woman, what kind of a joke are you playing on an old man?"

"Old?" she said. "Are you really old?"

"I'm old, old, old," he said. "I sit here in this pile of a house and watch the jackals gather to fight over my bones."

"It's the war," she said. "This horrible war. Everyone seems taken up in a kind of hysteria. The horrible bloodiness—"

"I hate the thought of the war," he said. "It is an idiot war. There is no end to it, and only the blood and the killing and the waste for what reason— It never was our war—"

"No," she said soothingly. "You must have lost someone very dear, but it is our war. It is our war, even though it's nearly over."

"It'll never be over," he said.

"Only a matter of days," she said "and then we can breathe in peace and be truly free of all the dreadfulness. They've crossed the Rhine and—"

"Crossed the Rhine?" he shouted. "Are you mad?"

"—only a matter of time—" the voice said, its quality suddenly tinny.

"What's crossing the Rhine got to do with a lot of backward Asiatics in a fifth-rate jungle nation, and the death of everything—of my nephew, who was the one good thing that came out of my flesh?"

"—the Nazis," she said. "The horrible Nazis—"

Then, *sputter . . . sputter . . . sputter . . .* from the phone and—

"When you hear the tone, the time will be exactly—"

He slammed the receiver to the carriage, and breathing heavily, stumbled to the bed. He lay weak and fearful.

The sense of being utterly alone swept over him. Alone, alone, alone—the words clattered off the walls, shattered against his inner ear, echoed down the flesh passages to the inner chambers of his being.

Alone.

Except for an insane voice from somewhere that still fought a war involving crossing the Rhine and Nazis as villains—a voice that recognized his with pleasure.

With pleasure, he thought in surprise—but only a voice. People did not acknowledge him with pleasure. They pretended and thought he didn't see through their transparent stratagems to ingratiate themselves with him. He knew. Knew. Knew. As he knew the doctors who told him there was nothing wrong with him.

"There's nothing wrong with you, Mr. Fleiker. Age, yes, with all the small degenerations of age, but you're sound as a dollar."

"That's not very damned sound," he would growl.

"Well, you know what I mean."

"I'm dying," he would say.

"You think you're dying," the doctors would say softly.

"It's the same thing."

"Perhaps." Pursed lips. "Perhaps. Perhaps."

What would they think now? The final delirium. Hearing voices on the phone that told him they were talking from the year after the Korean War. 1953 or 1954? When were armies crossing the Rhine? 1945? A voice that knew him. That spoke to him gently. (People had seldom spoken to him gently; even his dead wife, who had scarcely spoken at all.)

His ancient heart leaped for an instant. His eighty-two-year-old heart pounded for an instant, and he fell back against the pillow, blood coursing through the fine veining of his face, flushing his nose, lips, cheeks, with unexpected warmth.

"Oh, God," he said. "Oh, God, to play such an irony on me." Cruel, vicious God. (All gods are cruel and vicious. You've worshiped many of them.) Cruel and vicious God.

His quivering fingers found the phone. Dialed. Faltered. Dialed again. He held the receiver to his ear.

He waited.

*Click . . .*

"When you hear the tone, it will be—"

He sobbed. Pressed the button. Dialed again. Waited. Breathing. Breathing. Breathing.

"Hello?"

"Hello," he said excitedly. "Hello, it is you? Is it you?"

"Mark," she said. "Is it you? After eight years? Is it you?"

"Yes," he said. "Yes, it's Mark. It's Mark."

"I thought I would never hear your voice again. After so many years, to hear your voice again."

"It's Mark," he said, choking.

"You don't sound well," she said.

"I'm not well," he said.

"If I could come just once to you."

"If you could," he said. "If only you could."

"I don't even know your last name. We've spoken so few times, and I don't even know your last name."

"Of course you do," he said. "It's Fleiker. Mark Fleiker."

"That can't be right," she said. "There's a Mark Fleiker who's a presidential adviser. I met him once—at a reception. My, he was handsome—but so intense."

"That was I—that was years ago," he said.

"No, not the same at all," she said. "Mark, such a sense of humor. Not the same at all."

The voice carrying a frown . . . returning to a . . . a caress.

"That was years and years ago," he said. "That was just before the war."

"Will there be a war?" she asked. "Pray God there won't be a war."

"The year before the Japs bombed Pearl Harbor," he said. "In nineteen-forty-one, just before Pearl Harbor."

"Mark, I don't understand you," she said.

. . . *Sputter* . . . *sputter* . . . The connection was going, he knew.

"Don't go," he shouted.

"Mark," she said. "I can't hear you. I don't understand."

"Don't go," he shouted, "I love you. Don't go."

"Mark . . ." *Sputter* . . . "Mark, you know it's nineteen-forty-one now. You know it's December sixth, a Saturday, when school is out. You know it's . . ."

*Click* . . .

"When you hear the tone—"

December 6, 1941! When you hear the tone—1941—December 6!

His hand clawed at the sheets, made cabbage folds, knotted them. What was she? Where was she? Who was she?

He didn't even know her name. A voice without form, without body, without face, without name. They must have passed each other briefly once. Touched hands, perhaps. So long ago and he had not known.

In that single instant the sense of aloneness, of being lost on the edge of time-space, had made him say it. "I love you." The unknown emotion had welled inside his ancient frame, coursed through his sluggish blood, and suddenly he knew. He knew it with fear and hope and anger and a sense of utter loss.

Love?

Love doesn't come this way, he told himself. You don't fall in love with a phantom, with something that's a faint image projecting through time into the dying present. Youth is a time for love. Not love. Not now. Not now. Not with a phantom. Not this thing to torture me in my last hours, he thought. Oh, no, God, not this, not this, not this.

He heard them puttering in the hall, and he realized he was breathing heavily. The vultures were waiting. They heard him breathing his excited rasping breath, and they were flocking close. He heard the doorknob turn, and the door began to open silently.

"Stay out," he shouted. "God damn it, stay out. I'll let you know when I want you. Stay out."

The door closed, and he was alone again. Alone, as he had always been. Alone now except for the memory of a voice that stretched across years and years from the past and belonged to a woman he did not know and would never know.

What marvels, what magic, his little-boy mind in the old, old mind said. Magic that feeble electric currents over copper wires should span distances—and years. Alexander Graham Bell, magician. Mr.—what was his name—Mr. Watson, sorcerer's apprentice. Those two half a century ago with caldrons and eye of newt and wire of copper and oil of vitriol and certain discrete particles of carbon and . . .

And he didn't even know her name.

Delicate voice, tender voice, object mystical and unseen. Of love? One does not love a voice and cannot love a voice and you don't fit your aging ideal to a mere voice.

Only he had. In an impossible moment, in an insane working of the chemistry of his aged body.

And he didn't even know her name.

He lay for many minutes, looking at the cradled phone. Thinking, wondering, fearing, hoping, dreading, dreaming, then . . . He couldn't stop it. He couldn't halt his spotted hand with its lean, gray-bristled fingers; imbued with a life of their own, they drifted across the sheets, gained new strength, became purposeful, grasped, held the instrument tightly, lifted . . . and his other hand with sure touch was dialing. Any number. It made no difference. Any number. Dial the letters: 6 . . . N . . . 3 . . . E . . . 9 . . . W . . . 5 . . . L . . . 6 . . . 0 . . . 8 . . . V . . . 3 . . . Why not? Why not? The world is insane and dying, and I am insane—but suddenly terribly, impossibly, very much alive.

*Click . . .*

"When you hear the tone, the time will be—"

*Click . . click . . . click . . .*

"Hello," Firm, young, vigorous voice. Gentle, strong.

"It's Mark," he said.

"Mark? Mark?" she said.

"Mark," he said.

"Oh," she said. "I remember. It's been such a long time."

"It's been only minutes for me," he said.

"I don't understand," she said.

"What year is it?" he asked.

"Nineteen-thirty-three," she said. "You know that."

"Listen to me," he said excitedly. "I'm not insane, and I know you will think so—but listen to me. Here it's nineteen-seventy."

"Oh, my," she said. "That's a peculiar joke."

She didn't get angry, he thought. Nor annoyed. Marvelous.

"Believe me," he said. "Here it's nineteen-seventy. I've been calling you—talking with you all evening. Only it's you earlier and earlier."

"That's strange. What a lovely idea," she said.

"It's real," he told her. "It's real."

"A strange idea. A beautiful idea," she said.

"It's horrible. I can't even see you."

"I shouldn't do this," she said. "But I'll see you."

"I can't," he said. "I can't, I can't. Don't you understand? It's not the miles."

"Where are you?" she asked.

"San Francisco. Twin Peaks."

"I'm only blocks away. Jones Street! Nob Hill," she said. "I've lived here for years. My family before me. Only blocks away."

"Years away," he said.

"You sound so lost."

"You are so lost," he said.

"You sound so . . . I shouldn't but—"

*Sputter . . . sputter . . .*

"What's your name?" he asked.

*Sputter.*

"Your name?" he pleaded. "Your name."

"Angela; you know that. A fine pretty Victorian name. Angela—"

"Angela what?"

*Sputter.*

"When you hear the tone, it will be—"

*Click* . . .

He sobbed.

His fingers dialed frantically. Any number. Any number.

*Click* . . .

*Click* . . .

"Hello." Young voice.

"Angela?" he asked.

"Yes, who's this?"

"Mark," he said.

"What a nice name," she said. "I don't know any Mark, though."

"What's your last name?" he asked.

"I don't recall ever meeting a Mark."

"We've met," he told her. "But I don't know your last name."

"You have such a nice voice," she said. "So young. Oh, I really shouldn't say that—"

"Your last name," he pleaded.

*Sputter* . . .

"Why no harm in telling, I suppose. It's Haym—"

*Sputter* . . . *click* . . .

"When you hear—"

"Oh, dear God," he said aloud. Just one second more and he would have had it. One second more. Fingers dialed frantically.

*Click* . . .

"When you hear the—"

*Click* . . .

"Hello—hello?" A man's voice, deep, resonant.

"Hello," he shouted.

A grunt of displeasure.

"Hello," he shouted.

"Mr. Watson," the voice said. "Come here. I need you."

After that there was silence. Long, long, long, dread silence. Not even a sputter. Not even a click.

Only silence.

He returned the receiver to the hook, feeling tired and old and quite ready to close his eyes and never open them again.

It was too late. Rather, too early. Back to the very beginning, and beyond that year, that day, that moment, there would be nothing. The ancient copper would be dead, because before that instant when Mr. Bell had spilled the acid of the battery and called for his helper, there was nothing. No voices, no Angela, no hope—ever.

He felt like sobbing, but it required too much energy. He had little left. There was only lying in bed and staring at the wall and listening to the whisper of the doctors and the insipid questions of endless nephews and knowing that the days stretched out without hope, without feature, without pity.

Angela Haym—and something else. One syllable. Two syllables? He wasn't even sure he had the first one right. There had been so much static and the quality of the transmission from the primitive phone was so bad.

He grabbed the directory and thumbed to the H's. Impossible. Haymaker—Hayman (See also: Heyman—Heiman—Heimann —Heymann—Hyman). Then Haymend, Haymer, Haymond. An impossible task. He counted them. Thirteen, not counting commercial listings, under Haym . . . then Heym . . . then Heim . . .

Then seventy-eight listings. Impossible.

He didn't even know if she was still alive. Or still in the city. Or even that she still had the same last name. She could have married. She hadn't on the first call. At least she hadn't seem married. A schoolteacher.

Memory. What had she said? After she retired? She had gone to the class reunion. In Denver?

His fingers skipped to the yellow pages. Hopefully. Under "Associations." University of Denver . . . The Alumni Association. One impossible chance.

He called. A woman answered. He invented a story. He couldn't remember the exact last name. Could she help? After long moments he had three names that might be she.

He started to call. Praying.

On the third call a voice answered, and he said breathlessly, "Angela Haymeyer?"

"Yes," the voice said.

"This is Mark Fleiker."

"Who?"

His heart sank. This was the last one. There was no other. What would he do?

"Mark Fleiker," he said tiredly.

"Oh, Mark," she said. "After all these years. After all these years."

Breath caught in his throat. Suddenly panic, fear.

"Angela," he said, "can you entertain a gentleman caller? An old friend."

"After all these years? An old friend?"

"An old friend," he said.

"What a pleasure it would be!"

"It will be," he said, feeling suddenly alive, young-old—alive.

"It will be such a pleasure after all these years," he said.

And, not waiting for the click, he replaced the receiver and began to dress.

"After all these years," he said aloud to the empty room, and felt very, very good.

# LOVE AND TECHNOLOGY

# DANIEL F. GALOUYE

# SHARE ALIKE

*The late Daniel F. Galouye is best known for his remarkable post-holocaust novel* Dark Universe *(1961), although he was a frequent contributor to the science fiction magazines from 1952 to the mid-1960's.*

*Here he reminds us that one has to make judgments in life in order to function as an adult. But it is always nice to remember that you can never know all there is to know about someone else, which may or may not be dangerous. So if you keep your eyes open, as does the tempestuous Cherry O'Day in this story, just one new bit of information can sometimes cause you to radically change your feelings toward another person.*

When Cherry discovered there was a man in her apartment, she was quite righteously and understandably indignant.

Not that she was unduly puritanical in the matter of sharing her quarters with a man she didn't know. After all, residential facilities for the unmarried personnel in Rigel IV–Port were critically limited. And girls were expected to share apartments—with the chances being about even that the "other person" would be a man.

Disgustedly, she fluffed the cushion on the sofa to smooth out the imprint of his bulky frame—he must be a giant to have made that much of a hollow!—and slammed the window against the cold wind—fresh-air fiend, too!

Allowing her resentment no chance to abate, the stormed over to the videocom and punched the number for Housing.

"Expediter's office." The receptionist's voice came through buoyantly, even before her image formed on the screen. "Good morn—"

"It is *not* a good morning!" Cherry said, her red hair swirling as she shook her head emphatically.

"First," she thrust up a rigid finger to enumerate the point, "there are no mornings here.

"Second," another finger indicated, "none of them would be good with a gale blustering around outside and a man blustering around inside!"

"Oh, it's you, Miss O'Day," the receptionist said disappointedly as her face replaced the shifting pattern on the screen.

"Yes, it's me—Cherry O'Day, Coefficient B, Shift B. And there's still a man in my apartment!"

"Naturally," said the receptionist wearily. "You understood when you were assigned to the dormitory that—"

"I understood there would be a man or a woman. But I was also assured that regardless of whatever else it was, it would be Coefficient A, Shift A, and that it would be either working or at recreation during the twelve hours I am entitled to the apartment!"

"I know," the receptionist said impatiently. "And it—I mean he is Coefficient of Existence A, but Shift B—the same shift as yours."

"And every time I turn around in my apartment, there he is—or, rather, there he isn't. What space-happy idiot in your office assigned him to the right CE, but the wrong shift?"

Cherry stamped her foot and folded her arms so there would be no question as to the uncompromising nature of her indignation.

"We have your complaint on file, Miss O'Day," the receptionist began formally, "and—"

"Then do something about it! I don't care to spend any more sleep periods in bed with a man, however relatively immaterial he may be!"

The receptionist shrugged apathetically. "These things take time, you know."

"Is Art—is Mr. Edson in?"

"Not yet. The A-Shift Expediter is still on duty. Would you like to speak with him?"

"Never mind," Cherry answered stiffly. "I'll be in later."

Exasperated, she snapped off the videocom. If there was one thing she was sure of, it was that she would stand for no more delay in regaining unchallenged occupancy of her apartment during her B-Shift off-period.

This Mr. Whatever-His-Name-Is was imminently close to getting thrown out on his ear regardless of his unguessable bulk . . . provided she could improvise some means of locating his nonexistent ear.

Resolutely, she strode back into the hall and waited next to the bathroom door, focusing her rage on the mocking patter of shower water against porcelain and flesh.

Then she winced as his deep bass voice rose gratingly off key:

"Oh-h-h-h, the ship slipped out of Hyper
With-h-h-h the motions of a viper . . ."

Furiously, she beat on the door.

The spray stopped like the tail-end of a cloudburst.

"Still out there?" There was more amusement than annoyance in his tone.

"Sometime this morning," she said with forced control, "I am expected to report to work. Before then, however, there are some trifling personal necessities I must attend to—if you will concede," she was shouting now, "that I am entitled to the use of my bathroom!"

"Temper, temper!" he chided. "*Our* bathroom." His voice was mockingly placating as the doorknob turned. "After all, I'm as much inconvenienced as you. But do I go around shouting?"

The door swung open and a large white towel, briskly rubbing nothing, swept past her and into the bedroom.

"You could at least move out," she said, following the towel and squinting as though she might find something else to direct her words to, "before the whole base discovers I'm sharing my apartment with a Coefficient A man who's on the B-Shift!"

The towel fluttered down and draped itself across the back of a chair.

"It could be worse," he suggested. "Suppose I were Coefficient B, like you. Then they'd really have something to waggle their tongues about." The disembodied voice receded as its owner crossed the room.

"Please move out!" she begged.

"Back to the shuttle? Uh-uh. *You* move out."

"This is my apartment and you aren't going to tell me—"

"Ah-ah! Watch that blood pressure, sweetheart!"

A dresser drawer opened and, a moment later, closed. Then another. But, naturally, she couldn't see any of the things he was withdrawing; they were Displacemant A articles so they could co-exist in the same space with her clothes.

For a long while, she was silent, trying to control her rage, not caring that time was slipping by and she would be even later for work. If she could only do *something*!

The locker door opened and the light went on inside, il-luminating her clothes on the racks—the same racks that held his things, only on a different level of existence.

Smiling vengefully, she went stealthily forward, until she realized she and her personal effects were as immaterial and invisible to him as he was to her. Then she lunged across the remaining distance and slammed the door, locking it.

"Now," she said triumphantly, "you may come out when you agree to vacate!"

Silence.

"Otherwise you'll stay in there until the Expediter comes and straightens out this mess."

A sudden burst of laughter exploded behind her and she spun around, crying out apprehensively.

"I wondered when you'd try something like that," he chuckled.

She watched the broad impression return in the sofa cushion, straining her eyes as though she might force herself to negotiate, visually at least, the barrier between the two coefficients of existence.

Then, impulsively, she seized a vase from the dresser and hurled it.

Spilling artificial flowers, it jolted to a stop in midair above the sofa. The cushion's hollow smoothed out abruptly and the vase drifted back to its place on the dresser.

"Easy, honey! How'd you like it if I started throwing mutually existent things at you?"

Cherry waited until he left and then rushed through her shower, regaining some of the time she had lost, and hurriedly dressed with only token attention to detail.

She darted across the lobby and slammed into the Coefficient Booth. Using her B-type key, she activated the rectifiers and waited until her displacement was erased and until the door swung open. Then, once again on a normal plane of existence, she raced outside.

Fortunately there was a bus waiting at the stop. It whisked her to the Expediter's office, where she soon stood fuming in front of his desk.

"Art, how long is this going to last?"

"That man again?" Only half holding back a smile, he ran a hand over his closely cropped blond hair and came around the desk.

"You've *got* to do something!" she burst out.

"Look, Cherry—we're doing the best we can. It was the A-Shift Expediter's mistake. He's checking it through now."

"I've had enough! I'm going straight to the Coordinator!"

Art shrugged. "Can't. He's eighty-six million miles away on a survey of Rigel V–Port."

"And what am I supposed to do in the meantime?"

"You might try bearing with us and making the best of the situation. Anyway, even if we found out how the mistake was made, we couldn't do anything about it right now. The unmarried personnel quarters are all filled. We'd have to change his shift. That would upset the balance of the entire working force."

"You could make him move back aboard the shuttle," she insisted.

"The shuttle's been sent to V–Port. Don't you see, Cherry, we're helpless until the Coordinator returns? In any case, it can't be all that serious. You and this fellow are on different coefficients of existence, so it can't be a critical question of morals."

"Oh, it can't, can't it?" she said. "Just tell me who he is—how I can meet him face to face!"

Art spread his hands helplessly. "You know if he's in there by mistake, there's no way of tracking down his identity until we find out how the mistake was made. Housing assignments are restricted—a matter of preserving privacy under the apartment-sharing plan."

She drew herself up to her full five foot two. "If you thought anything of me, you'd find some way to dump him out on his neck."

"Now how can I do that?" he reasoned. "Like you, all I've got is a B-key, which makes him nonexistent to me, too, while we're in the dormitory. Taking a sock at nothing wouldn't do any good. And I don't think I could forcibly convince nothing to tell me who he is so I could settle with him outside.''

She let her chin and shoulders down. ''I give up. What am I supposed to do—place myself at the mercy of a practical joker for the rest of my time here?''

''You might try marrying me, you little hothead. Then we could move into the married persons' quarters and forget the whole thing.''

''For the twentieth time—*no*!''

''Why not, Cherry? What's wrong with me?''

She backed off and surveyed him. Actually, there wasn't anything wrong with him.

''For one thing, you don't love me,'' she accused. ''If you did, you wouldn't stand around and see me living in an apartment with another man.''

''If I clear up the mistake—if I find some way to get him out—will you marry me then?''

She turned away. ''No, Art. That's what they expect the pre-colonization force to do—marry among themselves and stay on as colonists after everything is prepared.''

''I'd forgotten,'' he said dejectedly. ''You're going to make a career out of pre-colonization.''

At Space plot, Cherry rushed across the large, circular room to her calculator console.

''Wish *I* had devastating looks,'' Madge said jokingly as she gathered up her things. ''Then I could throw away my clock, too.''

Cherry glanced up at the time. She hadn't expected to be an hour late to relieve the other girl.

''Same trouble,'' she explained. ''I went to see Art again.''

''Any results?''

She shook her head irritably and began punching coordinate figures onto the tape.

"Learn who he is?" Madge asked.

"Not yet. But I will," Cherry said resolutely. Then she drew back and stared incriminatingly at the keyboard as she surveyed a broken nail.

Madge squirmed into her coat. "I've heard of guys like that. They think it's fun—keeping a girl hopping when she can't see him any more than he can see her. Does something for their masculine ego. But just catch him away from the dormitory without his CE-A and your CE-B and he'll soon cower!"

Cherry's resolute expression slumped. "I can't find out who he is. He's protected by hidden-identity regulations."

She snatched open the top of the machine and jerked out the half-punched roll of tape. She had fed in data for at least three hyper-approach paths that would put incoming ships within frying distance of Rigel. She started over again with the first coordinates.

Madge leaned over and nudged her in the ribs. "If you can't get rid of the guy, why don't you marry him? You're already living with him, practically."

"Bright girl," Cherry said, not in the least amused.

"I'll bet *he* wouldn't frown on the suggestion if he knew his roommate was almost Miss Procyon VI."

Cherry hurled the role of tape and Madge ducked.

Then she frowned troubledly. "Why do they have to have this silly setup of Coefficient Displacements to complicate pre-colonization work?"

"Ultimate economy of space," Madge said, parroting a phrase from the Handbook. "They could put two girls in one apartment and two men in another. But then the IV–Port base would need twice as many drawers, chairs, lockers, dressers, desks and so forth. It's easier to have two shifts sharing the quarters at different times and separated on different planes of existence."

Pensively, Cherry stood before the range, watching the pot of water come to a boil. Maybe she could manage to ignore the man until the Coordinator returned. After all, she reminded herself, he wasn't really there at all, since they were assigned to different levels of existence while in the dormitory. She could hear him talk only because the air, which carried the vibrations of his voice, was mutually existent between them.

Something rammed sharply into her back and she whirled around.

"Sorry, darling," the rumbling bass voice apologized. "Didn't know you were here."

A frying pan, waist-high, circled wide around her and landed on a burner. She glared with her most annoyed expression for fully a minute before she realized the look was futile; as far as he was concerned, she wasn't really there at all.

The cupboard door swung out and a can of assorted vegetables made a descending arc to the range and began opening itself.

"Oh-h-h-h, the ship slipped out—"

"Please!" she shouted. "Please spare me that foghorn voice of yours!"

The voice stopped, but the tune continued—in a shrill, off-key whistle.

The can elevated, tipped over and poured its contents into the frying pan.

Just like a man—not knowing when to use a pot.

Eventually the whistling stopped and the fire was extinguished under the pan. A minute passed and she began hesitantly scanning the kitchen for moving articles that might betray his whereabouts.

The cupboard opened again and a canister floated over to the table and kicked off its lid. A small mound of flour levitated from the container and drifted over toward her. Puzzled, she wondered what sort of recipe would call for "a handful of flour" to be added to vegetables.

But the white mound steadied and hung motionless between her and the range.

"This is my first experience with CE-Displacement," he said thoughtfully.

She backed away. The flour advanced, following her in a half-circle around the kitchen. But how could he know where she was?

He laughed. "Imagine—you displaced a half-level above normal existence and me a half-level below."

"Three or four levels might be a better arrangement," she said uncertainly, her eyes riveted on the flour.

"Interesting, this CE-A and CE-B gimmick," he continued, "and mutually co-existent articles—like the furnishings in the apartment and the food in the kitchen."

Of course! The apron she was wearing—that was how he knew where she was! It was only one of the apartment's items that were as real to *both* of them as was the mound of flour in his hand.

"Ever consider," he suggested, "that there might be a way of seeing what you look like?"

"You wouldn't dare!"

His breath came out with a poof and the flour covered her face with a fine powder.

Stupefied, she stood staring in his direction.

"Small chin," he appraised, "upturned nose, rather high cheekbones. Hm-m-m . . . Blonde or brunette?"

Enraged, she fled from the room.

But it was only the beginning of a climactic night, she found out soon after she activated the light filters on the windows and turned on a table lamp in the living room.

She selected Brahms on the Central Relay Receiver. But

before she could return to the sofa, the Lullabye faded and a dissonant bit of syncopation replaced it.

Determinedly, she went back to the receiver and reset the dial. Even before she removed her hand, however, she felt the knob return to the other position.

Tightening her grip, she moved it back. But again it rotated in the opposite direction. Deciding she could present a better display of unruffled dignity by not creating a scene, she got a book and returned to the sofa.

But she had hardly read a paragraph before she felt the cushion under her sink considerably lower. An open magazine which she hadn't noticed before drifted up and positioned itself in front of her book.

She moved the book around in front of the magazine, but the magazine only leap-frogged over the book and once more blocked her vision.

"There are two ends to this sofa," she said with teeth-gritting politeness.

"But, darling," he protested facetiously, "there's hardly any light over there."

She snapped to her feet and stood facing the depression in the cushion. Then, in a flash of inspiration, she slammed the book shut and swung it sharply in front of her. That the volume was mutually co-existent was proved by the smack of paper against flesh.

But her satisfaction quickly melted in embarrassment before his laughter.

Frustrated, Cherry went to bed.

But only minutes later, she felt the mattress sag under his weight.

"Asleep, sweetheart?" he asked.

She didn't answer; she moved closer to the edge of the bed. There was no one there, she told herself. If she reached out, she would feel nothing except the empty space where his body—in another level of existence—held the top sheet up and away from the bottom one.

Still, it was so upsettingly real—being aware of his every move, the pull of the covers when he tugged on them, the sound of his breathing.

Abruptly, the section of the co-existent sheet that was folded back over the covers swung up and fluttered down on her face.

She started to spring erect. But his hands, given reciprocal reality by the sheet, clasped her cheeks. Then his lips pressed down firmly against hers through the cloth.

Fuming, she jumped from the bed, grapped her pillow and stomped out to the sofa, trying not to hear his chuckling.

If only she could come face to face with him outside! She would humiliate him so severely in front of everyone within earshot that he would become the laughingstock of the base and it would be impossible for him to stay on at IV–Port!

Suddenly, a plan began taking shape and a smile relaxed her face as she gave it serious consideration.

Cherry was up early the next morning and out through the Coefficient Displacement Stall before her phantom roommate was even awake. Hidden behind a plant in the outer lobby, she stood vigil with her eyes on the booth, secure in the knowledge that there was no exit from the dormitory except through the nucleo-polarizer.

There was the subtle glow of the rectifier field inside the enclosure and a small, lean man stepped out, glancing anxiously at his watch.

If she studied everyone who came through, she would at least provide herself with a list of possible suspects. And by eliminating those who didn't meet the physical specifications, she could narrow the field down to a handful.

Three women came through in quick succession, hardly allowing time for the glow to subside in the stall. Then a steady flow of workers was emerging. That was even better, Cherry realized. If she managed to spot him while the lobby was filled with witnesses, the ridicule that she would heap on him would be more humiliating.

Four more men, all the wrong sizes and shapes, and two women trailed out. Then came a stout man, but too short; next a tall man, but too thin.

She was just beginning to doubt her chance for success when she heard a whistled song coming through from somewhere on the other side of the booth. Excitedly, she added subvocal words to the tune: "The ship slipped out of . . ."

The whistling stopped. But at least she knew he would be coming through shortly.

The rectifier's glow flared, then the next suspect stepped out. He was tall and muscular, heavy but not stout. And bald, with a fringe of hair circling his head like a horseshoe . . .

Just the type! She had known all along that he would look something like that, even down to his almost contemptuous smile!

She plunged from her hiding place, swinging her handbag. It caught him full in the chest and he fell back with a grunt of surprise.

"*You're* the one, you miserable sneak!" Cherry brought the bag up in an overhanded swing and down on his head.

The last dozen or so persons who had come through the booth crowded around.

"Hide out in a girl's apartment, will you?" Her tongue worked like a lash as she aimed the bag at his face. "Try to take advantage of a clerical error!"

He retreated, but she gave him no quarter. Her bag broke and spilled; she tossed it aside and used her hard little fists.

Suddenly someone had her hands locked behind her and was pulling her away.

"Cherry, you little hot pepper!" It was Art. "You don't *know* who that is!"

She turned around. "I—I don't?"

Her confounded victim had finally recovered and was brushing himself off.

"Who is this girl, Mr. Edson?" he asked.

Art hesitated, then shrugged futilely. "This is Miss O'Day . . . Cherry, Coordinator Barton. He got back from V– Port late yesterday."

"Miss O'Day," the man repeated thoughtfully. "This is a coincidence. I was just at your apartment."

"You—you were?" Cherry smiled weakly.

"I was hoping I could catch you before you checked out on your shift."

He straightened his coat and tie. "I thought I might find a way out of your difficulty."

"That's very kind—"

"As a matter of fact, I still think I might." He turned stiffly. "Drop by at my office and we'll talk it over—say, in five or six weeks?"

Rigidly, Cherry watched the Coordinator stride off. Then, numbly, she let Art lead her to the bus stop.

"That temper is going to get you into trouble one of these days." He shook his head solicitously.

She felt frustration and despair sweep over her; then, all at once, she was crying against his chest.

"Marry me," he pleaded. "Then they'll have to put us in the permanent residence quarters. I love you, Cherry."

She blinked up angrily into his face. "Prove it! Get that—that despicable thing out of my quarters!"

"*Then* will you marry me?"

She hesitated before giving him her twenty-first no. For a moment, she had remotely considered accepting—abandoning her plans for a pre-colonization career. After all, there wouldn't be anyone like Art around when she reached the top.

"I couldn't possibly marry you now, even if I wanted to. How could I be sure I wouldn't be doing it just to escape the man in my apartment?"

"All right, Cherry. I'll see what I can do about getting him out—even if it means sidestepping some of the regulations."

But Cherry was in no mood to wait until retribution, plodding at its customary snail's pace, caught up with her immaterial room-mate—not if she could help it along.

At the end of her next recreation period, she waited on the handball court until she caught Madge reporting for physical culture before starting her day's work.

"Lend me your A-Displacement key," she urged.

Madge drew back. "Oh, no, you don't! If you're going to get in a jam, you're going to do it without my help. The Handbook says it's against regulations to swap Coefficients of Existence."

"But, Madge, don't you see that's the only way I can trap him—by cornering him in the apartment on *his* level of existence?"

The other girl's frown gave way to a mischievous grin. "Then you'll let him have it?"

"But good!"

Madge handed over the A-key. "Good luck, kid!" she applauded.

Cherry had wasted almost an hour off-shift finding Madge. But that was to her advantage. It would give Mr. What's-His-Name time to get settled in the apartment before she descended on him.

She hurried back to the dormitory and through the CE stall. Displaced on the new A-level, she strode across the inner lobby. As she turned into the corridor where her quarters were located, she saw a tall, muscular man twisting the key in her lock and entering.

Quelling her anxiety, she slowed to give him a chance to become occupied so she could take him by complete surprise.

At the door, she waited another minute, then noiselessly let herself in. He was on the other side of the room, bending down over the Central Relay Receiver!

She crept across the carpet, sweeping up a straight-back chair as she advanced.

Then she let out a triumphant cry and started the chair swinging down toward her now-material adversary. In the final second before it struck, he started to turn around.

It was Art!

The chair crashed against him and he collapsed in front of the receiver.

Confounded, she stood staring down at him, vaguely wondering . . .

No—the man's voice was a deep bass; Art's was a moderate baritone.

Then she was on her knees beside him as he sat up and shook his head groggily.

"Little hellcat," he muttered.

She steadied his head between her hands. "Art, darling—I didn't know . . . What were you doing?"

"Told you I'd see what I could manage," he mumbled. "Broke into the files to find out where your quarters were. Then got an A-Displacement key. Figured I'd catch him here. But he wasn't in, after all."

"He'll show up," she promised. "We'll get him!"

She seized his arm to help him up.

But he grunted in pain and grasped his shoulder. "Not now, we won't get him."

His fingers gingerly explored the lump on his head. "I—I— Say, you're A-Displacement too. How—"

He toppled over.

In the hospital, the doctor slipped out of his smock and came over to where Cherry stood anxiously in the corridor.

"You did a real good job on him," he said sarcastically.

"Is he badly hurt?" she asked.

"Slight concussion—plus a dislocated shoulder—plus scalp lacerations."

She started toward the room into which they had wheeled Art.

But the doctor stopped her. "He's resting now. You won't be able to see him until tomorrow."

She started slowly across Rigel IV–Port base for the dormitory, realizing remorsefully that she might have seriously hurt Art . . . and all on account of the man in her apartment!

Her regret simmered into indignation and then deepened into a glowing rage as she hastened her steps. She covered the final block in a determined stride, her arms swinging and her fists clenched.

It had gone far enough! Now she would end it. And when she got through, this Whoever-He-Was would sorely regret the day he had moved in with her!

In the Displacement Booth, she used Madge's key again, then went storming into her quarters.

"Come on out!" she challenged as she crossed the living room.

In the bedroom, she shouted, "Where are you?"

She swept into the kitchen. "I know you're somewhere!"

But there was only silence.

She *had* used Madge's A-key, hadn't she?

Jerking open the closet door, she saw only his clothes on the rack—reassurance that she was now on his level of existence.

But he was nowhere in the apartment.

Very well, then, she would find something to do until he arrived—like ripping his clothes to shreds and destroying all his personal effects.

She started with the top drawer of the dresser.


Art sat up, speechless. "That's what I said," Cherry was repeating, "I'm in love with him."

Groaning, he sank back down in the hospital bed.

"I hated him so much, I guess it backfired," she explained. "Anyway, he's the man I want to marry."

He sprang upright again. "But you can't do that!"

She paced, looking blithesomely at the ceiling. "It's his aggressiveness—his forcefulness—the way he takes over. And he's so good-natured all the time. Do you suppose he'll want to marry me, Art?"

He swung his legs over the side of the bed and sent his feet groping for his slippers.

Smiling wistfully, she returned to the bedside. "Just think, he almost drove me into marrying you. Maybe I would have, if I hadn't been afraid I was being forced into it to get away."

"But—but, Cherry, you don't understand! I love you! And—"

"He does, too. I know it. Besides, I've been living with him over a week."

"But he *doesn't* love you! I mean—look, you don't even know who he is!"

"Oh, but I do. Furthermore, I know he purposely *arranged* it so that he'd be A-Displacement but B-Shift. He was in a position to swing it that way."

"He what?"

"I went back to the apartment after I left here. I was going to tear up his clothes, just for spite." She reached into her handbag. "I found his identity card in the dresser."

She handed it to him.

He reached out with his good arm and pulled her to him. He didn't have to look at the photograph to know it was his own.

# RAYMOND E. BANKS

# THE LITTLEST PEOPLE

*At the age of ten boys and girls don't like each other very much, but ten years later (at least for most), it's a different story. People change over time, and probably one of the greatest causes of unhappiness is that the once contented partners have grown apart through change. But it is also possible that commonly shared experiences, like those of John and Gleam in this story, can promote changes that bring people even closer together.*

*Raymond E. Banks never published a science fiction novel, which may be one of the reasons that his great skill in the genre has been generally unrecognized. He certainly deserves a "Best of . . ." collection, and you should make a point of looking for his stories in anthologies and back issues of science fiction magazines.*

Whenever Old Mott came to the asteroid with his little people, I always made Dad take me with him. I was fascinated with the little people. I was too fascinated. It finally made trouble.

My father was Personnel Director of the local Asteroid Mines, Inc. diggings on our tiny planet. He was one of the most important persons under the Dome. The workers and families of Point Montana always lifted their hats and smiled to him, and it was fun to be walking beside him and see the respect he got. Only the General Manager got more, and he was bald and they kidded about "Old Hat." But no one ever kidded with my father.

We climbed up the steps of Mott's space-burned old craft with a feeling of importance, at least on my part, because no one was allowed aboard an Employment rocket except the Personnel Director of the asteroid and one or two other high officials.

Old Mott met us at the entrance and bowed and grinned, his funny, old-fashioned glasses glittering and his almost toothless mouth shapeless in the smile. Then there was a long waste of talk while they had a glass of wine together. Meanwhile I was anxiously waiting, watching the door that burned so bright in my imagination. On the other side of its prosaic gray metal the little people rested.

"No technicians," apologized Mott. "I can give you some cooks, and some helpers and some housewife-hopefuls this trip. Many fine ones."

My father shook his head. "Unskilled labor is a drug here, Mott. Like everywhere. I feel sorry for the poor devils, but I can't take any, especially the housewife-hopefuls."

Old Mott looked disappointed. "Some of these people have been in space for many years," he muttered. "Too many. It ain't fair, Chet."

"Send them back to Earth."

Old Mott shook his head and sighed. Finally he and my father rose, and we went into the heavily locked room where the little people were.

Old Mott had them arranged by profession. It was a small room, not over ten by ten, and three walls were filled with shelves. The little people were propped up along the shelves, with tiny name-plates beneath each one. They were about seven inches high and stood rigid like so many dolls. Only they weren't dolls; they were real people.

They were the poor, the unskilled, the have-not hopefuls. They couldn't get jobs on Earth. They couldn't pay their way to the planets. So they signed contracts with Greater New York Employment or one of those outfits and traveled from planet to planet and out through the asteroids looking for work. In one of these Employment ships, when they were reduced in size, you could get a couple of hundred; and as little people they needed very little food or oxygen. Full-sized in life, the ship wouldn't take two dozen. And so they traveled, in a fitful sleep, reduced in size, reduced in hope, trying to find a place to work and settle down and make a home.

Old Mott covered his stocks of little people with cellophane. That was so when Father or anybody picked one up, it wouldn't get dirty from handling. Sometimes you almost thought their tiny eyes watched you. Other times, you couldn't be sure. In reduction they were supposed to sleep, with the agent doing all of the interviewing for them.

I wandered down the aisles, staring at the little people from Earth, while my father and Old Mott argued about a handful of laborers—all that Dad was going to buy this trip.

I was never allowed to touch the stock. It was a very important rule. Everybody felt a little ashamed about the little people and was sorry because they couldn't find a place to live. You were very careful not to handle them unnecessarily.

But down on the end one of them had fallen on the floor. I picked it up. It was a woman, maybe a girl. She was staring right at me with bold blue eyes and a smile. I would swear that she looked at me and winked. Hands trembling to feel that unspeakable warm life in my hand, I hastened to put her back on the shelf.

There was no place for her. Old Mott was getting pretty old at the time, and, I guess, careless. All the spots were filled and he must have let her fall to the floor and his weak old eyes didn't see her.

I wondered how long she'd been there.

I walked back to where my father and Old Mott were. My father and the old man had selected three laborers and were studying them through magnifying glasses, my father telling Old Mott how defective they were, and Old Mott insisting that they were real good merchandise. Just as I came up to them there was a commotion outside the ship. Some men yelled. I was curious; but I wanted to tell Old Mott about the tiny woman first.

"Father—"

"Please, son," said my father. "Don't interrupt."

He was always touchy in the little room. It was, I think, the aura of failure and hopelessness. It was the embarrassment of having to touch and handle and scan the tiny bodies of other people less fortunate than him, and deciding their fates in dollars and cents.

"Mr. Mott—"

"Go see who's climbing the ship, son," he ordered without looking. "I haven't got much time left. I'm due back on Mars Friday—"

I should have put the tiny figure on the table. But there was an unholy fascination in holding that hot little figure in my hand—a person born before me, an adult, and here she was a tiny foot-ruler of life in my hand. So I went out to see what the trouble was about, still holding her.

It was the Sheriff. He was herding along two men who hadn't worked out well on the asteroid. He had them in handcuffs, and they were fighting and cursing as he prodded them into the ship. My father and Old Mott came out and set down on the table the three tiny figures my father had chosen.

Then Old Mott and the Sheriff and my father dragged the two men into the Converter and shut the door. I could hear the explosive cries of the rejected men who had gotten into trouble on our asteroid. Then the machinery cut over them, whining with a scary sound that made me shake all over. Once I heard a scream.

Pretty soon they all came out again. The Sheriff went away, saying, "I hope you pick better ones this time, Mr. Blake."

Old Mott had two tiny figures in his hands. He wrapped them in cellophane and put them in his pocket.

"It'll be a cold day in January before I sell *them* two again," he said. "They been getting into trouble everywhere I take 'em. Let 'em cool for a while."

Then he and my father took the three new little figures and went back in the Converter. The machinery whined again, but this time it sounded different. Pretty soon they came out, and I blinked. I always blinked when I saw those tiny figures go into the Converter and come out twice as big as me, full-sized and smiling and being real deferential to Father.

"This is wonderful, Mr. Blake," said one. "We'll sure work hard, Mr. Mott."

"It was real kind of you to take us on, Mr. Blake," said another. "We ain't never had a chance before."

They looked at my father with smiles that tried too hard, and held their hats in their hands and bobbed their heads. You could see the whites of their eyes like a dog's. They wore the faded blues and reds of workers, and they were clumsy on their feet after so many months of being little. They were young, but they looked old and tired, and I had to swallow in my throat when they looked out of the window and saw how small and gray our little asteroid was, and how they kept on smiling and bowing, and swallowing their disappointment at their new home.

Father smiled back at them, but he'd heard it all before. Some of them would start drinking. Some of them would get in trouble with women. Some of them would get bored and make trouble. Not one in ten ever really liked our asteroid and really became one of us.

Maybe it was partly our fault, because it made a big difference how you came to the asteroid. If you came in a regular rocket, full-sized and with luggage, it was easier. Those were the engineers and doctors and scientists, and they were important in the Dome. But the little people made big lived on the sides of the Dome, where there was less oxygen, and they didn't ever make much or have much.

My father and I said good-bye to Mr. Mott and climbed down the loading ladder. Old Mott peered after us through his glasses and smiled and waved, and my father waved the contracts up at him—the contracts that said that Father would deduct Old Mott's money from the laborers' wages every month, and also pay the Greater New York Employment its fee.

Then we started back for Point Montana, the new workers unsteady on their legs and still trying to be nice. My father walked between them, bracing them with his arms, and answered their questions, I brought up the rear.

And that night, nearly eight years ago, when I got home, I found Gleam in my pocket. I had forgotten to give her back to Old Mott, I had stolen one of the little people.

Naturally, I didn't know what to do with her—until I went in my sister's playroom and saw her dolls. Then I gave her to my sister Kate and told her that it was a new kind of doll, a used-up little person that Old Mott had given me on the promise that I wouldn't tell the folks. I swore her to secrecy.

Kate jumped up and down, hugging the little figure in cellophane. "She gleams," she cried, "I'll call her Gleam."

For a while she played with Gleam like her other dolls, and our folks didn't notice because on Point Montana there was less power and fewer appliances and we all had to work—even my mother had to do her own washing by hand—and so we kids were left pretty much to entertain ourselves.

I figured Kate would get tired of Gleam and I could return her to Old Mott on his next trip. I worried quite a lot in the meantime, because I knew they had rigid laws about handling the little people.

The very day Old Mott came back, Kate brought Gleam to me.

"Look," she said. "I was dumping my stuff in the toy box, and your dump-truck fell on her."

There was something wrong with one of the legs. Gleam had straight, slim legs—but now one of them was oddly crooked. I ran to Dad's library and got the magnifying glass.

Gleam was good-looking, with a curved generous mouth that smiled and blue eyes that always had a far-off look of waking sleep. But now she was turning the lips in, and the cheek hollows stood out in pain, and there was sweat on her forehead. The blue eyes were closed. I got scared. I knew she was going to die.

"I'm going to tell Mother," said Kate, looking at my face and beginning to whimper. "I didn't bring her here, and I don't like her any more."

"All right, stupid, tell her," I said in misery. I was thinking what it would be like to go to prison—but Kate wouldn't understand that.

"Mom will probably stop our going to the videopix for three months," I said. That was something she could understand.

Kate stopped whimpering. "You can have her," she said. "You can do whatever you want. I won't say anything."

I didn't plan to give her back to Old Mott before I asked some questions. I casually asked him about the whole process, and then about injuries to the little people. He'd been reduced once himself, a long time ago.

"Don't feel a thing," he said. "The Converter goes on, and you go to sleep while your molecules close up and a lot of water is taken out of you. Then you just drift and dream, slow, lazy, easylike, until you get your full size again."

"What if they got hurt?"

"It might wake 'em up," he chuckled. "But ain't nobody gonna buy damaged goods, so they just better not get hurt."

That scared me more. If I gave her back to him, he couldn't get her a job now.

"Say, Chet," he asked my father, "I didn't leave a girl with you last time, did I? I got one missin'. Cute little blonde, she was.''

My father smiled and shook his head. ''You know I never take the cute ones. They only get the men to fighting, and make trouble. You probably bootlegged her to some slave-trader.''

Old Mott laughed and winked and said he'd filled out a missing persons report, but, for all of him, one missing was just one less to worry about.

''Won't they—won't they send you to prison for that?'' I asked, round-eyed.

Old Mott roared. ''Prison? Naw, son, who cares about the little people?''

After that, I was determined not to give her back to him.

I got a first aid book and set Gleam's leg, using some of Mom's nailboards for splints. Then I put her in a pigeon-hole in my desk in my room, so I could check up on her. I even fed her with an eye-dropper like I'd seen Old Mott do once.

''Sugar and water once every month,'' he had once said. ''God, ain't it a shame us reliable folk got to eat so much expensive stuff when they get by on sugar and water?''

It was about two weeks after that when I got my next shock. I had checked on Gleam and found her eyes open and her face back to normal. Since she didn't move at all, I figured her leg was healing.

Then one night I sat down to do my homework and found a scrap of paper on my desk in front of the pigeon-hole. I could see some tiny scratches on it—some writing. I got the magnifying glass, my heart thumping.

''An injury might wake 'em up,'' Old Mott had said. I read the note: *Littl boy. You brok my leg. Give me bak to the Mployment.*

With trembling hands, I pulled her out of the pigeon-hole. I could feel the warmth of her body, and felt that I could even see her breathe. She was awake! I looked at her through the magnifying glass and tried to talk to her, but I could see the tiny head shake. She kept trying to raise her hand, and at last I saw she wanted the pencil.

*Littl boy*, she wrote in tiny, tiny script. *I cant heer you. Rite me note. Reel small note.*

I guessed then that my voice must sound like roaring in her ears.

I wrote her: *I can't give you back till the next employment rocket. Are you all right?*

She wrote: *I hurt. Im lonly. I want to go home.*

At that point I felt very sorry for her, and I felt guilty too. I held my breath while she took off the splint and tried her leg.

She moved slowly and with a limp. She walked the whole length of the desk, but the limp didn't go away. She put her hands to her tiny blond head and shook as if in terror.

Wide-eyed, I pushed the writing pad to her.

*I'm rooned*, she wrote in panic. *I limp. Littl boy youve rooned my life.*

*Maybe it'll get better*, I told her, sick myself.

*I was beetiful*, she wrote, *but whos gone marry a crippld girl?*

I was utterly miserable. Her leg looked all right, but the limp wouldn't go away. In my childlike reasoning, I had ruined her life, and in my guilt I didn't know what to do. I couldn't tell Old Mott; I couldn't tell my father. Through damaging her leg, I had deprived her of a chance to get hired through Employment, and my father was the kind of man who took grim satisfaction in his principles.

"We are leaders," he would say, "and we must have principles. I would as soon send my own son to prison as allow injustice to pass."

It was this shuddery thought of his detached anger that imprisoned me with my problem. The only thing I could think of was to make Gleam into a schoolteacher. Miss Griswold, our teacher, had a withered arm and was very old. She was saving up to return to Earth. I figured that when I got to be a little older and understudied my father in his job as Personnel Director, I could take care of Gleam, and it wouldn't matter if she limped. Such is the selfish judgment of tender years.

I told Gleam of my idea.

*No*, she wrote. *I was waittres. I dont want scool. I will kill you if you dont let me go.*

I thought her threat was idle.

Late at night, there is a change of machinery in the asteroid Dome. All the lights go off, and the oxygen goes up, and they blow the scent of mountain pine trees through the ventilators. I remember waking in the middle of the night with a weight on my chest, and drawing the pure air into my lungs and feeling that something was horribly wrong.

Gleam stood on my chest. Her figure was silhouetted against the dim starlight outside my window. She had my pocketknife. She was throwing her whole weight on it to stab me with the open blade, and before I could stop her, it plunged into my chest.

I screamed. Stupid, ignorant, revengeful Gleam—she had meant her threat of killing me!

When my parents came running, I clutched her hot body in my hand under the covers. I could feel my own blood on my pajamas and I was scared and sick and angry. But the act of pulling up the covers had dislodged the knife, and I realized that I was not seriously hurt.

I told my parents I'd had a nightmare.

"Dreaming of the little people," my mother said to my father. "You see, I told you he was too young to go on the Employment Rocket!"

My father shrugged and insisted that a son of his should be strong-minded, and they went back to bed.

I got up on the edge of my bed and leaned over and vomited,

feeling hatred and an underlying abysmal guilt toward the soft, squirming thing I held in my hands.

From the moment she plunged the knife blade in me, I was filled with anger and determination that she would not ruin my life, even by revealing her existence to my parents, who, I thought, would send me to prison. My idea of making her into a schoolteacher and hiring her to replace Miss Griswold, when I should have the power in a few years, grew from a promise snatched out of the air into real purpose.

She objected violently, first crying and then cursing me so loudly that I could faintly hear the words. As I heard the squeaking vileness pour from her tiny lips, my hate toward her deepened into an almost holy reverence for my mission. She had been a poor girl; she had not had much education; she only wanted to marry and settle down, or at least get a job as a waitress, which was the only thing she knew.

My feeling of pity for all the little folk, embarrassment at their poor possessions and awkward ways and helplessness, centered on her—her shallow and vile being. As I chained her to the desk with a solid gold-plated watch-chain that night, I had accepted the problem of her existence.

Next evening I went to work.

*You are still good-looking*, I wrote her, *but you are stupid. I will make you less stupid. I will teach you how to be as smart and polite as Mrs. Ellensberg, the Chief Chemist's wife.*

Thus stirred by my emotions of fear, anger and pity, I laid out her schedule. When she refused to cooperate, I took the tiny arm and twisted it until she screamed. After that, she did what I wanted.

The period of childhood has a prisonlike quality of do's and don'ts and my own discipline had been no less severe than that which I passed on to her. I made her do my homework with me; I made her take exercise; and every night promptly at nine, I shut her in my bureau drawer.

In no other home on Point Montana could I have gotten away

with it. But my parents were very busy people, and they left their children to amuse themselves, seldom even coming into our rooms. My sister Kate, of course, knew all about Gleam; but she was under my control, as younger sisters often are, and the secret was kept.

Of course, there were crises. One time my parents found the cat with its throat slit. I had to talk fast to get out of that one. I was going to put Gleam on bread and water for that sin, but when I saw the long, deep scratches that the cat had given her in its playful way, I said nothing.

Then there was the time that she got loose and filled her thimble with Father's wine. I usually fed her with scraps from the table, for sugar and water wouldn't do for Gleam now that she moved around and was awake. I kept the thimble in her drawer for her to have her milk in.

She came weaving into the study, slopping wine out of her thimble and singing a song that astounded my unsophisticated ears.

"Little boy," she said in her tiny voice, "I'm going to spit in your eye." She stood on her tiptoes, her blond hair hanging loose, laughing. "Wow, what a party," she cried enthusiastically. "What a crime!"

I barely had time to scoop her up and hide her in the bureau before my father came snooping suspiciously into the room.

He smiled when he saw me with a thimbleful of wine.

"The young must learn by imitation," he said, "but you'll never get in much trouble if you only take a thimbleful at a time, John."

Then he gave me my first real wineglass full of wine, and I knew I was growing up.

We had a man-to-man talk in his study that night, about my future and my relations with Lucy Ellensberg, whom I had dated at school, and how I would go to work in Employment after I had been to school on Ceres. I almost told him about Gleam then, but when I started to talk about the little people, he got a pained look in his eye.

"I'm sorry, John," he said, "but you mustn't go overboard for them. They're people—but they're ignorant, superstitious and undisciplined. They must be treated differently."

Afterward, back in my room, I found Gleam crying in the bureau drawer. She was still drunk.

"I am going to kill myself, little boy," she wept. "Nobody loves me."

"You have a home here," I told her. "You are being trained for a good job. Soon you'll be able to teach school and marry someone who doesn't mind your limp."

She shook her head. "Someday you'll pay for this, little boy," she said, and then hiccuped and fell over and went to sleep. I couldn't help grinning. I reached in and brushed back her hair and eased her tiny figure into a more comfortable position.

It was when I went to school on Ceres that the change took place. Up until that time Gleam was like a pet, very little more to me than a frog or dog. But on Ceres, I had my first real drunk and my first real date; on Ceres it was I who didn't want to work, feeling the freedom of a real city, strange people, exciting things.

Gleam became my conscience. And I didn't particularly like it.

I had taken her to Ceres with many misgivings, not because I wanted to but because I was afraid to leave her behind. There were many other little people there, kept by the people of Ceres as pets just as I kept Gleam. Most of them were alcoholics or the demented who did not wish to become big again. So I was able to keep Gleam openly.

And now, at least, I began to think of getting rid of her.

The second day, I was walking down the astonishingly wide street with its gash of neon red and blue and green signs. Gleam, as usual, was standing in my pocket and leaning her elbows on the edge as she looked out. We came to the Ceres office of the Greater New York Employment. Suddenly, I stopped.

"Gleam," I said, speaking softly and a little high-pitched, the way I'd found she could best understand me. "Maybe it's time for you to be big again."

"No! Not now, little boy, it isn't time."

The tiny voice was almost a cry of terror. Something about it puzzled me.

When I asked her what was wrong, she wouldn't talk to me.

That night, I told my roommate, Rand, about it.

He shrugged. "They get afraid. They get used to being taken care of. She won't ever want to be big again."

Now, for the first time, I was eager to get rid of Gleam; and she wouldn't go. She put on airs on Ceres. She acted very strangely, insisting on complete privacy for dressing and undressing, and when we traveled she preferred to ride on my neck, holding onto my ear and shouting wry comments at me.

"That Alice you been eyeing," she said one day. "She's a common slut. You've got a future at Point Montana; she's after you. Better watch out, little boy."

"I can take care of myself."

"Those clothes!" she laughed, pointing to another girl that I had been trying to be introduced to. "She dresses like a waitress. And listen to her language! Split infinitives and dangling participles all over the place. One would do well to ignore these street-women, little boy!"

After that, I didn't dare ask the girl for a date.

Gleam helped me with my lessons. She goaded me into doing them. She criticized my clothes and my manners and, since she knew cities and I did not, even told me where to go around the town. This was annoying to me—but with her help I did well in school, and, due to her knowledge of the seamier side of life, achieved a certain fame among my contemporaries as a man of the world.

She became increasingly meddlesome, and we had arguments often. Especially when I had dates and left her behind I would come home to find her pacing my desk. "Well," she would sneer, "did the little darling find out how much you will make and how big a home you own and how much money your family has in the bank?"

"Never mind."

"You're an idiot, little boy. You have apples for brains."

We finally had it out on my last week at school.

"Gleam," I said, "when I go back, I'll have to get married, you know. That is, I can't hold a job in Employment unless I'm married. And Lucy Ellensberg is sort of—"

"What happens to me?" she cried.

"You'll have to get big and get a job. I kept you because I ruined your life. But in our house you've learned enough to get by as a schoolteacher or a governess. You've learned how the other half lives. I've paid for my sin in stealing you and breaking your leg."

"You could do better than Lucy Ellensberg!"

"I don't want to do better."

She picked up her thimble and tossed off the spate of beer I'd poured for her.

"There's me, for instance," she said. "After all, I know your habits—"

I burst into laughter. "You! Marry you! Why, Gleam, I think of you as a sister, with your bad leg and—"

Then I stopped laughing. Because she was staring at me with something in her tiny eyes that I'd never seen before. All the years, we'd fought every step of the way. I had found her vile and obscene. She had found me childishly cruel. I had made her life hell at home, and she had made mine hell on Ceres. Always it had been with a veiled contempt on both sides.

But this time her look was different.

"I'm sorry, John. I'm sorry you said that."

Before, I had always been "Little Boy." And I had always

called her Gleam, because I knew her real name was impossibly corny.

My chest felt hot. I was embarrassed. "I'm sorry too, Millicent," I said. "But this is as far as we can go together."

The next day I took her to Employment, and she didn't complain. A thick distance lay between us.

They accepted her. The last time I ever saw tiny Gleam was as she strode importantly up and down the Director's desk, limping but waving her hands in earnest and giving them complete instructions on the important job she wanted. Somewhere far away.

"As far away as possible from provincial bumpkins like John Blake!" she cried to the Director. "You will make a good deal of money from me, my good man!"

His jaw dropped, and the others in the room gathered around the self-important, strutting little figure as I slipped out to freedom.

I was oddly disturbed at the parting, yet oddly pleased. The years of discipline had paid off for Gleam. She'd always had a good brain, just an undeveloped one; now she was fast, capable, bursting with confidence. I knew she'd get along.

The next months were exceedingly enjoyable. For the first time in more than seven years, I didn't have to worry about Gleam. At first, I missed the business of feeding her and taking care of her wants; but far more than that I enjoyed being able to exercise privacy. I read what I wanted, kept the hours that I wanted, and dated the girls I wanted.

Finally I returned to start my new job in Employment on Point Montana.

"I won't ask too many questions about Ceres," smiled my father, who was noticeably older. "You seem to have matured astonishingly for your age. Ceres was good for you, John. By the way, Lucy Ellensberg is coming over for supper tonight."

I had anticipated that night for a long time. Lucy seemed

lovely; she had charm and manners; I was only a little disappointed to see how much her thoughts revolved around petty matters of the Point, and how soft and selfish she seemed.

It was all very routine. We were alone; the night lights of Point Montana gleamed in fuzzy softness; we stood in my parents' tiny garden and smelled the pine scent of the ventilators, and I proposed and was accepted.

"We'll live in a small house by the edge of the Dome at first," I told her. "I want to get the feel of the workmen's lives, since I'll be hiring them."

"Well," she said dubiously. "Only for a very short time, John. After all, there's our part of the social calendar to keep up!"

"And then we'll have to get started on a family."

She laughed: "Later, John. It's all right for you—you've been out to see the world and had your fling. But for me it's the first time away from home. I want parties! I want to learn to get drunk and have some real fun—"

It went on that way, and suddenly I saw Lucy as she really was. Suddenly I realized that Gleam had left her mark on me, despite her ignorance of social ways. In day-to-day close contact with Gleam's adult mind, I had gone a long way past the kids of my own age on the Point.

Lucy would be fine when she grew up a little more.

After she left, I noted that we had been standing near the spot where I had buried the cat Gleam had killed many years before. Alone in the garden, smoking a cigarette, I stared up through the Dome at the stars and wondered what Gleam was doing that night. It was certain that she wasn't worrying about the size of house she lived in—Gleam hungered for any sort of shack of her own.

What would I do if Gleam should come this way again? I didn't know. Up until tonight, I'd thought I had planned my life with Lucy.

I remembered then that the Greater New York Employment rocket was due next week, and I put out my cigarette and went in, a sort of expectant fear surging inside.

My father and I were there when the rocket landed. Old Mott was dead, of course, but young Billy Stanger grinned and poured the wine, and we sat and talked while I leafed through the list of names and occupations on the printed sheets. Trying to look casual, I turned to the "Schoolteachers" section.

*Millicent Hamm* leaped out of the page at me.

I kept my voice steady, but I couldn't keep excitement out of it.

"I need a schoolteacher," I said. I thrust the paper at him. "Try this one. I'm sure she'll be all right. I won't go in the room if you don't mind. Just put her through the Converter."

Employment people see much, say little. Stanger nodded and went out. Presently he came out of the stock room, carrying something in his hand, and went into the Converter. I heard the machinery squeal and slowly got to my feet. The door opened.

For comfort she was wearing briefies of pleasing black and white, bootlets, and a ribbon in her hair. The eyes were hard and suspicious, stuffed with a knowledge of me. The legs were youthful and graceful, but there was a slight limp. She was tall, a walking dream from my memories, barely three inches shorter than I, moving with assurance and poise.

The Gleam I had made stood and stared at the John Blake she had made.

"Well, little boy," she said in a voice that sounded loud because I'd always heard it thinner, "I see you got trapped in this forlorn dump for the rest of your life."

"So have you," I said, walking toward her. My father and Stanger were staring.

She raised her arms. Her eyes got wet.

"So have I," said the new Gleam.

# JOHN D. MACDONALD

# RING AROUND THE REDHEAD

*Many readers will recognize John D. MacDonald as a world-famous author of mystery novels, but relatively few are aware that in the late 1940's and early 1950's he was one of the finest science fiction writers. "Ring Around the Redhead" is an outstanding example of his great talent.*

*Adversity is not something we look forward to, but it does have certain benefits. It helps us realize the value of many things we take for granted, and overcoming it gives us a feeling of self-confidence. Seeing how another person reacts to adversity, especially if we have strong emotional feelings toward him or her, can (as in this story) provide us with important clues about what kind of a person we are involved with.*

The prosecuting attorney was a lean specimen named Amery Heater. The buildup given the murder trial by the newspapers had resulted in a welter of open-mouthed citizens who jammed the golden oak courtroom.

Bill Maloney, the defendant, was sleepy and bored. He knew he had no business being bored. Not with twelve righteous citizens who, under the spell of Amery Heater's quiet, confidential oratory were beginning to look at Maloney as though he were a fiend among fiends.

112 • LOVE 3000


The August heat was intense and flies buzzed around the upper sashes of the dusty windows. The city sounds drifted in the open windows, making it necessary for Amery Heater to raise his voice now and again.

But though Bill Maloney was bored, he was also restless and worried. Mostly he was worried about Justin Marks, his own lawyer.

Marks cared but little for this case. But, being Bill Maloney's best friend, he couldn't very well refuse to handle it. Justin Marks was a proper young man with a Dewey mustache and frequent daydreams about Justice Marks of the Supreme Court. He somehow didn't feel that the Maloney case was going to help him very much.

Particularly with the very able Amery Heater intent on getting the death penalty.

The judge was a puffy old citizen with signs of many good years at the brandy bottle, the hundreds of gallons of which surprisingly had done nothing to dim the keenness of eye or brain.

Bill Maloney was a muscular young man with a round face, a round chin and a look of sleepy skepticism. A sheaf of his coarse, corn-colored hair jutted out over his forehead. His eyes were clear, deep blue.

He stifled a yawn, remembering what Justin Marks had told him about making a good impression on the jury. He singled out a plump lady juror in the front row and winked solemnly at her. She lifted her chin with an audible sniff.

No dice there. Might as well listen to Amery Heater.

" . . . and we, the prosecution, intend to prove that on the evening of July tenth, William Howard Maloney did murderously attack his neighbor, James Finch and did kill James Finch by crushing his skull. We intend to prove there was a serious dispute between these men, a dispute that had continued for some time. We further intend to prove that the cause of this dispute was the dissolute life being led by the defendant.''

Amery Heater droned on and on. The room was too hot. Bill Maloney slouched in his chair and yawned. He jumped when Justin Marks hissed at him. Then he remembered that he had yawned and he smiled placatingly at the jury. Several of them looked away, hurriedly.

Fat little Doctor Koobie took the stand. He was sworn in and Amery Heater, polite and respectful, asked questions which established Koobie's name, profession and presence at the scene of the ''murder'' some fifty minutes after it had taken place.

''And now, Dr. Koobie, would you please describe in your own words exactly what you found.''

Koobie hitched himself in his chair, pulled his trousers up a little over his chubby knees and said, ''No need to make this technical. I was standing out by the hedge between the two houses. I was on Jim Finch's side of the hedge. There was a big smear of blood around. Some of it was spattered on the hedge. Barberry, I think. On the ground there was some hunks of brain tissue, none of them bigger than a dime. Also a piece of scalp maybe two inches square. Had Jim's hair on it all right. Proved that in the lab. Also found some pieces of bone. Not many.'' He smiled peacefully. ''Guess old Jim is dead all right. No question of that. Blood was his and the hair was his.''

Three jurors swallowed visibly and a fourth began to fan himself vigorously.

Koobie answered a few other questions and then Justin Marks took over the cross-examination.

''What would you say killed Jim Finch?''

Many people gasped at the question, having assumed that the defense would be that, lacking a body, there was no murder.

Koobie put a fat finger in the corner of his mouth, took it out again. ''Couldn't rightly say.''

''Could a blow from a club or similar weapon have done it?''

''Good Lord, no! Man's head is a pretty durable thing. You'd have to back him up against a solid concrete wall and bust him with a full swing with a baseball bat and you still wouldn't do that much hurt. Jim was standing right out in the open.''

"Dr. Koobie, imagine a pair of pliers ten feet along and proportionately thick. If a pair of pliers like that were to have grabbed Mr. Finch by the head, smashing it like a nut-cracker, could it have done that much damage?''

Koobie pulled his nose, tugged on his ear, frowned and said, ''Why, if it clamped down real sudden like, I imagine it could. But where'd Jim go?''

"That's all, thank you,'' Justin Marks said.

Amery Heater called other witnesses. One of them was Anita Hempflet.

Amery said, ''You live across the road from the defendant?''

Miss Anita Hempflet was fiftyish, big-boned, and of the same general consistency as the dried beef recommended for Canadian canoe trips. Her voice sounded like fingernails on the third grade blackboard.

"Yes I do. I've lived there thirty-five years. That Maloney person, him sitting right over there, moved in two years ago, and I must say that I . . .''

"You are able to see Mr. Maloney's house from your windows?''

"Certainly!''

"Now tell the court when it was that you first saw the redheaded woman.''

She licked her lips. ''I first saw that . . . that woman in May. A right pleasant morning it was, too. Or it was until I saw her. About ten o'clock, I'd say. She was right there in Maloney's front yard, as bold as brass. Had on some sort of shiny silver thing. You couldn't call it a dress. Too short for that. Didn't half cover her the way a lady ought to be covered. Not by half. She was . . .''

"What was she doing?''

"Well, she come out of the house and she stopped and looked

around as though she was surprised at where she was. My eyes are good. I could see her face. She looked all around. Then she sort of slouched, like she was going to keel over or something. She walked real slow down toward the gate. Mr. Maloney came running out of the house and I heard him yell to her. She stopped. Then he was making signs to her, for her to go back into the house. Just like she was deaf or something. After a while she went back in. I guessed she probably was made deaf by that awful bomb thing the government lost control of near town three days before that.''

''You didn't see her again?''

''Oh, I saw her plenty of times. But after that she was always dressed more like a girl should be dressed. Far as I could figure out, Mr. Maloney was buying her clothes in town. It wasn't right that anything like that should be going on in a nice neighborhood. Mr. Finch didn't think it was right either. Runs down property values, you know.''

''In your knowledge, Miss Hempflet, did Mr. Maloney and the deceased ever quarrel?''

''They started quarreling a few days after that woman showed up. Yelling at each other across the hedge. Mr. Finch was always scared of burglars. He had that house fixed up so nobody could get in if he didn't want them in. A couple of times I saw Bill Maloney pounding on his door and rapping on the windows. Jim wouldn't pay any attention.''

Justin cross-examined.

''You say, Miss Hempflet, that the defendant was going down and shopping for this woman, buying her clothes. In your knowledge, did he buy her anything else?''

Anita Hempflet sniggered. ''Say so! Guess she must of been feeble minded. I asked around and found out he bought a blackboard and chalk and some kids' books.''

''Did you make any attempt to find out where this woman came from, this woman who was staying with Mr. Maloney?''

"Should say I did! I know for sure that she didn't come in on the train or Dave Wattle would've seen her. If she'd come by bus, Myrtle Gisco would have known it. Johnny Farness didn't drive her in from the airport. I figure that any woman who'd live openly with a man like Maloney must have hitchhiked into town. She didn't come any other way."

"That's all, thank you," Justin Marks said.

Maloney sighed. He couldn't understand why Justin was looking so worried. Everything was going fine. According to plan. He saw the black looks the jury was giving him but he wasn't worried. Why, as soon as they found out what had actually happened, they'd be all for him. Justin Marks seemed to be sweating.

He came back to the table and whispered to Bill, "How about temporary insanity?"

"I guess it's okay if you like that sort of thing."

"No. I mean as a plea!"

Maloney stared at him. "Justy, old boy. Are you nuts? All we have to do is tell the truth."

Justin Marks rubbed his mustache with his knuckle and made a small bleating sound that acquired him a black look from the judge.

Amery Heater built his case up very cleverly and very thoroughly. In fact, the jury had Bill Maloney so definitely electrocuted that they were beginning to give him sad looks—full of pity.

It took Amery Heater two days to complete his case. When it was done, it was a solid and shining structure, every discrepancy explained—everything pinned down. Motive. Opportunity. Everything.

On the morning of the third day, the court was tense with expectancy. The defense was about to present its case. No one knew what the case was, except, of course, Bill Maloney, Justin

Marks, and the unworldly redhead who called herself Reja-pachalandakeena. Bill called her Keena. She hadn't appeared in court.

Justin Marks stood up and said to the hushed court, "Your Honor. Rather than summarize my defense at this point, I would like to put William Maloney on the stand first and let him tell the story in his own words."

The court buzzed. Putting Maloney on the stand would give Amery Heater a chance to cross-examine. Heater would rip Maloney to tiny shreds. The audience licked its collective chops.

"Your name?"

"William Maloney, Twelve Braydon Road."

"And your occupation?"

"Tinkering. Research, if you want a fancy name."

"Where do you get your income?"

"I've got a few gimmicks patented. The royalties come in."

"Please tell the court all you know about this crime of which you are accused. Start at the beginning, please."

Bill Maloney shoved the blond hair back off his forehead with a square, mechanic's hand and smiled cheerfully at the jury. Some of them, before they realized it, had smiled back. They felt the smiles on their lips and sobered instantly. It wasn't good form to smile at a vicious murderer.

Bill slouched in the witness chair and laced his fingers across his stomach.

"It all started," he said, "the day the army let that rocket get out of hand on the seventh of May. I've got my shop in my cellar. Spend most of my time down there.

"That rocket had an atomic warhead, you know. I guess they've busted fifteen generals over that affair so far. It exploded in the hills forty miles from town. The jar upset some of my apparatus and stuff. Put it out of kilter. I was sore.

"I turned around, cussing away to myself, and where my coal

bin used to be, there was a room. The arch leading into the room was wide and I could see in. I tell you, it really shook me up to see that room there. I wondered for a minute if the bomb hadn't given me delusions.

"The room I saw didn't have any furniture in it. Not like furniture we know. It had some big cubes of dull silvery metal, and some smaller cubes. I couldn't figure out the lighting.

"Being a curious cuss, I walked right through the arch and looked around. I'm a great one to handle things. The only thing in the room I could pick up was a gadget on top of the biggest cube. It hardly weighed a thing.

"In order to picture it, you've got to imagine a child's hoop made of silvery wire. Then right across the wire imagine the blackest night you've ever seen, rolled out into a thin sheet and stretched tight like a drumhead on that wire hoop.

"As I was looking at it I heard some sort of deep vibration and there I was, sumbling around in my coal bin. The room was gone. But I had that darn hoop in my hand. That hoop with the midnight stretched across it.

"I took it back across to my workbench where the light was better. I held it in one hand and poked a finger at that black stuff. My finger went right through. I didn't feel a thing. With my finger still sticking through it, I looked on the other side.

"It was right there that I named the darn thing. I said, 'Gawk!' And that's what I've called it ever since. The Gawk. My finger didn't come through on the other side. I stuck my whole arm through. No arm. I pulled it back out. Quick. Arm was okay. Somehow it seemed warm on the other side of the gawk.

"Well, you can imagine what it was like for me, a tinkerer, to get my hands on a thing like that. I forgot all about meals and so on. I had to find out what it was and why. I couldn't see my own hand on the other side of it. I put it right up in front of my face, reached through from the back and tried to touch my nose. I couldn't do it. I reached so deep that without the gawk there, my arm would have been halfway through my head . . ."

"Objection!" Amery Heater said. "All this has nothing to do with the fact . . ."

"My client," Justin said, "is giving the incidents leading up to the alleged murder."

"Overruled," the judge said.

Maloney said, "Thanks. I decided that my arm had to be someplace when I stuffed it through the gawk. And it wasn't in this dimension. Maybe not even in this time. But it had to be someplace. That meant that I had to find out what was on the other side of the gawk. I could use touch, sight. Maybe I could climb through. It intrigued me, you might say.

"I started with touch. I put my hand through, held it in front of me and walked. I walked five feet before my hand rammed up against something. I felt it. It seemed to be a smooth wall. There wasn't such a wall in my cellar.

"There has to be some caution in science. I didn't stuff my head through. I couldn't risk it. I had the hunch there might be something unfriendly on the other side of the gawk. I turned the thing around and stuck my hand through from the other side. No wall. There was a terrible pain. I yanked my hand back. A lot of little blood vessels near the surface had broken. I dropped the gawk and jumped around for a while. Found out I had a bad case of frostbite. The broken blood vessels indicated that I had stuffed my hand into a vacuum. Frostbite in a fraction of a second indicated nearly absolute zero. It seemed that maybe I had put my hand into space. It made me glad it had been my hand instead of my head.

"I propped the thing up on my bench and shoved lots of things through, holding them a while and bringing them back out. Made a lot of notes on the effect of absolute zero on various materials.

"By that time I was bushed. I went up to bed. Next day I had some coffee and then built myself a little periscope. Shoved it through. Couldn't see a thing. I switched the gawk, tested with a thermometer, put my hand through. Warm enough. But the periscope didn't show me a thing. I wondered if maybe something happened to light rays when they went through that blackness. Turns out that I was right.

"By about noon I had found out another thing about it. Every time I turned it around I was able to reach through into a separate and distinct environment. I tested that with the thermometer. One of the environments I tested slammed the mercury right out through the top of the glass and broke the glass and burned my hand. I was glad I hadn't hit that one the first time. It would have burned my hand off at the wrist.

"I began to keep a journal of each turn of the gawk, and what seemed to be on the other side of it. I rigged up a jig on my work bench and began to grope through the gawk with my fireplace tongs.

"Once I jabbed something that seemed to be soft and alive. Those tongs were snatched right through the gawk. Completely gone. It gave me the shudders, believe me. If it had been my hand instead of the tongs, I wouldn't be here. I have a hunch that whatever snatched those tongs would have been glad to eat me.

"I rigged up some grappling hooks and went to work. Couldn't get anything. I put a lead weight on some cord and lowered it through. Had some grease on the end of the weight. When the cord slacked off, I pulled it back up. There was fine yellow sand on the bottom of the weight. And I had lowered it thrity-eight feet before I hit sand.

"On try number two hundred and eight, I brought an object back through the gawk. Justy has it right there in his bag. Show it to the people, Justy."

Justin looked annoyed at the informal request, but he unstrapped the bag and took out an object. He passed it up to the judge who looked at it with great interest. Then it was passed through the jury. It ended up on the table in front of the bench, tagged as an exhibit.

"You can see, folks, that such an object didn't come out of our civilization."

"Objection!" Heater yelled. "The defendant could have made it."

"Hush up!" the judge said.

"Thanks. As you can see that object is a big crystal. That thing in the crystal is a golden scorpion, about five times life size. The corner is sawed off there because Jim Finch sawed it off. You notice that he sawed off a big enough piece to get a hunk of the scorpion's leg. Jim told me that leg was solid gold. That whole bug is solid gold. I guess it was an ornament in some other civilization.

"Now that gets me around to Jim Finch. As you all know, Jim retired from the jewelry business about five years ago. Jim was a pretty sharp trader. You know how he parlayed his savings across the board so that he owned a little hunk of just about everything in town. He was always after me to let him in on my next gimmick. I guess those royalty checks made his mouth water. We weren't what you'd call friends. I passed the time of day with him, but he wasn't a friendly man.

"Anyway, when I grabbed this bug out of the gawk, I thought of Jim Finch. I wanted to know if such a thing could be made by a jeweler. Jim was home and his eyes popped when he saw it. You know how he kept that little shop in his garage and made presents for people? Well, he cut off a section with a saw. Then he said that he'd never seen anything like it and he didn't know how on earth it was put together. I told him that it probably wasn't put together on earth. That teased him a little and he kept after me until I told him the whole story. He didn't believe it. That made me mad. I took him over into my cellar and showed him a few things. I set the gawk between two boxes so it was parallel to the floor, then dropped my grapples down into it. In about three minutes I caught something and brought it up. It seemed to be squirming.''

Maloney drew a deep breath.

"That made me a shade cautious. I brought it up slow. The head of the thing came out. It was like a small bear—but more like a bear that had been made into a rug. Flat like a leech, and instead of front legs it just seemed to have a million little sucker disks around the flat edge. It screamed so hard, with such a high note, that it hurt my ears. I dropped it back through.

"When I looked around, old Jim was backed up against the cellar wall, mumbling. Then he got down on his hands and knees and patted the floor under the gawk. He kept right on mumbling. Pretty soon he asked me how that bear-leech and that golden bug could be in the same place. I explained how I had switched the gawk. We played around for a while and then came up with a bunch of stones. Jim handled them, and his eyes started to pop out again. He began to shake. He told me that one of the stones was an uncut ruby. You couldn't prove it by me. It would've made you sick to see the way old Jim started to drool. He talked so fast I could hardly understand him. Finally I got the drift. He wanted us to go in business and rig up some big machinery so we could dig through the gawk and come back with all kinds of things. He wanted bushels of rubies and a few tons of gold.

"I told him I wasn't interested. He got so mad he jumped up and down. I told him I was going to fool around with the thing for a while and then I was going to turn it over to some scientific foundation so the boys could go at it in the right easy.

"He looked mad enough to kill me. He told me we could have castles and cars and yachts and a million bucks each. I told him that the money was coming in faster than I could spend it already and all I wanted was to stay in my cellar and tinker.

"I told him that I guessed the atomic explosion had dislocated something, and the end product belonged to science. I also told him very politely to get the devil home and stop bothering me.

"He did, but he sure hated to leave. Well, by the morning of the tenth, I had pretty well worn myself out. I was bushed and jittery from no sleep. I had made twenty spins in a row without getting anything, and I had begun to think I had run out of new worlds on the other side of the gawk.

"Like a darn fool, I yanked it off the jig, took it like a hoop and scaled it across the cellar. It went high, then dropped lightly, spinning.

"And right there in my cellar was this beautiful redhead. She was dressed in a shiny silver thing. Justy's got that silver thing in his bag. Show it to the people. You can see that it's made out of some sort of metal mesh, but it isn't cold like metal would be. It seems to hold heat and radiate it."

The metal garment was duly passed around. Everybody felt of it, exclaimed over it. This was better than a movie. Maloney could see from Amery Heater's face that the man wanted to claim the metal garment was also made in the Maloney cellar.

Bill winked at him. Amery Heater flushed a dull red.

"Well, she stood there, right in the middle of the gawk which was flat against the floor. She had a dazed look on her face. I asked her where she had come from. She gave me a blank look and a stream of her own language. She seemed mad about something. And pretty upset.

"Now what I should have done was pick up that gawk and lift it back up over her head. That would have put her back in her own world. But she stepped out of it, and like a darn fool, I stood and held it and spun it, nervous like. In spinning it, I spun her own world off into some mathematical equation I couldn't figure.

"It was by the worst or the best kind of luck, depending on how you look at it, that I made a ringer on her when I tossed the gawk across the cellar. Her makeup startled me a little. No lipstick. Tiny crimson beads on the end of each eyelash. Tiny emerald green triangles painted on each tooth in some sort of enamel. Nicely centered. Her hairdo wasn't any wackier than some you see every day.

"Well, she saw the gawk in my hands and she wasn't dumb at all. She came at me, her lips trembling, her eyes pleading, and tried to step into it. I shook my head, hard, and pushed her back and set it back in the jig. I shoved a steel rod through, holding it in asbestos mittens. The heat beyond the blackness turned the whole rod cherry red in seconds. I shoved it on through the rest of the way, then showed her the darkened mitten. She was quick. She got the most horrified look on her face.

"Then she ran upstairs, thinking it was some sort of joke, I guess. I noticed that she slammed right into the door, as though she expected it to open for her. By the time I got to her, she had figured out the knob. She went down the walk toward the gate.

"That's when nosey Anita must have seen her. I shouted and she turned around and the tears were running right down her face. I made soothing noises and she let me lead her back into the house. I've never seen a prettier girl or one stacked any . . . I mean her skin is translucent, sort of. Her eyes are enormous. And her hair is a shade of red that you never see.

"She had no place to go and she was my responsibility. I certainly didn't feel like turning her over to the welfare people. I fixed her up a place to sleep in my spare room and I had to show her everything. How to turn on a faucet. How to turn the lights off and on.

"She didn't do anything except cry for four days. I gave her food that she didn't eat. She was a mess. Worried me sick. I didn't have any idea how to find her world again. No idea at all. Of course, I could have popped her into any old world, but it didn't seem right.

"On the fourth day I came up out of the cellar and found her sitting in a chair looking at a copy of See Magazine. She seemed very much interested in the pictures of the women. She looked up at me and smiled. That was the day I went into town and came back with a mess of clothes for her. I had to show her how a zipper worked, and how to button a button.''

He looked as if that might have been fun.

''After she got all dressed up, she smiled some more and that evening she ate well. I kept pointing to things and saying the right name for them.

''I tell you, once she heard the name for something, she didn't forget it. It stayed right with her. Nouns were easy. The other words were tough. About ten that night I finally caught her name. It was Rejapachalandakeena. She seemed to like to have me call her Keena. The first sentence she said was, 'Where is Keena?'

''That is one tough question. Where is here and now? Where is this world, anyway? On what side of what dimension? In which end of space? On what twisted convolution of the time stream? What good is it to say 'This is the world'? It just happens to be our world. Now I know that there are plenty of others.

''Writing came tougher for her than the sounds of the words. She showed me her writing. She took a piece of paper, held the pencil pointing straight up and put the paper on top of the rug. Then she worked that pencil like a pneumatic hammer, starting at the top right corner and going down the page. I couldn't figure it until she read it over, and made a correction by sticking in one extra hole in the paper. I saw then that the pattern of holes was very precise—like notes on a sheet of music.

''She went through the grade school readers like a flash. I was buying her some arithmetic books one day, and when I got back she said, 'Man here while Billy gone,' She was calling me Billy. 'Keena hide,' she said.

''Well, the only thing missing was the gawk, and with it, Keena's chance to make a return to her own people. I thought immediately of Jim Finch. I ran over and pounded on his door. He undid the chain so he could talk to me through a five-inch crack, but I couldn't get in. I asked him if he had stolen the little item. He told me that I'd better run to the police and tell them exactly what it was that I had lost, and then I could tell the police exactly how I got it. I could tell by the look of naked triumph in his eyes that he had it. And there wasn't a thing I could do about it.

"Keena's English improved by leaps and bounds and pretty soon she was dipping into my texts on chemistry and physics. She seemed puzzled. She told me that we were like her people a few thousand years back. Primitives. She told me a lot about her world. No cities. The houses are far apart. No work. Everyone is assigned to a certain cultural pursuit, depending on basic ability. She was a designer. In order to train herself, she had had to learn the composition of all fabricated materials used in her world.

"I took notes while she talked. When I get out of this jam, I'm going to revolutionize the plastics industry. She seemed bright enough to be able to take in the story of how she suddenly appeared in my cellar. I gave it to her slow and easy.

"When I was through, she sat very still for a long time. Then she told me that some of the most brilliant men of her world had long ago found methods of seeing into other worlds beyond their own. They had borrowed things from worlds more advanced than their own, and had thus been able to avoid mistakes in the administration of their own world. She told me that it was impossible that her departure should go unnoticed. She said that probably at the moment of her disappearance, all the resources of a great people were being concentrated on that spot where she had been standing talking to some friends. She told me that some trace of the method would be found and that they would then scan this world, locate her and take her back.

"I asked her if it would be easier if we had the gawk, and she said that it wasn't necessary, and that if it was, she would merely go next door and see Jim Finch face to face. She said she had a way, once she looked into his eyes, of taking over the control of his involuntary muscles and stopping his heartbeat.

"I gasped, and she smiled sweetly and said that she had very nearly done it to me when I had kept her from climbing back through the gawk. She said that everybody in her world knew how to do that. She also said that most adults knew how to create, out of imagination, images that would respond to physical tests. To prove it she stared at the table. In a few seconds a little black box slowly appeared out of misty nothingness. She told me to look at it. I picked it up. It was latched. I opened it. Her picture smiled out at me. She was standing before the entrance of a white castle that seemed to reach to the clouds.

"Suddenly it was gone. She explained that when she stopped thinking of it, it naturally disappeared, because that was what had caused it. Her thinking. I asked her why she didn't think up a doorway to her own world and then step through it while she was still thinking about it. She said that she could only think up things by starting with their basic physical properties and working up from there, like a potter starts with clay.

"So I stopped heckling Jim Finch at about that time. I was sorry, because I wanted the gawk back. Best toy I'd ever had. Once I got a look in Jim's garage window. He'd forgot to pull the shade down all the way. He had the gawk rigged up on a stand, and had a big arm, like the bucket on a steam shovel rigged up, only just big enough to fit through the hoop. He wasn't working it when I saw him. He was digging up the concrete in the corner of his cellar. He was using a pick and he had a shovel handy. He was pale as death. I saw then that he had a human arm in there on the floor and blood all over. The bucket was rigged with jagged teeth. It didn't take much imagination to figure out what Jim had done.

"Some poor innocent character in one of those other worlds had had a massive contraption come out of nowhere and chaw his arm off. I thought of going to the police, and then I thought of how easy it would be for Jim Finch to get me stuck away in a padded cell, while he stayed on the outside, all set to pull more arms off more people."

Heater glanced uneasily at the jury. They were drinking it in.

"I told Keena about it and she smiled. She told me that Jim was digging into many worlds and that some of them were pretty advanced. I gradually got the idea that old Jim was engaging in as healthy an occupation as a small boy climbing between the bars and tickling the tigers. I began to worry about old Jim a little. You all know about that couple of bushels of precious stones that were found in his house. That's what made him tickle the tigers. But the cops didn't find that arm. I guess that after he got the hole dug, Jim got over his panic and realized that all he had to do was switch the gawk around and toss the arm through. Best place for old razor blades I ever heard of.

"Well, as May turned into June and June went by, Keena got more and more confident of her eventual rescue. As I learned more about her world, I got confident of it too. In a few thousand years we may be as bright as those people. I hope we are. No wars, no disease.

"And the longer she stayed with me, the more upset I got about her leaving me. But it was what she wanted. I guess it's what I'd want, if somebody shoved me back a thousand years B.C. I'd want to get home, but quick.

"On the tenth of July, I got a phone call from Jim Finch. His voice was all quavery like a little old lady. He said, 'Maloney, I want to give that thing back to you. Right away.' Anything Jim Finch gave anybody was a spavined gift horse. I guessed that the gobblies were after him like Keena had hinted.

"So I just laughed at him. Maybe I laughed to cover up the fact that I was a little scared, too. What if some world he messed with dropped a future type atomic bomb back through the gawk into his lap? I told him to burn it up if he was tired of it.

"I didn't know Jim could cuss like that. He said that it wouldn't burn and he couldn't break it or destroy it anyway. He said that he was coming out and throw it across the hedge into my yard right away.

"As I got to my front door, he came running out of his house. He carried the thing like it was going to blow up.

"Just as he got to the hedge, I saw a misty circle in the air over his head. Only it was about ten feet across. A pair of dark blue shiny pliers with jaws as big as the judge's desk there swooped down and caught him by the head. The jaws snapped shut so hard that I could hear sort of a thick, wet, popping sound as all the bones in old Jim's head gave way all at once.

"He dropped the gawk and hung limp in those closed jaws for a moment, then he was yanked up through that misty circle into nothingness. Gone. Right before my eyes. The misty circle drifted down to grass level, and then faded away. The gawk faded right away with it. You know what it made me think of? Of a picnic where you're trying to eat and a bug gets on your arm and bothers you. You pinch it between your thumb and forefinger, roll it once and throw it away. Old Jim was just about as important to those blue steel jaws as a hungry red ant is to you and me. You could call those gems he got crumbs, I guess.

"I was just getting over being sick in my own front yard when Timmy came running over, took one look at the blood and ran back. The police came next. That's all there is to tell. Keena is still around and Justy will bring her in to testify tomorrow."

Bill Maloney yawned and smiled at the jury.

Amery Heater got up, stuck his thumbs inside his belt and walked slowly and heavily over to Bill.

He stared into Bill's smiling face for ten long seconds. Bill shuffled his feet and began to look uncomfortable.

In a low bitter tone, Amery Heater said, "Gawks! Golden scorpions! Tangential worlds! Blue jaws!" He sighed heavily, pointed to the jury and said, "Those are intelligent people, Maloney. No questions!"

The judge had to pound with his gavel to quiet the court. As soon as the room was quiet, he called an adjournment until ten the following morning.

When Bill Maloney was brought out of his cell into court the next morning, the jurors gave each other wise looks. It was obvious that the young man had spent a bad night. There were puffy areas under his eyes. He scuffed his heels as he walked, sat down heavily and buried his face in his hands. They wondered why his shoulders seemed to shake.

Justin Marks looked just as bad. Or worse.

Bill was sunk in a dull lethargy, in an apathy so deep that he didn't know where he was, and cared less.

Justin Marks stood up and said, ''Your Honor, we request an adjournment of the case for twenty-four hours.''

''For what reason?''

''Your Honor, I intended to call the woman known as Keena to the stand this morning. She was in a room at the Hotel Hollyfield. Last night she went up to her room at eleven after I talked with her in the lounge. She hasn't been seen since. Her room is empty. All her possessions are there, but she is gone. I would like time to locate her, your Honor.''

The judge looked extremely disappointed.

He pursed his lips and said, in a sweet tone, ''You are sure that such a woman actually exists, counsellor?''

Justin Marks turned pale and Amery Heater chuckled.

''Of course, your Honor! Why, only last night . . .''

''Her people came and got her,'' Bill Maloney said heavily. He didn't look up. The jury shifted restlessly. They had expected to be entertained by a gorgeous redhead. Without her testimony, the story related by Maloney seemed even more absurd than it had seemed when they had heard it. Of course, it would be a shame to electrocute a nice clean young man like that, but really you can't have people going about killing their neighbors and then concocting such a fantasy about it . . .

"What's that?" the judge asked suddenly.

It began as a hum, so low as to be more of a vibration than a sound. A throb that seemed to come from the bowels of the earth. Slowly it increased in pitch and in violence, and if the judge had any more to say on the subject, no one heard him. He appeared to be trying to beat the top of his desk in with the gavel. But the noise couldn't be heard.

Slowly climbing up the audible range, it filled the court. As it passed the index of vibration of the windows, they shattered, but the falling glass couldn't be heard. A man who had been wearing glasses stared through empty frames.

The sound passed beyond the upper limits of the human ear, became hypersonic, and every person in the courtroom was suddenly afflicted with a blinding headache.

It stopped as abruptly as a scream in the night.

For a moment there was a misty arch in the solid wall. Beyond it was the startling vagueness of a line of blue hills. Hills that didn't belong there.

She came quickly through the arch. It faded. She was not tall, but gave the impression of tallness. Her hair was the startling red of port wine, her skin so translucent as to seem faintly bluish. Her eyes were half-way between sherry and honey. Tiny crimson beads were on the tip of each eyelash. Her warm full lips were parted, and they could all see the little green enameled triangles on her white teeth. Her single garment was like the silver metallic garment they had touched. But it was golden. Without any apparent means of support, it clung to her lovely body, following each line and curve.

She looked around the court. Maloney's eyes were warm blue fire. "Keena!" he gasped. She ran to him, threw herself on him, her arms around his neck, her face hidden in the line of jaw, throat and shoulder. He murmured things to her that the jury strained to hear.

Amery Heater, feeling his case fade away, was the first to recover.

"Hypnotism!" he roared.

It took the judge a full minute of steady pounding to silence the spectators. "One more disturbance like this, and I'll clear the court," he said.

Maloney had come to life. She sat on his lap and they could hear her say, "What are they trying to do to you?"

He smiled peacefully. "They want to kill me, honey. They say I killed Jim Finch."

She turned and her eyes shriveled the jury and the judge.

"Stupid!" she hissed.

There was a little difficulty swearing her in. Justin Marks, his confidence regained, thoroughly astonished at finding that Bill Maloney had been telling the truth all along, questioned Keena masterfully. She backed up Maloney's story in every particular. Maloney couldn't keep his eyes off her. Her accent was odd, and her voice had a peculiar husky and yet liquid quality.

Justin Marks knuckled his mustache proudly, bowed to Amery Heater and said, "Do you wish to cross-examine?"

Heater nodded, stood up, and walked slowly over. He gave Keena a long and careful look. "Young woman, I congratulate you on your acting ability. Where did you get your training? Surely you've been on the stage."

"Stage?"

"Oh, come now! All this has been very interesting but now we must discard this dream world and get down to facts. What is your real name?"

"Rejapachalandakeena."

Heater sighed heavily. "I see that you are determined to maintain your silly little fiction. That entrance of yours was somehow engineered by the defendant, I am sure." He turned and smiled at the jury—the smile of a fellow conspirator.

"Miss So-and-so, the defense has all bene based on the idea

that you come from some other world, or some hidden corner of time, or out of the woodwork. I think that what you had better do is just prove to us that you do come from some other world." His voice dripped with sarcasm. "Just do one or two things for us that we common mortals can't do, please."

Keena frowned, propped her chin on her fist. After a few moments she said, "I do not know completely what you are able to do. Many primitive peoples have learned through a sort of intuition. Am I right in thinking that those people behind that little fence are the ones who decide whether my Billy is to be killed?"

"Correct."

She turned and stared at the jury for a long time. Her eyes passed from face to face, slowly. The jurors were oddly uncomfortable.

She said, "It is very odd. That woman in the second row. The second one from the left. It is odd that she should be there. Not very long ago she gave a poison, some sort of vegetable base poison, to her husband. He was sick for a long time and he died. Is that not against your silly laws?"

The woman in question turned pale green, put her hands to her throat, rolled her eyes up and slid quietly off the chair. No one made a move to help her. All eyes were on Keena.

Some woman back in the courtroom said shrilly, "I knew there was something funny about the way Dave died! I knew it! Arrest Mrs. Watson immediately!"

Keena's eyes turned toward the woman who had spoken. The woman sat down suddenly.

Keena said. "This man you call Dave. His wife killed him because of you. I can read that in your eyes."

Amery Heater chuckled. "A very good trick, but pure imagination. I rather guess you have been prepared for this situation, and my opponent has briefed you on what to do should I call on you in this way."

Keena's eyes flashed. She said, "You are a most offensive person."

She stared steadily at Amery Heater. He began to sweat. Suddenly he screamed and began to dance about. Smoke poured from his pockets. Blistering his fingers, he threw pocketknife, change, moneyclip on the floor. They glowed dull red, and the smell of scorching wood filled the air.

A wisp of smoke rose from his tie clip, and he tore that off, sucking his blistered fingers. The belt buckle was next. By then the silver coins had melted against the wooden floor. But there was one last thing he had to remove. His shoes. The eyelets were metal. They began to burn the leather.

At last, panting and moaning he stood, surrounded by the cherry red pieces of metal on the floor.

Keena smiled and said softly, "Ah, you have no more metal on you. Would you like to have further proof?"

Amery Heater swallowed hard. He looked up at the open-mouthed judge. He glanced at the jury.

"The prosecution withdraws," he said hoarsely.

The judge managed to close his mouth.

"Case dismissed," he said. "Young woman, I suggest you go back wherever you came from."

She smiled blandly up at him. "Oh, no! I can't go back. I went back once and found that my world was very empty. They laughed at my new clothes. I said I wanted Billy. They said they would transport him to my world. But Billy wouldn't be happy there. So I came back."

Maloney stood up, yawned and stretched. He smiled at the jury. Two men were helping the woman back up into her chair. She was still green.

He winked at Keena and said, "Come on home, honey."

They walked down the aisle together and out the golden oak doors. Nobody made a sound, or a move to stop them.

Anita Hempflet, extremely conscious of the fact that the man who had left her waiting at the altar thirty-one years before was buried just beyond the corn hills in her vegetable garden, forced her razor lips into a broad smile, beamed around at the people sitting near her and said, in her high, sharp voice:

"Well! That girl is going to make a lovely neighbor! If you folks will excuse me, I'm going to take her over some fresh strawberry preserves."

# LOVE
# AND OTHER
# WORLDS

# ROBERT SHECKLEY

# HUMAN MAN'S BURDEN

*Romance is not always an accidental happening. Sometimes it is the result of a carefully planned campaign with specific goals in mind. However, one of the key elements in any conspiracy of this nature is to position oneself in an advantageous location, as Sheila trys to do in this excellent story.*

*Robert Sheckley has been delighting science fiction readers for almost thirty years, and he is still going strong. One of his many stories, "Seventh Victim," was made into an interesting and successful film called* The Tenth Victim, *which starred Ursula Andress and Marcello Mastroianni.*

Edward Flaswell bought his planetoid, sight unseen, at the Interstellar Land Office on Earth. He selected it on the basis of a photograph, which showed little more than a range of picturesque mountains. But Flaswell loved mountains and as he remarked to the Claims Clerk, "Might be gold in them thar hills, mightn't thar, pardner?"

"Sure, pal, sure," the clerk responded, wondering what man in his right mind would put himself several light-years from the nearest woman of any description whatsoever. No man in his right mind would, the clerk decided, and gave Flaswell a searching look.

But Flaswell was perfectly sane. He just hadn't stopped to consider the problem.

Accordingly, Flaswell put down a small sum in credits and made a large promise to improve his land every year. As soon as the ink was dry upon his deed, he purchased passage aboard a second-class drone freighter, loaded it with an assortment of second-hand equipment and set out for his holdings.

Most novice pioneers find they have purchased a sizable chunk of naked rock. Flaswell was lucky. His planetoid, which he named Chance, had a minimal manufactured atmosphere that he could boost to breathable status. There was water, which his well-digging equipment tapped on the twenty-third attempt. He found no gold in them thar hills, but there was some exportable thorium. And best of all, much of the soil was suitable for the cultivation of dir, olge, smis and other luxury fruits.

As Flaswell kept telling his robot foreman, "This place is going to make me rich!"

"Sure, Boss, sure," the robot always responded.

The planetoid had undeniable promise. Its development was an enormous task for one man, but Flaswell was only twenty-seven years old, strongly built and of a determined frame of mind. Beneath his hand, the planetoid flourished. Months passed and Flaswell planted his fields, mined his picturesque mountains and shipped his goods out by the infrequent drone freighter that passed his way.

One day, his robot foreman said to him, "Boss Man, sir, you don't look too good, Mr. Flaswell, sir."

Flaswell frowned at this speech. The man he had bought his robots from had been a Human Supremicist of the most rabid sort, who had coded the robots' responses according to his own ideas of the respect due Human People. Flaswell found this annoying, but he couldn't afford new response tapes. And where else could he have picked up robots for so little money?

"Nothing wrong with me, Gunga-Sam," Flaswell replied.

"Ah! I beg pardon! But this is not so, Mr. Flaswell, Boss. You have been talking to yourself in the fields, you should excuse my saying it."

"Aw, it's nothing."

"And you have the beginning of a tic in your left eye, sahib. And your fingers are trembling. And you are drinking too much. And—"

"That's enough, Gunga-Sam. A robot should know his place," Flaswell said. He saw the hurt expression that the robot's metal face somehow managed to convey. He sighed and said, "You're right, of course. You're always right, old friend. What's the matter with me?"

"You are bearing too much of the Human Man's Burden."

"Don't I know it!" Flaswell ran a hand through his unruly black hair. "Sometimes I envy you robots. Always laughing, carefree, happy—"

"It is because we have no souls."

"Unfortunately I do. What do you suggest?"

"Take a vacation, Mr. Flaswell, Boss," Gunga-Sam suggested, and wisely withdrew to let his master think.

Flaswell appreciated his servitor's kindly suggestion, but a vacation was difficult. His planetoid, Chance, was in the Throcian System, which was about as isolated as one could get in this day and age. True, he was only a fifteen-day flight from the tawdry amusements of Cythera III and not much farther from Nagondicon, where considerable fun could be obtained for the strong in stomach. But distance is money, and money was the very thing Flaswell was trying to make on Chance.

He planted more crops, dug more thorium and began to grow a beard. He continued to mumble to himself in the fields and to drink heavily in the evenings. Some of the simple farm robots grew alarmed when Flaswell lurched past and they began praying to the outlawed Combustion God. But loyal Gunga-Sam soon put a stop to this ominous turn of events.

"Ignorant mechanicals!" he told them. "The Boss Human, he all right. Him strong, him good! Believe me, brothers, it is even as I say!"

But the murmurings did not cease, for robots look to Humans to set an example. The situation might have gotten out of hand if Flaswell had not received, along with his next shipment of food, a shiny new Roebuck-Ward catalogue.

Lovingly he spread it open upon his crude plastic table and, by the glow of a simple cold-light bulb, began to pore over its contents. What wonders there were for the isolated pioneer! Home distilling plants, and moon makers, and portable solidovision, and—

Flaswell turned a page, read it, gulped and read it again. It said:

## MAIL ORDER BRIDES!

Pioneers, why suffer the curse of loneliness alone? Why bear the Hu-Man's Burden singly? Roebuck-Ward is now offering, for the first time, a limited selection of *Brides for the Frontiersman*!

The Roebuck-Ward Frontier Model Bride is carefully selected for strength, adaptability, agility, perseverance, pioneer skills and, of course, a measure of comeliness. These girls are conditioned to any planet, since they possess a relatively low center of gravity, a skin properly pigmented for all climates, and short, strong toe and fingernails. Shapewise, they are well-proportioned and yet not distractingly contoured, a quality which the hardworking pioneer should appreciate.

The Roebuck-Ward Frontier Model comes in three general sizes (see specifications below) to suit any man's taste. Upon receipt of your request, Roebuck-Ward will quick-freeze one and ship her to you by third-class Drone

Freight. In this way, your express charges are kept to an absolute minimum.

Why not order a Frontier Model Bride *TODAY*?

Flaswell called for Gunga-Sam and showed him the advertisement. Silently the mechanical read, then looked his master full in the face.

"This is surely it, effendi," the foreman said.

"You think so, huh?" Flaswell stood up and began to pace nervously around the room. "But I wasn't planning on getting married just yet. I mean what kind of a way is this to get married? How do I know I'll like her?"

"It is proper for Human Man to have Human Woman."

"Yeah, but—"

"Besides, do they quick-freeze a preacher and ship *him* out, too?"

A slow smile broke over Flaswell's face as he digested his servant's shrewd question. "Gunga-Sam," he said, "as usual, you have gone directly to the heart of the matter. I guess there's a sort of moratorium on the ceremony while a man makes up his mind. Too expensive to quick-freeze a preacher. And it would be nice to have a gal around who could work her share."

Gunga-Sam managed to convey an inscrutable smile.

Flaswell sat down and ordered a Frontier Model Bride, specifying the small size, which he felt was plenty big enough. He gave Gunga-Sam the order to radio.

The next few weeks were filled with excitement for Flaswell and he began to scan the skies anxiously. The robots picked up the mood of anticipation. In the evenings, their carefree songs and dances were interspersed with whispering and secret merriment. The mechanicals said to Gunga-Sam over and over again, "Hey, Foreman! The new Human Woman Boss, what will she be like?"

"It's none of your concern," Gunga-Sam told them. "That's

Human Man business and you robots leave it alone." But at the end, he was watching the skies as anxiously as anyone.

During those weeks, Flaswell meditated on the virtues of Frontier Woman. The more he thought about it, the more he liked the idea. No pretty, useless, helpless painted woman for him! How pleasant it would be to have a cheerful, common-sense, down-to-gravity gal who could cook, wash, pretty up the place, boss the house robots, make clothes, put up jellies. . . .

So he dreamed away the time and bit his nails to the quick.

At last the drone freighter flashed across the horizon, landed, jettisoned a large packing case, and fled in the direction of Amyra IV.

The robots brought the case to Flaswell.

"Your new bride, sir!" they shouted triumphantly, and flung their oilcans in the air.

Flaswell immediately proclaimed a half-day holiday and soon he was alone in his living room with the great frigid box marked *"Handle with Care. Woman Inside."*

He pressed the defrosting controls, waited the requisite hour, and opened the box. Within was another box, which required two hours to defrost. Impatiently he waited, pacing up and down the room and gnawing on the remnants of his fingernails.

And then the time was up, and with shaking hands, Flaswell opened the lid and saw—

"Hey, what is this?" he cried.

The girl within the box blinked, yawned like a kitten, opened her eyes, sat up. They stared at each other and Flaswell knew that something was terribly wrong.

She was clothed in a beautiful, impractical white dress and her name, *Sheila*, was worked upon it in gold thread. The next thing Flaswell noticed was her slenderness, which was scarcely suitable for hard work on outplanet conditions. Her skin was a creamy white, obviously the kind that would blister under his planetoid's fierce summer sun. Her hands were long-fingered, red-nailed, elegant—completely unlike anything the Roebuck-Ward Company had promised. As for her legs and other parts, Flaswell decided they would be very well on Earth, but not here, where a man must pay attention to his work.

She couldn't even be said to have a low center of gravity. Quite the contrary.

Flaswell felt, not unreasonably, that he had been swindled, duped, made a fool of.

Sheila stepped out of the crate, walked to a window and looked out over Flaswell's flowering green fields and his picturesque mountains beyond them.

"But where are the palm trees?" she asked.

"Palm trees?"

"Of course. They told me that Srinigar V had palm trees."

"This is not Srinigar V," Flaswell said.

"But aren't you the Pasha of Srae?" Sheila gasped.

"Certainly not. I am a Frontiersman. Aren't you a Frontier Model Bride?"

"Do I *look* like a Frontier Model Bride?" Sheila snapped, her eyes flashing. "I am the Ultra Deluxe Luxury Model Bride and I was supposed to go to the subtropical paradise planet of Srinigar V."

"We've both been cheated. The shipping department must have made an error," Flaswell said gloomily.

The girl looked around Flaswell's crude living room and a wince twinged her pretty features. "Oh, well. I suppose you can arrange transportation for me to Srinigar V."

"I can't even afford to go to Nagondicón," Flaswell said. "I will inform Roebuck-Ward of their error. They will undoubtedly arrange transportation for you, when they send me my Frontier Model Bride."

Sheila shrugged her shoulders. "Travel broadens one," she said.

Flaswell nodded. He was thinking hard. This girl had, it was obvious, no pioneering qualities. But she was amazingly pretty. He saw no reason why her stay shouldn't be a pleasant one for both.

"Under the circumstances," Flaswell said, with an ingratiating smile, "we might as well be friends."

"Under what circumstances?"

"We are the only two Human People on the planet." Flaswell rested a hand lightly on her shoulder. "Let's have a drink. Tell me all about yourself. Do you—"

At that moment, he heard a loud sound behind. He turned and saw a small, squat robot climbing from a compartment in the packing case.

"What do *you* want?" Flaswell demanded.

"I," said the robot, "am a Marrying Robot, empowered by the government to provide legal marriages in space. I am further directed by the Roebuck-Ward Company to act as guardian, duenna and protector for the young lady in my charge, until such time as my primary function, to perform a ceremony of marriage, has been accomplished."

"Uppity damned robot," Flaswell grumbled.

"What did you expect?" Sheila asked. "A quick-frozen Human preacher?"

"Of course not. But a robot duenna—"

"The very best kind," she assured him. "You'd be surprised at how some men act when they get a few light-years from Earth."

"I would?" Flaswell said disconsolately.

"So I'm told," Sheila replied, demurely looking away from him. "And after all, the promised bride of the Pasha of Srae should have a guardian of some sort."

"Dearly beloved," the robot intoned, "we are here gathered to join—"

"Not now," Sheila said loftily. "Not this one."

"I'll have the robots fix a room for you," Flaswell growled, and walked away, mumbling to himself about Human Man's Burden.

He radioed Roebuck-Ward and was told that the proper model Bride would be sent at once and the interloper shipped elsewhere. Then he returned to his farming and mining, determined to ignore the presence of Sheila and her duenna.

Work continued on Chance. There was thorium to be mined out of the soil and new wells to dig. Harvest time was soon at hand, and the robots toiled for long hours in the green-blossomed fields, and lubricating oil glistened on their honest metal faces, and the air was fragrant with the perfume of the dir flowers.

Sheila made her presence felt with subtle yet surprising force. Soon there were plastic lampshades over the naked cold-light bulbs and drapes over the stark windows and scatter rugs on the floors. And there were many other changes around the house that Flaswell felt rather than saw.

His diet underwent a change, too. The robot chef's memory tape had worn thin in many spots, so all the poor mechanical could remember how to make was beef Stroganoff, cucumber salad, rice pudding and cocoa. Flaswell had, with considerable stoicism, been eating these dishes ever since he came to Chance, varying them occasionally with shipwreck rations.

Then Sheila took the robot chef in hand. Patiently she impressed upon his memory tape the recipes for beef stew, pot roast, tossed green salad, apple pie, and many others. The eating situation upon Chance began to improve markedly.

But when Sheila put up smis jelly in vacuum jars, Flaswell began to have doubts.

Here, after all, was a remarkably practical young lady, in spite of her expensive appearance. She could do all the things a Frontier Wife could do. And she had other attributes. What did he need a regular Roebuck-Ward Frontier Model for?

After mulling this for a while, Flaswell said to his foreman, "Gunga-Sam, I am confused."

"Ah?" said the foreman, his metal face impassive.

"I guess I need a little of that robot intuition. She's doing very well, isn't she, Gunga-Sam?"

"The Human Woman is taking her proper share of Human Person's Burden."

"She sure is. But can it last? She's doing as much as any Frontier Model Wife could do, isn't she? Cooking, canning—"

"The workers love her," Gunga-Sam said with simple dignity. "You did not know, sir, but when that rust epidemic broke out last week, she toiled night and day, bringing relief and comforting the frightened younger robots."

"She did all that?" Flaswell gasped, shaken. "But a girl of her background, a luxury model—"

"It does not matter. She is a Human Person and she has the strength and nobility to take on Human Person's Burden."

"Do you know," Flaswell said slowly, "this has convinced me. I really believe she is fit to stay here. It's not her fault she isn't a Frontier Model. That's a matter of screening and conditioning, and you can't change that. I'm going to tell her she can stay. And then I'll cancel the other Roebuck order."

A strange expression glowed in the foreman's eyes, an expression almost of amusement. He bowed low and said, "It shall be as the master wishes."

Flaswell hurried out to find Sheila.

She was in the sick bay, which had been constructed out of an old toolshed. With the aid of a robot mechanic, she was caring for the dents and dislocations that are the peculiar lot of metal-skinned beings.

"Sheila," Flaswell said, "I want to speak to you."

"Sure," she answered absently, "as soon as I tighten this bolt."

She locked the bolt cleverly into place, and tapped the robot with her wrench.

"There, Pedro," she said, "try that leg now."

The robot stood up gingerly, put weight on the leg, found that it held. He capered comically around the Human Woman, saying, "You sure fixed it, Boss Lady. Gracias, ma'am."

And he danced out into the sunshine.

Flaswell and Sheila watched him go, smiling at his antics. "They're just like children," Flaswell said.

"One can't help but love them," Sheila responded. "They're so happy, so carefree—"

"But they haven't got souls," Flaswell reminded her.

"No," she agreed somberly. "They haven't. What did you wish to see me about?"

"I wanted to tell you—" Flaswell looked around. The sick bay was an antiseptic place, filled with wrenches, screwdrivers, hacksaws, ballpeen hammers and other medical equipment. It was hardly the atmosphere for the sort of announcement he was about to make.

"Come with me," he said.

They walked out of the hospital and through the blossoming green fields, to the foot of Flaswell's spectacular mountains. There, shadowed by craggy cliffs, was a still, dark pool of water overhung with giant trees, which Flaswell had force-grown. Here they paused.

"I wanted to say this," Flaswell said. "You have surprised me completely, Sheila. I expected you would be a parasite, a purposeless person. Your background, your breeding, your appearance all pointed in this direction. But I was wrong. You have risen to the challenge of a Frontier environment, have conquered it triumphantly, and have won the hearts of everybody."

"Everybody?" Sheila asked very softly.

"I believe I can speak for every robot on the planetoid. They idolize you. I think you belong here, Sheila."

The girl was silent for a very long while, and the wind murmured through the boughs of the giant force-grown trees, and ruffled the black surface of the lake.

Finally she said, "Do *you* think I belong here?"

Flaswell felt engulfed by her exquisite perfection, lost in the topaz depths of her eyes. His breath came fast, he touched her hand, her fingers clung.

"Sheila. . . ."

"Yes, Edward. . . ."

"Dearly beloved," a strident metallic voice barked, "we are here gathered—"

"Not now, you fool!" Sheila cried.

The Marrying Robot came forward and said sulkily, "Much as I hate to interfere in the affairs of Human People, my taped coefficients are such that I must. To my way of thinking, physical contact is meaningless. I have, by way of experiment, clashed limbs with a seamstress robot. All I got for my troubles was a dent. Once I thought I experienced something, an electric something that shot through me giddily and made me think of slowly shifting geometric forms. But upon examination, I discovered the insulation had parted from a conductor center. Therefore, the emotion was invalid."

"Uppity damned robot," Flaswell growled.

"Excuse my presumption. I was merely trying to explain that I personally find my instructions unintelligible—that is, to prevent any and all physical contact until a ceremony of marriage has been performed. But there it is; those are my orders. Can't I get it over with now?"

"No!" said Sheila.

The robot shrugged his shoulders fatalistically and slid into the underbrush.

"Can't stand a robot who doesn't know his place," said Flaswell. "But it's all right."

"What?"

"Yes," Flaswell said, with an air of conviction. "You are as good as any Frontier Model Wife and far prettier. Sheila, will you marry me?"

The robot, who had been thrashing around in the underbrush, now slid eagerly toward them.

"No," said Sheila.

"No?" Flaswell repeated uncomprehendingly.

"You heard me. No! Absolutely no!"

"But why? You fit so well here, Sheila. The robots adore you. I've never seen them work so well—"

"I'm not interested in your robots," she said, standing very straight, her hair disheveled, her eyes blazing. "And I am not interested in your planetoid. And I am most emphatically not interested in you. I am going to Srinigar V, where I will be the pampered bride of the Pasha of Srae!"

They stared at each other, Sheila white-faced with anger, Flaswell red with confusion.

The Marrying Robot said, "Now should I start the ceremony? Dearly beloved. . . ."

Sheila whirled and ran toward the house.

"I don't understand," the Marrying Robot said plaintively. "It's all very bewildering. When does the ceremony take place?"

"It doesn't," Flaswell said, and stalked toward the house, his brows beetling with rage.

The robot hesitated, sighed metallically and hurried after the Ultra Deluxe Luxury Model Bride.

All that night, Flaswell sat in his room, drank deeply and mumbled to himself. Shortly after dawn, the loyal Gunga-Sam knocked and slipped into the room.

"Women!" Flaswell snarled to his servitor.

"Ah?" said Gunga-Sam.

"I'll never understand them," Flaswell said. "She led me on. I thought she wanted to stay here. I thought. . . ."

"The mind of Human Man is murky and dark," said Gunga-Sam, "but it is as crystal compared to the mind of Human Woman."

"Where did you get that?" Flaswell asked.

"It is an ancient robot proverb."

"You robots. Sometimes I wonder if you *don't* have souls."

"Oh, no, Mr. Flaswell, Boss. It is expressly written in our Construction Specifications that robots are to be built with no souls, to spare them anguish."

"A very wise provision," Flaswell said, "and something they might consider with Human People, too. Well, to hell with her. What do you want?"

"I came to tell you, sir, that the drone freighter is landing."

Flaswell turned pale. "So soon? Then it's bringing my new bride!"

"Undoubtedly."

"And it will take Sheila away to Srinigar V."

"Assuredly, sir."

Flaswell groaned and clutched his head. Then he straightened and said, "All right, all right. I'll see if she's ready."

He found Sheila in the living room, watching the drone freighter spiral in. She said, "The very best of luck, Edward. I hope your new bride fulfills all your expectations."

The drone freighter landed and the robots began removing a large packing case.

"I had better go," Sheila said. "They won't wait long." She held out her hand.

Flaswell took it.

He held her hand for a moment, then found he was holding her arm. She did not resist, nor did the Marrying Robot break into the room. Flaswell suddenly found that Sheila was in his arms. He kissed her and felt exactly like a small sun going nova.

Finally she said, "Wow," huskily, in a not quite believing voice.

Flaswell cleared his throat twice. "Sheila, I love you. I can't offer you much luxury here, but if you'd stay—"

"It's about time you found out you love me, you dope!" she said. "Of course I'm staying!"

The next few minutes were ecstatic and decidedly vertiginous. They were interrupted at last by the sound of loud robot voices outside. The door burst open and the Marrying Robot stamped in, followed by Gunga-Sam and two farm mechanicals.

"Really!" the Marrying Robot said. "It is unbelievable! To think I'd see the day when robot pitted himself against robot!"

"What happened?" Flaswell asked.

"This foreman of yours *sat* on me," the Marrying Robot said indignantly, "while his cronies held my limbs. I was merely trying to enter this room and perform my duty as set forth by the government and the Roebuck-Ward Company."

"Why, Gunga-Sam!" Flaswell said, grinning.

The Marrying Robot hurried up to Sheila. "Are you damaged? Any dents? Any short-circuits?"

"I don't think so," said Sheila breathlessly.

Gunga-Sam said to Flaswell, "The fault is all mine, Boss, sir. But everyone knows that Human Man and Human Woman need solitude during the courtship period. I merely performed what I considered my duty to the Human Race in this respect, Mr. Flaswell, Boss, sahib."

"You did well, Gunga-Sam," Flaswell said. "I'm deeply grateful and—oh, Lord!"

"What is it?" Sheila asked apprehensively.

Flaswell was staring out the window. The farm robots were carrying the large packing case toward the house.

"The Frontier Model Bride!" said Flaswell. "What'll we do, darling? I canceled you and legally contracted for the other one. Do you think we can break the contract?"

Sheila laughed. "Don't worry. There's no Frontier Model Bride in that box. Your order was canceled as soon as it was received."

"It was?"

"Certainly." She looked down, ashamed. "You'll hate me for this—"

"I won't," he promised. "What is it?"

"Well, Frontiermen's pictures are on file at the Company, you know, so Brides can see what they're getting. There is a choice—for the girls, I mean—and I'd been hanging around the place so long, unable to get unclassified as an Ultra Deluxe, that I—I made friends with the head of the order department. And," she said all in a rush, "I got myself sent here."

"But the Pasha of Srae—"

"I made him up."

"But why?" Flaswell asked puzzledly. "You're so pretty—"

"That everybody expects me to be a toy for some spoiled, pudgy idiot," she finished with a good deal of heat. "I don't want to be! I want to be a wife! And I'm just as good as any chunky, homely female!"

"Better," he said.

"I can cook and doctor robots and be practical, can't I? Haven't I proved it?"

"Of course, dear."

She began to cry. "But nobody would believe it, so I had to trick you into letting me stay long enough to—to fall in love with me."

"Which I did," he said, drying her eyes for her. "It's all worked out fine. The whole thing was a lucky accident."

What looked like a blush appeared on Gunga-Sam's metallic face.

"You mean it wasn't an accident?" Flaswell exclaimed.

"Well, sir, Mr. Flaswell, effendi, it is well known that Human Man needs attractive Human Woman. The Frontier

Model sounded a little severe and Memsahib Sheila is a daughter of a friend of my former master. So I took the liberty of sending the order directly to her. She got her friend in the order department to show her your picture and ship her here. I hope you are not displeased with your humble servant for disobeying.''

"Well, I'll be damned," Flaswell finally got out. "It's like I always said—you robots understand Human People better than anyone." He turned to Sheila. "But what *is* in that packing case?"

"My dresses and my jewelry, my shoes, my cosmetics, my hair styler, my—"

"But—"

"You want me to look nice when we go visiting, dear," Sheila said. "After all, Cythera III is only fifteen days away. I looked it up before I came."

Flaswell nodded resignedly. You had to expect something like this from an Ultra Deluxe Luxury Model Bride.

"Now!" Sheila said, turning to the Marrying Robot.

The robot didn't answer.

"Now!" Flaswell shouted.

"You're quite sure?" the robot queried sulkily.

"Yes! Get started!"

"I just don't understand," the Marrying Robot said. "Why now? Why not last week? Am I the only sane one here? Oh, well. Dearly beloved. . . ."

And the ceremony was held at last. Flaswell proclaimed a three-day holiday and the robots sang and danced and celebrated in their carefree robot fashion.

Thereafter, life was never the same on Chance. The Flaswells began to have a modest social life, to visit and be visited by couples fifteen and twenty days out, on Cythera III, Tham and Randico I. But the rest of the time, Sheila was an irreproachable Frontier Wife, loved by the robots and idolized by her husband.

The Marrying Robot, following his instruction manual, retrained himself as an accountant and bookkeeper, skills for which his mentality was peculiarly well suited. He often said the whole place would go to pieces if it weren't for him.

And the robots continued to dig thorium from the soil, and the dir, olge and smis blossomed, and Flaswell and Sheila shared together the responsibility of Human People's Burden.

Flaswell was always quite vocal on the advantages of shopping at Roebuck-Ward. But Sheila knew that the real advantage was in having a foreman like the loyal, soulless Gunga-Sam.

# RICHARD McKENNA

# HOME THE HARD WAY

*Why does the grass look greener on the other side of the fence?*
*Psychologists believe it is because in casual relationships we*
*tend to notice and overgeneralize a person's good points. But*
*the closer we get to another, the more likely it is that we will*
*notice his/her bad points. There is always a tendency then, like*
*Chief Biotech Skinner Webb, to think we might be happier with*
*someone else. So it's important to consider both present*
*strengths and potential disadvantages before making hasty*
*choices.*

*The late Richard McKenna (1913–1964) is best known as the*
*author of* The Sand Pebbles, *a best-selling novel that was made*
*into an excellent film starring Steve McQueen. In science fic-*
*tion, he is remembered as a stylist who died before he could*
*fulfill his great promise. The best of his stories were collected as*
Casey Agonistes and Other Science Fiction and Fantasy Stories.

Chief Biotech Skinner Webb, balding and burly in the gray
coverall working uniform of the Galactic Patrol, walked in front
of his assistant down the path of Crystal Gorge. On either hand
phytos of all sizes detached themselves from their twigs and
branches and swept into the twittering, multicolored swirl above
his head. Phytos were always curious.

Webb sat down on a translucent ledge overlooking white and blue water cascading through milky quartz boulders a hundred feet below. It had become a favorite spot of his in the past month of this rescue mission, and you couldn't pick a prettier place for a drowning. He motioned his assistant to sit down also.

"Vry," he told her, "there's something I want to talk to you about."

Vry Chalmers looked at him gravely. She was small and trim in her Patrol coverall. Compact black curls framed the upper part of her heart-shaped face. Her large and wide-set black eyes were faintly shadowed. She said nothing.

Webb raised his gruff voice above the noise of the water. "Vry, I been thinking I'll jump ship here."

"No!" she said, sitting erect. "Don't joke about such things."

"No joke, Vry. When you lift ship three days from now, I'll be long gone."

"But why are you telling me?"

"Because I want you to come along. We're a team and I need you with me."

She leaned toward him, small fists clenched on her knees. "But however could we get away with it, Skinner? There's only this one settlement. Captain Kravitz would find us in an hour."

"The Conovers will hide us. We can fake a drowning here in the gorge, throw our boots in or something. I've been planning it with Clay and Celia Conover."

Vry's lips quivered. "Oh Skinner, I . . . I . . . but the Patrol will come back . . ."

"Way out here past the edge of nothing? Not for years, maybe a generation. By then we'll both be Conovers."

Vry sat upright again and raised her black eyebrows. "How do you mean, be Conovers?"

"Marry in. I bet you could trap Clay Conover in a month. And old King Conover as good as told me already I could have Celia along with ten thousand square miles of land."

Vry stood up. Her face was suddenly flushed.

"No!" she said, eyes sparkling. "We swore an oath, remember?"

Webb stood up too, hulking his barrel torso above her slightness. "Yes, I remember it. I remember something in it about helping humanity in trouble on strange planets and between the stars."

"Well?"

"Well, they need us here. They were near starving when we got their signal and came. A year after we're gone they'll be starving again and likely there won't be a Patrol ship within a kiloparsec."

"Let Captain Kravitz judge that."

"His hands are tied. Only Prime Reference can reassign a critical rating like biotech. You know that. I even think Kravitz might not be too hard to fool if we faked a drowning . . ."

"Yes he would so too. He's loyal, if you know what that means."

Webb sat down again and inhaled deeply. Sweat beaded his bald spot. He rubbed the back of a thick wrist against his broken nose.

"Sit down, Vry. Don't get excited. I'm being loyal to these six-hundred-something poor devils trying to make themselves a world way out here in nowhere."

She remained standing. "Pooh to that. Conover is trying to start a dynasty. That's why he came so far. Except for the Brecks and Spinellis the people are all morons. Conover chose them so on purpose. And that's why we can't teach them to work a third order bio field." She was panting.

"They're human and they're in the soup."

"Well, I'm not getting in with them and neither are you."

Webb jumped to his feet, heavy jaw set grimly.

"Now Vry," he said, frowning, "you don't mean you'd tell Kravitz what I been saying . . .?"

"It's my duty to tell him. You were trying to get me to desert. But I won't if you won't."

"Well, dammit, Vry, we've been shipmates, and I taught you all you know about biotechnics, and I thought you liked this planet and . . ."

"It's the loveliest planet I've ever seen, and I hope I never see it again," she said angrily.

She turned and marched back up the path toward the settlement shops where the gray, cylindrical form of GPS Carlyle bulked through tree tops. A gay aureole of phytos swooped and whispered above her. She looked small and determined. Webb gazed after her, seething.

"Chalmers!" he shouted suddenly. She halted and looked back.

"Move your stuff aboard and start annual in-grav checks on the bio units. I want it done before we lift out."

"It's not due for months yet. You said we'd do it in Planet Belconti," she protested. "Why . . ."

"Because I'm chief biotech and you're only second class, that's why. You swore an oath, remember?"

"Aye aye, sir," she said in a small voice almost lost in the noise of the tumbling water.

Music eddied among the tree trunks on the Conover lawn the night before lift-out. Clouds of phytos overhead danced in shifting chromatic splendor through the beams of scattered floodlights, leaving the branches almost bare. The phytos liked Mozart. Captain Kravitz and the Carlyle's officers mingled with the Brecks and Spinellis in a group around King Conover. Skinner Webb, resplendent in his blue and gold dress uniform, walked apart with Celia Conover.

She was blond and plump and pink and ivory, and Webb could see her wide blue eyes even when he wasn't looking at them. She wore a brief white sleeveless dress with the barred comet of Conover worked in blue on one shoulder, and she was sweetly rounded in whatever whole or partial aspect Webb chose to gaze at. He rubbed his sweating palms and stubby fingers on his hips.

"You see how it is, Skinno," she was saying. "We had to liquidate everything to get here and now we're stranded. We can't go back except as paupers. The planet is too far out in the void to commercialize it. But if we stay we starve."

"Well, no, I don't think that, Celia," Webb said haltingly. "You've got the wood digesters I set up, and sooner or later your people are bound to develop or find some native protein they can restructure under a first order field . . ."

She grasped his arm.

"The digesters will break down and we won't be able to fix them," she said sharply. "Besides, who wants to eat that dismal stuff year after year anyway? If you go away we'll starve, Skinno. I just know it!"

"Now Celia . . ."

"We'll starve, I tell you. Next time we won't be lucky enough to contact a Patrol ship. Skinno, you've just got to stay here with us. With me." She was clutching his upper arm with both hands.

"Blue space, girl, I want to stay! I want to! I like to went on my knees to Kravitz about it. But he won't lift on it, and now that rat of an assistant of mine has soured the other plan."

"Damn her! Just damn her!" Celia spat.

"Why in hell I ever told her . . ."

"My fault too, Skinno. I should have told you. Clay asked her about it before you did. He even proposed to marry her."

They started walking again across the blue padweed. Webb looked at her bare feet and rounded ankles.

"There's this, and it ain't much," he said. "Captain Kravitz told me he might recommend that a Patrol biotech group be sent out here, and he also said I could request Prime Reference for a special order discharge. One way or another I'll get back here."

"If you leave I'm afraid you'll never come back, Skinno. If you got a discharge, how would you get here?"

"Mail capsule. Weaker men than I have done it before now. I'll steal the capsule if I can't afford to charter one."

"Oh Skinno, could you . . .?"

"I always do things the hard way, seems like. But I do 'em. I'll come back here, Celia."

"Father has some Solarian credits left that are just so much plastic to us now. I'll give them to you before we say goodbye."

"Get me a copy of the sub-space coordinates and the landing tape. I'll need them too."

"Yes Skinno. Oh, you're brave and strong and good, and I believe you will come back even if nobody else could do it."

She steered him toward the group around King Conover and the refreshments. He swelled his biceps under her hand.

"Oh Skinno," Celia said as they approached the others, "I don't see your assistant anywhere. I know Clay invited her."

"She's aboard running in-grav checks," Webb said morosely. "She'll be lucky if she's finished by morning."

He took a few steps and looked at Celia's profile.

"If she doesn't finish, I'll give her blue space worms!" he added savagely.

Four months later, when the Carlyle was space-cruising in the mining region offshore from Planet Belconti, Captain Kravitz called Webb into his office. The captain was a lean, sharp-featured man with grizzled hair and a close clipped gray mustache.

"Chief," he said, "I'm sorry to have to tell you that your request for discharge has just come back from Prime Reference disapproved. Now I don't want you to feel bad . . ."

"Excuse me, Captain," Webb broke in, glowering, "but I can't help feeling bad. I want that discharge something awful."

"Well, PR says you can't have it, Chief. Not until you complete seven more years of service. You knew about that when you put in to go back to Earth for your special third order training."

Then, more kindly, "Seven years isn't a long time, Webb. You're not much past thirty. Remember how Jacob worked for Rachel."

Webb would not be comforted. "How about your recommendation that Patrol biotechs go out there on duty? What came of that . . . sir?" he asked.

"I didn't make it."

"Didn't make it? But you told me . . ."

"I said I might, not that I would. But it wouldn't have done any good.

"In the first place there aren't a dozen Patrol biotechs with third order training in this whole sector as yet. It's too new."

"But those people are going to starve, Captain."

"No, they won't starve. I left them three emergency capsules preset for Prime Reference. They can request evacuation."

"But they'll lose everything, be paupers."

"Most of them always were."

"I mean the Conovers and the Spinellis . . ."

"Damn them and the Brecks too. They want to set up for nobility. Chief, don't let the Conovers fool you. They don't give a damn about you; all they want is your skill. They're setting up an unhealthy social situation on that planet. In a few hundred years there'll be revolution there and good Patrolmen will be killed trying to square it away."

"I don't know anything about politics . . ."

"Well, I do," the captain said with a note of finality. "I hope they starve out. Go back to your work, Chief."

The Belconti drinkhouse was smoky and red, with grimy pearl shell paneling. Raucous music echoed through it.

"Ish the most beau'ful planet in the galaxy or out of it," Webb said joyfully, "and I'm gonna go there and live happily ever after."

"You're not going anywhere, spacer," the girl sitting opposite said. "You missed your ship." She was fleshy and dark, a professional spaceport entertainer.

"I missed the GPS Carlyle. Now I'll charter a mail capsule, and I'll go home, home, home from the spaceways . . . ." Webb, leering at her under his sandy brows, roared tunelessly into the song.

"Watch out the surface patrol don't catch you," she said.

"If they do, I'll get a kickout for missing my ship, and then I'll still go home," he chortled. "I can't lose, don't you shee?"

"Costs money to charter a mail capsule," the girl said, yawning.

"I got it, jetty. They give me a whole wad of Solarian credits to work the deal. I got it, all right." He slapped his ample stomach.

The girl punched out the formula for two more drinks.

"You better hide out at my place for a while, spacer," she said. "If the surface patrol noses around, I can stall 'em off for you." She stroked his bald spot.

Webb, standing stiffly at attention, faced Lieutenant Hathaway across the green table. He was thinking that Hathaway looked like a pink rabbit. The young officer held a paper in his hand. Four other officers sat around the table.

"Chief Biotechnician Webb," the lieutenant said formally, "this court martial board finds you guilty by plea of willfully missing your ship on Planet Belconti. In accordance with the subjoined references to Articles for the Government of the Galactic Patrol, you are sentenced to be reduced to the rating of space apprentice third class and to be released from your service with a bad conduct discharge."

The night stick scar still visible on Webb's bald spot flushed angrily and his heavy jaw set more firmly. The corners of his mouth twitched, but he said nothing. The lieutenant smiled slightly and read from the paper:

"Approved by convening authority except that the discharge is remitted unconditionally, and the reduction in rating is remitted to petty officer first class on the condition of one year's probation. Signed, L. G. Kravitz, Captain, GP, commanding GPS Carlyle, Galactic Three Twenty-seven Fourteen Forty."

Webb turned crimson. He could feel the half-healed scar throbbing on his scalp.

"Aye aye, sir," he choked.

A few minutes later the chief jimmylegs found Webb in the cramped CPO quarters. She was a graying, hard-faced woman.

"You'll have to move out of here now, Skinhead," she said, "and I don't know where I'm going to berth you. There's only one first class PO sleeper left."

"What's wrong with it?" he growled.

"Nothing's wrong, only Vry Chalmers was promoted to first class today, and I don't know which one of you is senior in rate."

Webb looked at her somberly.

"Of course you're senior in service . . ." the jimmylegs said.

"Give it to Vry," Webb said. "I'll take one of the three-shifters in the common room."

That afternoon, sealed in the sleeper for the eight-hour period that was his, Webb could not sleep.

"You donkey!" he thought bitterly. "You damned, slobbering space worm! Rolled for your credits by that Belconti flea-bag, beat up by the patrol she whistled onto you, busted down level with your own helper, and stuck into a hot sleeper for who knows how long? I've got to run away. Oh, blast it . . ."

Webb was the first man ashore on Planet Crim Leggar. The deck hands in the duty section were just starting to erect staging to stellite the Carlyle's worn and pitted bow plates. Webb felt thankful that he was a technician as he lumbered along past them in the high gravity under the two hot suns. His columnar legs and thick body were designed for a high grav planet. He knew Crim Leggar from way back, and this time he would make it good.

Too bad he only had first class PO liberty now. They would start looking for him right after turn-to went tomorrow morning. But he was playing it cold this time. No drinking. No celebration until he got there. Celebrate with Celia Conover.

He took a helio into town and there caught a tube out to an industrial suburb. He bought civilian clothes in a pawn shop and changed into them in a public refresher station. He hid his ID tracer packet in an air vent. Then he took a tube to the rocket port and caught a rocket to the city of Ishikawa on the opposite side of Crim Leggar's one continent. In Ishikawa, two hours later, he rented a room in a shabby district and sat on the edge of the bed.

Good enough! Let 'em find him now! No drinking. Not one drink until he saw Celia Conover. He turned on the stereo. Only one or two of the programs were in Galactic English. The others were in some sort of oriental jabber. One program seemed to be a night club show. The dancing girls were scantily dressed and cute, for oriental types, but he wouldn't swap Celia Conover for the whole planetful.

For two days he took his food packaged through the automat in his room. He didn't know when the Carlyle would lift out. He paced the floor before the stereo thinking about Planet Conover and Celia. Play it cold, no drinking. He watched the night club program on the stereo, and on the third night he saw a party eating what might be Bengdorf.

He adjusted the spot magnifocus to see their table more clearly and it was Bengdorf. Bengdorf! He didn't know they even knew what it was on Planet Crim Leggar. What d'ya know! Bengdorf!

Webb sat at a small table in the shadow of the balcony and far from the stage. Play it cold. No drinking.

"Bengdorf," he ordered, "and a pot of coffee."

It was good Bengdorf, and he spooned it greedily. Suddenly, he was aware of four small, inoffensive-looking men standing by his table.

"He looks like an ape," said one.

"He has a crescent-shaped scar on a bald head," said another.

"He is eating Bengdorf," said a third.

"You are Skinner Webb, a straggler from GPS Carlyle in New Tokyo," said the fourth, addressing Webb directly. "You must come with us, please."

Webb glared at them, thrusting out his lips.

"My name is Smith," he said.

"You must come, please," the man repeated.

Webb upset the table, sending the Bengdorf flying.

"Not for fifty of you monkeys!" he howled.

"You've been to mast before, Ape Shape," the chief jimmylegs said crisply. "Take off your hat!"

Webb took it off.

"Want me to take off the bandages too?" he asked sourly.

"I wouldn't blame the skipper if he took off your whole damned head," the jimmylegs said. "Go on in now." She pushed his shoulder.

Mast was enough. The captain executed the remitted bust to space apprentice third and put Webb on half pay and ship restriction for six months.

"Well, you can't kick me no lower than the three-shift sleeper I got already, sheriff," Webb said as they walked aft.

"No, but you lose the privilege of the petty officer detergent cabinet. You use the common room detergent cabinet from now on," she reminded him.

Next morning, Webb mustered with the prisoners-at-large and then went to the bio shop. He saw with a start that Vry was wearing a CPO uniform. She looked pretty under the CPO hat.

"Congratulations, Vry," he said awkwardly. "When did it come through?"

"While you were gone . . ." she blushed and looked away.

"In my wild goose chase," he finished for her bitterly. "Well, you can hold the rate, Vry. I taught you myself. You're a good biotech."

He looked around the shop. Everything was shipshape and dustless. There were only two small medical units on the repair bench.

"We won't do much today," he said. "I don't feel so good. Let's see if we can structure a pot of coffee out of some of this ifil wood."

"Skinner," she said, blushing still more, "I'm sorry . . . I don't know how to tell you . . . you have to go on a working party."

"Working party!" he shouted. "I'm a technician!"

"Not any more on paper," she said. "You're a space apprentice third class, and your name went on the working party roster right at the top."

He looked at her, flushing with rising anger.

"I tried to get you off," she said. "I lied and told them I had a tough repair job I couldn't do alone. But jimmylegs said let it wait until tomorrow."

"Well," he said, "I guess if I gotta . . ." He turned toward the door.

Vry put her small hand on his arm. "I'm sorry Skinner, for everything," she said softly.

He remembered another hand on his arm and jerked away.

"Stow it!" he snapped. "No favors, Chief, now or another time. Let me do it the hard way."

Before he had sat an hour on the high bow staging, the heavy stelliting cable had worn a blister on his right shoulder. Sweat soaked him. He clicked off the stellite gun and thought.

"How in hell did they know I would go for Bengdorf? Nobody knew I used to make the stuff in the bio units. Nobody except . . . By God! I wonder . . .? Might as well have sewed a tracer packet in my coat!"

Shaking his bandaged head, he lifted the heavy stellite gun and started it spitting the vaporized metal. It seemed to express his own obscure feelings.

Webb caught working parties three times before the Carlyle lifted out from Crim Leggar. Underway there were no working parties, but life in the common room irked him. He hated the compulsory check-in system on the detergent cabinet, as if they couldn't trust him to keep himself clean. The times were always inconvenient, and he could never have a bath when he wanted one. Each time he mustered with the prisoners-at-large, it was like a knife thrust into him.

He couldn't act naturally with anybody. His old drinking partners from the CPO quarters treated him gingerly, as if they were afraid of hurting his feelings. Some of the deck hands he lived among tended to defer to him on account of his former status, and that hurt his feelings. Others, tough punks like he himself had once been, tried to patronize him and to push him around. These he beat up, and that relieved his feelings. Nothing was the same any more. Nobody was the same.

All but Vry. She hadn't changed. They were still a team, able to work up a ten-element third order bio field like two skilled pianists playing a duet. Vry let him run the shop, just like always, and she did it without hurting his feelings. She had to sign all the report forms, of course, but she always waited until he had initialed them. The bio shop was his refuge, his sanctuary, in the ship he sometimes thought he hated. But in spite of everything, when Webb thought about Bengdorf, he found himself hating Vry too. He never made any more Bengdorf, and she never suggested doing so.

He never got used to it. During the six months of his restriction, the Carlyle cruised through the Rim stars making planetfall after planetfall. All it meant to Webb was working parties. On Planet Hopkins he handled stores. On Planet Graufels he stellited bow plates. On Planet Tristan he fumed the intra-skin compartments. Even if he had rated liberty, his apprentice's half pay would hardly have taken him through the third drink.

"If I could only make it to Planet Conover," he often thought, "I would be a king. Almost a king."

Webb had always made a little alcohol in the bio units, just enough for the chiefs. He began making more and more. One of the deck hands brought him back a bubble of Tristanian kresch, and when the Carlyle was underway again, he templated a tube of it into a third order bio field and synthesized a gallon. That made for quite a drunk in the common room, and Webb began thinking that some of the deck hands weren't such hopeless punks after all.

Then one day after working hours, he tried to make another batch of kresch and it went sour. He tried two other bio units with no luck. Something was wrong. He pulled off the inspection panels on one and after some probing found the trouble. A jumper circuit had been added, and he could tell from the location and the color code that it would function as a hydroxyl inhibitor.

"Now dammit," he thought, puzzled. "Vry must've done it. Slick job, too. Can see I trained that girl."

All of the units were similarly guarded. He tried to remove one inhibitor, but it was set in plasteel and secured with a garson lock. He ransacked the shop and found no keys. Dull anger began churning. He had to go back to the common room without anything to drink. The deck hands were expecting some more kresch. He'd be damned if he'd tell them he was no longer master in his own shop. Oh well, tell 'em something . . .

He was still angry next morning when he came into the shop.

"Vry," he said ominously, "why in hell did you put in those hydroxyl inhibitor circuits?"

She looked frightened but game. Her heart-shaped face was pale under the clustering black curls and the black eyebrows.

"I had to, Skinner. The exec has been after me to stop alky getting into the common room. It seemed to me easier than telling you."

"Every trick I ever taught you, Vry, I know another worth two of it," he said. "I can piece in a neutralizer around that inhibitor in no time flat." He jerked open a tool drawer.

"No, you can't!" She pushed the drawer closed again and leaned her slight body against it, facing him. She was paler than ever, leaner backward a little and supporting herself with her hands clutching the edge of the workbench.

"The hell I can't!" he said thickly. "This is my shop. Get out of the way."

"No," she said. "I'll call the master-at-arms."

"Yes, you would, wouldn't you?" he growled. "Like you tipped the apple on how I liked Bengdorf. Shipmate Chalmers! Well, you got chief out of it . . ."

Tears spilled down her cheeks, but her voice was firm. "Listen to what the exec told me, Skinner Webb! He gave me a direct order to lock the shop after working hours and to oversee everything you did during working hours. I thought I could get around that by putting in the inhibitors. I know what this shop means to you . . ."

"Yeah, you know, and so you stole it from me. I trained you, Chalmers, and you bite me with my own teeth."

"Get out!" she snapped, standing erect. "Get back to the common room with the other deck hands! I don't have any work for you today."

Webb stood stupefied. Vry reached toward the intercom. Her pallor had given way to a hectic flush, but she was still crying.

"I'll call jimmylegs," she threatened.

Webb walked out, shaking his head. There was nothing left for him now. He'd almost sooner be dead than stay on aboard this hell ship.

Locked out of his own shop! That really put the iron into him like nothing before. A grim purpose came into his brooding. He would desert again, next chance he had. That would be when his restriction expired, and it would be on Planet Bigorne. Three weeks from now. He asked a few questions about Bigorne, but nobody knew much about it. Fairly well settled, they said. Well, all the easier to hide out.

No money. He would have to find work right off. But even a biotech who could only handle first order stuff pulled down big money on the outside. With his skill there was no limit. But maybe third order stuff was so new that they wouldn't even have the units on Bigorne yet. Okay, all the better. He would steal the Carlyle's spare bio elements, and he could improvise the rest. They would be a kind of stake: each one had cost the Patrol more than a thousand Solarian credits.

Good enough. It was going to be do or die this time. If they caught him it would mean prison. He'd die fighting before he let the Patrol haul him back again. No lone wolf stuff; have to plug in with some kind of organization. Well, beam in, Bigorne! Let's go!

Webb came on the quarterdeck with a bundle under his arm. Inside it were seven bio elements and a flame pistol that he had stolen from the small arms locker in the CPO quarters after liberty call on the previous day. He saluted the OOD and asked permission to leave the ship.

The OOD was Ensign Whittaker, blond, roly-poly and very

young. He returned Webb's salute with the familiar embarrassment and asked, "What do you have in the bundle, Webb?"

"It's my CPO dress uniform and my medals. I thought I might sell 'em for the price of a couple of drinks."

The ensign looked more embarrassed. "Don't you know that apprentices don't rate drink liberty, Webb?" he asked.

"Yes sir, I know. I know, all right," Webb said.

"Permission granted," said the ensign.

They wouldn't sell him a drink in the first bar because of his apprentice stripes. He asked the houseman in what part of town they overlooked such niceties and, on receiving directions, went there. He had to act fast. Sometime tomorrow they would have a pickup out on him. Maybe even sooner if Vry found out about the bio elements. She had changed the lock on them, must have been suspicious. Lucky he was able to slug the new lock.

He chose a shabby-looking place with only a few people in it and sat down in a booth. He tipped a signal to the oldest and hardest-looking entertainer at the back table. She joined him.

"Let me punch out the drinks," she said. "This dispenser is cranky sometimes."

"Get me Earth whisky and plain water," he said, dropping a ten credit piece into the bank slot. It was half his funds.

"You look pretty grown up to be an apprentice, spacer," she commented. "Don't they like you topside?"

"No," he said, "and I don't like them."

There was a pause while the drinks were delivered. Then she said, "Something's on your mind, spacer. You aren't over-leave, are you?"

"Will be in about twelve hours," he said. "Look, I need your help."

"How?"

"I gotta trust you. I don't know anybody on Bigorne. I got no time."

"Time for what?"

"Make the right contact. Look, here in this bundle I got seven bio elements worth about ten thousand Solarian credits. I stole 'em from the ship."

"What are bio elements? Who buys them?"

He told her briefly. She was impressed but doubtful. Finally she said, "I know a man . . . but I can't get to him this time of day."

Webb persuaded her to try. After several calls she came back to the table and said, "Let's go." Webb picked up his bundle and followed her out.

The man, seated at a shabby desk in a small office, was grossly fat and hairless. He heard Webb's story with considerably more interest and comprehension than the woman had shown. Then he too made several calls, talking in a strange language to a blanked telescreen. When he was finished, he took a handful of credits from a drawer and gave them to the woman.

"You bow out now," he said.

She hesitated, looking at Webb. "Good luck, spacer," she said.

"Thanks, jetty," Webb answered. "It's time I had some, and maybe you brought it to me."

"I hope I did," she said thoughtfully. "Good-bye, spacer." She went out of the room.

The fat man rose and opened another door.

"They're coming for you, but it will be three or four hours yet," he said. "You can wait in here. There's a drink machine and a stereo."

Webb entered the room. The fat man closed the door and locked it. Webb whirled around to face the door, then shrugged and walked over to switch on the stereo.

It was night outside when they finally came for him, two dark-clad men who did not introduce themselves. They took his

ID tracer and his flame pistol and gave him civilian clothes to put on. They had a plastic bag for the bio elements. A private helio on the roof took them to a darkened rocket port where they boarded a small six-place rocket. They flew west, overhauling the sun, and it was twilight when the rocket sat down on what looked to be an island a good way offshore. It was hilly and wooded. There was a clump of gray buildings in a clearing.

The two men led Webb into a building and into a room with a table and half a dozen chairs. A tall, saturnine man with craggy features and thin lips stood by a window. Webb was holding the plastic bag.

"Here's that Patrol spacer, boss," one of the men said. They left, closing the door.

The black-haired man by the window looked at Webb silently for a moment. He had deep-set black eyes and bushy eyebrows. Then he spoke.

"My name's Crego. Captain Crego, to you. I don't have much spare time for palaver. Can you take these bio elements you've got and fix up a first order bio unit to make food out of plain rock?"

"Yes, depending on the rock. But nothing fancy. Starches and sugars."

"How long to rig it?"

"Four, five days. I'll need tools and materials."

"You'll get what you need. And you're what I've been needing—bad."

"What kind of a project are you working up?" Webb asked.

Crego sat down and waved Webb to a chair.

"I don't trust you Patrol spacers," he said. "In fact, I hate the linings of your stinking hearts. Something about this doesn't track for me yet. Give me the whole story."

Webb shot out his lips and frowned. "I ain't a Patrol spacer. I run away. But I knew some good men in the Patrol . . ."

Crego laughed mirthlessly. "The story," he commanded.

Webb told him. He warmed up as he reviewed his grievances and thumped on the table. Crego nodded from time to time and smiled thinly, with his lips only.

"Sounds like a straight story," he commented finally. "Those are just the kinds of things that would happen to an ape-brain like you."

Webb squirmed uneasily and glowered.

"Now I'll give you the layout," Crego continued. "I head up a Free Company, about a hundred men just now. We've got a small ship, powered for sub-space, but old and unreliable. Your damned Patrol knocked over our base out in Regius last year and we're still trying to get back on our feet."

Webb licked his lips and gulped. "That was GPS Konoye. I heard about it."

"Yes, and someday I'll blast GPS Konoye or one like her. But for now—we've got the coordinates, never mind how, of an asteroid stuffed with Weidmann matrices like raisins in a pudding. The discoverers are a small legitimate outfit. They're waiting until they can get some third order biotechs from Earth sector. With you, we can go out there now and loot the claim. It's the break I've been waiting for."

"Well, sounds good I guess," Webb said uncomfortably. "What will you pay me?"

"You get a lay of one-half percent for now. More later, if I like you after the Patrol stink wears off."

"Well, one-half percent of even a couple of Weidmann matrices ought to get me to Planet Conover," Webb said with a heartiness he did not feel.

Crego laughed harshly. "Get it square, spacer. You've just enlisted in a Free Company. If you don't know what that means, I'll tell you. You're in for life. How long a life partly depends on you. You already know too much."

Webb pondered that silently. His guts were churning. Crego spoke again.

"That doesn't mean you won't see Planet Conover," he said. "What you told me sounds like it might be a good hideout, even a base. Maybe worth looting the settlement too."

"They haven't got a thing," Webb said hurriedly. "They broke themselves getting out there."

"Got pretty women, maybe. The comrades would like that too. Give me the coordinates."

Webb jumped to his feet. "No!" he growled.

Crego stood up too and produced a flame pistol. A contemptuous grin shaped itself on the thin lips.

"You think you've got discipline in your damned Patrol," he said, almost whispering, "by God, you've really got it in a Free Company. Give me those coordinates, or I'll fry that bald spot for you."

Webb hesitated, feeling the red rage boil up, feeling the berserker battle grin twitching at his lips.

"Quick now!" Crego barked. "Don't be any more stupid than God made you, if that's possible. There's nowhere left you can run to and you know it. Hand it over!"

Webb handed over the plastic card. A slow fire began to burn in his stomach.

Webb was a prisoner in the ship. It was hardly a fifth the size of the Carlyle, perhaps a hundred feet long and twenty in diameter, but it carried a wicked armament of Kingross launchers. It was concealed in a shallow pit in the heavily wooded center of the island. Webb worked for several days on the ancient Mark II bio units, sleeping on deck in the locked bio shop. Guards brought him food at irregular intervals and twice Crego came urging him to hurry the job.

He tried to be fatalistic, but regrets kept nipping at him. He despised himself. What rankled most was his suspicion that he was afraid of Crego, afraid of him as a plain two-legged man and not as the embodiment of a thousand-year-old tradition, like

Captain Kravitz. Webb couldn't live with that. He might kill Crego before they burned him down, but Planet Conover would still be wide open. Maybe the thing was to wait until the ship was in sub-space and then try to blow it up and himself with it. He worked in a daze under a kind of paralysis of will.

Then, early on the morning of the fourth day, Webb was awakened by an alarm. Hatches banged, men ran and shouted, a main field generator whined into the upper registers. It sounded as if they were going to lift ship. Two guards unlocked the bio shop, not speaking, and hustled Webb off the ship, running him double time along a forest path to a small stone building. They kicked him through the door and clanked it shut.

Scarcely awake yet, Webb blinked in the darkness and rubbed his bald spot. He turned around slowly, making out the shape of a wooden table and some posts set in the floor. As his eyes adjusted he saw another figure in the room, crouched in a corner. It looked to be a woman. She had on a Patrol uniform. She was looking at him. It was Vry. No! Yes! Space devils! Vry!

"Vry," he said, "how . . . what . . . God above, *is* it you, Vry?"

"Yes," she said rising, "It's me, your loyal little helper."

Webb took her by the shoulders. "Vry, I don't get it," he said. Then he noticed that her right eye and upper lip were swollen and he saw the blood on her torn uniform.

"Are you hurt, Vry?" he asked anxiously.

"No," she said. "They thought I was a scout for a Patrol party at first and handled me around a little. But now they think I'm just a spy."

"Damn their guts. But are you spying?"

"No," she told him, speaking dully. Suspecting he might steal the bio elements, she had put tracer packets into four of them. One of the quartermasters, a friend of hers, had helped her to set up a search field and get a fix on them, and she had looked up the island on a map. She had come to get the bio elements back, that was all, and that was why she had come alone. Not being able to charter a helio in the nearest coastal city, she had had someone put her ashore from a skim boat.

"I wanted you to get away this time, Skinner," she said. "I was going to give you the money you needed. I drew all my savings from the paymaster."

"Bless you, Vry, my head's going around. It seems fantastic. How did the paymaster come to let you have your savings before your enlistment was up?"

"I told him it was an emergency."

"Lord, Lord, it sure is one now. Do you know what you got yourself into the middle of?"

"I think maybe a Free Company."

"Yes, what's left of that outfit the Konoye broke up last year. They're mean and dangerous and they hate us."

"I know."

"What in hell are we gonna do? Let's hide your ID tracer somewhere in here and tell 'em you lost it."

"They took it when they searched me."

"Who knows you were coming here, Vry?"

"Nobody. I wanted to protect you."

"How about that quartermaster?"

"Beacon? She might figure it. But she won't try until I'm a day or two overleave and the regulation search field fails."

"How long? Are you on leave?"

"Yes, ten days. I've got a week left."

Webb pondered for a moment. He could see her better now and she looked small and scared and helpless. On impulse, he put an arm around her shoulders.

"Vry, in some ways you're as dumb as I am. How did you figure to get back off the island if you let the skim boat go?"

She stiffened a little and there was a touch of returning spirit in her voice. "They told me in Port Omphale that it was a private estate. I thought the people here might have transportation or that I could signal for a helio. After all, I had a week, and how could I know . . .''

"You couldn't, Vry. I'm the stupid one, and now I've dragged you into bad trouble. I don't know what to do about you . . .''

"I do," broke in a metallic voice from the wall. "Bring 'em aboard, comrades.'' The door scraped open again.

It was still early dawn. The guards prodded them up the gangplank of the ship into the narrow central passageway and along it single file past the bio shop and into main control. Crego and another man were there. Crego was laughing sardonically.

"You're just stupid enough to ask all the right questions, Webb. I wouldn't trust that story if I had beaten it out of her.''

Crego looked from one to the other. Webb realized with a start that Vry's hand had crept into his own. He squeezed it gently.

"Just the same," Crego went on, "I'll take no chances. We lift out in forty-eight hours, just as soon as I can pull in all the comrades. And you, Webb, can you finish your conversion job with the material on hand?''

"Yes," Webb said. "With her helping me I can finish before you lift out. We're a team. I trained her, taught her all she knows.''

"Good," Crego said, cocking an eyebrow. "She can work with you.''

"Will you let her go when we lift out . . . sir?" Webb asked, knowing the answer.

Crego laughed again.

"Shame to break up a team," he said solicitously. "Besides, the Patrol got most of our women when they knocked over our base, and she'll be a peculiarly appropriate recruit. Do you know the Free Company rule about women, Comrade Webb?''

"Don't tell me," Webb said.

Locked in the bio shop, Webb and Vry used the tools and instruments there to assure themselves that no spy units were installed. Then they talked as they worked, in whispers.

"You can't go with this gang, Vry," Webb said.

"What can we do?"

"I don't know. I wish I could think. Vry, *you* think of something."

"We've got to break out of here. Could we, do you suppose?"

"Well . . . yes. At night, maybe. I think they leave the skin doors open at the gangplank because I never hear 'em operate. But likely there's a sentry there. Probably a watch in main control too, and the regular guard outside in the passageway. That's three . . ."

"Is three too many?"

"No, maybe not. But there's a hundred more of them, and we're on an island. I guess . . . Vry, I got it!"

"What?"

"I'll do what damage I can and let 'em blast me down. Then with me gone they won't dare bother you too much because they have to have a biotech . . ."

"No. Both of us or neither, Skinner."

"It's only common sense, Vry. I'm shot already. There's nowhere left for me to go . . ."

"No. Listen, Skinner. It was a lie I told you—and them— about the skim boat. I came in a chartered helio, and it may still be hidden where I left it. I had to walk a long way before . . ."

Webb hugged her to him and kissed her on the swollen eye. "Vry, I love you," he cried. "I'm alive again. I'm a man again."

"Hush! Even if the room's clear, they'll hear you through the door."

"Sorry. But see what it means, Vry! We'll get away!"

"Maybe they've already found the helio. We still have to get off the ship . . ."

"Easy as eating Bengdorf, Vry. Trust old Skinner. You've never seen me in action."

"First things first," she said, slipping out of his embrace. "You'll have yourself on Planet Conover in another ten seconds."

Webb sobered suddenly.

"No, Vry. I been thinking in circles for three days and just now it come to me. King Conover is a Crego type. If I did get out there, Conover would have me cold rivets just like Crego has me now. All either of 'em wants is a dog with third order bio training, and up until a minute ago Crego had me kind of thinking I was a dog."

"But isn't Celia a pretty little . . .?"

"Say it," he said. "Bitch. Only I just found out I ain't a dog."

"I'm glad, Skinner."

"We'll rig an arc to burn out that lock," he said. "We'll make the break early tomorrow morning, like when they caught you. People don't think fast that time of day."

"Show me what you want me to do, Skinner."

At noon a guard brought two bowls of food on a tray.

"Cap'n Crego says by tomorrow morning you better be able to make your own food with that thing, Patroller," he said.

"I can make better stuff than that slop out of sawdust," Webb said.

The guard spat in the tray. Webb felt Vry's hand on his arm and restrained himself. After a moment the guard locked the door.

"Let's finish rigging the arc," Webb whispered. "I hope that damn space worm is on duty out there tomorrow morning."

Webb worked on the arc while Vry tinkered with the bio units. He saw that she was dismantling them again, undoing his work.

"Go ahead, Vry," he told her. "That kind of undoes the past. Crego had me under a spell."

A different guard brought the supper tray, and there was only one bowl on it. Crego stood behind the guard in the narrow door.

"You, Chalmers, come along with me," he said. "The comrades want to induct you into the Company."

Vry looked at Webb, pale, lips parted. Webb pressed the switch on the arc, and the resultant sputter and flash gave him the diversion he needed. He broke Crego's gun arm and smashed the guard's head savagely against the steel door frame. Then, grunting obscenities, he wrestled Crego into the passageway and took the blast from the second guard's pistol in Crego's body. He dropped Crego to club the guard down with his fists, and the passageway was clear. Six strides took him to the gangplank. He looked back and saw Vry at his heels.

"Here," she said, thrusting a flame pistol into his hand.

"Out you go, Vry." He pushed her down the gangplank. Turning again, he fired a blast at a head peering above the coaming of the hatch to main drive and another for good measure into the open door of main control. Then he pulled the emergency closing lever for the skin doors and leaped through them as they clanged together. He focused the pistol down and spot welded the doors at their juncture before joining Vry at the foot of the gangplank.

"Hurry," she said.

"We've got a few minutes now. Which way? You lead."

She ran through the woods, angling up a slope. "I hope I can find it," she panted. "There was a big meadow with yellow flowers and a rock."

"It was too easy," he puffed, pounding along behind her. "I wanted a fight. I needed a fight."

"There's blood on your face," she panted back. "You had a kind of a fight. Don't be greedy."

"Anyway, I got Crego. Vry, I'm a man again."

"Save your breath. It's a long way."

They heard an alarm siren and distant shouts. Webb patted the flame pistol in his pocket.

"I wish it was darker," he grunted. "When we take off they might get a Kingross on the helio."

"It will be dark. It's a long way yet. Let's walk now."

"Okay. Let me break trail."

It was then that he first saw the plastic bag slung round her neck. "Let me carry that," he said. "What's in it?"

"The bio elements," she said. "You didn't think I'd leave them, did you? They're charged out to us."

"Good girl, Vry. You got a head. Can see I trained you."

"We're fairly safe now, I think," she said. "Since they don't know about the helio, they'll probably concentrate on the beaches."

It was quite dark before they finally found the helio, intact. Webb worried about a search field and Kingross projectiles but said nothing to Vry. Since it was a charter helio, the controls were preset for a Port Omphale helio center. There was nothing to do but ride and hope. They took off with running lights darkened, and Webb figuratively held his breath until he could see the loom of the island well behind them in the faintly starlit water. He was thinking, too. Thinking hard.

Vry borke the silence.

"We shouldn't lose any time getting the planetary authorities after those pirates," she said. "They're going to lift out and run."

"I been thinking that. We ought to call Captain Kravitz on the helio telescreen."

"Let's do, now."

"No. We gotta have a story first. Besides, he'll see me."

"Why shouldn't he?"

"Space worms, girl! I'm a deserter. I gotta drop out of sight first in this Port Omphale—is that the name?—and then you can fix up a story and call him.''

''You're not a deserter, Skinner,'' she said, out of the darkness.

''Tell that to Captain Kravitz. He's got the book in his blood.''

''I mean it,'' she said earnestly. ''I made a false muster for you every morning until I checked out on leave, and when I did, I checked you out on a ten day leave too.''

''No! How did you work it?''

''I've got friends in the Carlyle and so have you, whatever you may think. I told everybody it was an emergency. Lots of people know something unofficially, but on paper you're still all squared away.''

''Well. Well . . . what kind of a dummy am I, you didn't tell me that before?''

''I was afraid, Skinner. You get enthusiastic too easily. I wanted to keep you desperate and with your feet on the ground until we got clear. I'm sorry, maybe I was wrong . . .''

''No, maybe I do, Vry. Vry, I . . . let me turn on the light.''

He turned on the cabin light and looked at her, sitting there small and disheveled, looking at him apprehensively out of wide eyes. He put his hand on her shoulder, then dropped it.

''We still gotta think of a story,'' he said. ''All the more now, if I gotta be in it.''

She was silent. He shuffled his feet and cocked his head, thinking.

''We can almost tell the truth,'' he said finally. ''Tell 'em that we were kidnapped for our skills. All the rest can be true.''

''Tell them you killed Crego,'' she murmured.

''Yes. I killed Crego. Damn him, wish I could do it again. I ought to get a medal for that.''

''You probably will,'' she said. ''For sure, you'll get your CPO rating back.''

"Sure I will! Hell, yes, why didn't I think of that? Tip the apple on those damned pirates, and I'll be all the way back to battery. Vry, what would I ever do without you?"

"Get lumps on your head," she said. "As a matter of fact, you've got one now, a nasty cut. Let me clean it up." She pulled open the helio's first aid box.

"Ouch!" he cried. "Blazes! Take it easy, that's tender."

She continued daubing at the dried blood. "Do you still have that flame pistol?" she asked.

"Yes. Right here."

"Better slip it in the bag with the bio elements. I'll have to smuggle it back into the CPO arms locker and hope nobody checks the serial number."

"All right. Vry, I can't keep up with you. Ouch! That stuff stings!"

"Good for you."

Both the small hands were busy bandaging his head. All at once he wanted powerfully to press his face against her neck and shoulder. He pulled away and sat erect.

"I'm not done," she said.

"Neither am I," he said, pushing a loop of bandage off his eye. "Vry, we still got a week's leave. Let's use it to get married."

"Spacers shouldn't get married," she said in a small voice. "They don't have homes."

"Spacers are the only people who can really pick their homes," he countered. "What about homesteading on Planet Conover when my time is up?"

"I do love Planet Conover," she said musingly.

"Is that an answer? Say you will, Vry. We're a team, Vry. I taught you everything you know."

"Aye aye, sir," she murmured.

Webb kissed her soundly, then laid his cheek against hers and whispered in her ear, "I got the best idea yet. When we call

Captain Kravitz about the pirates, we'll ask for a week's extension on our leaves. I'll tell him it's a new emergency just come up, we're getting married.''

Her hands sought the loose ends of bandage.

''I'm afraid we can't tell him that, Skinner,'' she said softly. ''That was the emergency excuse I used to get our leaves approved in the first place.''

''Put your hat on, Skinhead,'' the jimmylegs said. ''You're not going to mast this time, you're getting the Patrol Bronze.''

''It won't fit over the bandages,'' Webb objected.

''Well, set it on top any old how. You're going to have to salute,'' the jimmylegs said sharply. ''Go on in now.''

# JOAN D. VINGE

# TIN SOLDIER

*Joan Vinge is one of the outstanding new talents in science fiction and the winner of the 1979 Hugo Award for her story "Eyes of Amber."*

*Here she projects one of the most beloved of all Hans Christian Andersen's tales into the far future, where a man who is more than a man finds love in the form of one of the most memorable characters in science fiction.*

The ship drifted down the ragged light-robe of the Pleiades, dropped like a perfect pearl into the midnight water of the bay. And reemerged, to bob gently in a chain of gleaming pearls stretched across the harbor toward the port. The port's unsleeping Eye blinked once, the ship replied. New Piraeus, pooled among the hills, sent tributaries of light streaming down to the bay to welcome all comers, full of sound and brilliance and rash promise. The crew grinned, expectant, faces peering through the transparent hull; someone giggled nervously.

The sign at the heavy door flashed a red one-legged toy; TIN SOLDIER flashed blue below it. EAT. DRINK. COME BACK AGAIN. In green. And they always did, because they knew they could.

"Soldier, another round, please!" came over canned music.

The owner of the Tin Soldier, also known as Tin Soldier,

glanced up from his polishing to nod and smile, reached down to set bottles out on the bar. He mixed the drinks himself. His face was ordinary, with eyes that were dark and patient, and his hair was coppery barbed wire bound with a knotted cloth. Under the curling copper, under the skin, the back of his skull was a plastic plate. The quick fingers of the hand on the goose-necked bottle were plastic, the smooth arm was prosthetic. Sometimes he imagined he heard clicking as it moved. More than half his body was artificial. He looked to be about twenty-five; he had looked the same fifty years ago.

He set the glasses on the tray and pushed, watching as it drifted across the room, and returned to his polishing. The agate surface of the bar showed cloudy permutations of color, grain-streak and whorl and chalcedony depths of mist. He had discovered it in the desert to the east—a shattered imitation tree, like a fellow traveler trapped in stasis through time. They shared the private joke with their clientele.

"—come see our living legend!"

He looked up, saw her coming in with the crew of the *Who Got Her–709*, realized he didn't know her. She hung back as they crowded around, her short ashen hair like beaten metal in the blue-glass lantern light. *New*, he thought. Maybe eighteen, with eyes of quicksilver very wide open. He smiled at her as he welcomed them, and the other women pulled her up to the agate bar. "Come on, little sister," he heard Harkané say, "you're one of us too." She smiled back at him.

"I don't know you . . . but your name should be Diana, like the silver Lady of the Moon." His voice caught him by surprise.

Quicksilver shifted. "It's not."

*Very new.* And realizing what he'd almost done again, suddenly wanted it more than anything. Filled with bitter joy he said, "What is your name?"

Her face flickered, but then she met his eyes and said, smiling, "My name is Brandy."

"Brandy . . ."

A knowing voice said, "Send us the usual, Soldier. Later, yes—?"

He nodded vaguely, groping for bottles under the counter ledge. Wood screeked over stone as she pulled a stool near and slipped onto it, watching him pour. "You're very neat." She picked nuts from a bowl.

"*Long* practice."

She smiled, missing the joke.

He said, "Brandy's a nice name. And I think somewhere I've heard it—"

"The whole thing is Branduin. My mother said it was very old."

He was staring at her. He wondered if she could see one side of his face blushing. "What will you drink?"

"Oh . . . do you have any—brandy? It's a wine, I think; nobody's ever had any. But because it's my name, I always ask."

He frowned. "I don't . . . hell, I do! Stay there."

He returned with the impossible bottle, carefully wiped away its gray coat of years and laid it gleaming on the bar. Glintings of maroon speared their eyes. "All these years, it must have been waiting. That's where I heard it . . . genuine vintage brandy, from Home."

"From Terra—really? Oh, thank you!" She touched the bottle, touched his hand. "I'm going to be lucky."

Curving glasses blossomed with wine; he placed one in her palm. "*Ad astra*." She lifted the glass.

"*Ad astra*; to the stars." He raised his own, adding silently, *Tonight . . .*

They were alone. Her breath came hard as they climbed up the newly cobbled streets to his home, up from the lower city where the fluorescent lamps were snuffing out one by one.

He stopped against a low stone wall. "Do you want to catch

your breath?'' Behind him in the empty lot a weedy garden patch wavered with the popping street lamp.

''Thank you.'' She leaned downhill against him, against the wall. ''I got lazy on my training ride. There's not much to do on a ship; you're supposed to exercise, but—'' Her shoulder twitched under the quilted blue-silver. He absorbed her warmth.

Her hand pressed his lightly on the wall. ''What's your name? You haven't told me, you know.''

''Everyone calls me Soldier.''

''But that's not your name.'' Her eyes searched his own, smiling.

He ducked his head, his hand caught and tightened around hers. ''Oh . . . no, it's not. It's Maris.'' He looked up. ''That's an old name, too. It means 'soldier,' consecrated to the god of war. I never liked it much.''

''From 'Mars'? Sol's fourth planet, the god of war.'' She bent back her head and peered up into the darkness. Fog hid the stars.

''Yes.''

''Were you a soldier?''

''Yes. Everyone was a soldier—every man—where I came from. War was a way of life.''

''An attempt to reconcile the blow to the masculine ego?''

He looked at her.

She frowned in concentration. '' 'After it was determined that men were physically unsuited to spacing, and women came to a new position of dominance as they monopolized this critical area, the Terran cultural foundation underwent severe strain. As a result, many new and not always satisfactory cultural systems are evolving in the galaxy. . . . One of these is what might be termed a backlash of exaggerated *machismo*—' ''

'' '—and the rebirth of the warrior/chattel tradition.' ''

''You've read that book too.'' She looked crestfallen.

''I read a lot. *New Ways for Old*, by Ebert Ntaka?''

''Sorry . . . I guess I got carried away. But, I just read it—''

"No." He grinned. "And I agree with old Ntaka, too. Glatte—what a sour name—was an unhealthy planet. But that's why I'm here, not there."

"Ow—!" She jerked loose from his hand. "Ohh, oh . . . God, you're strong!" She put her fingers in her mouth.

He fell over apologies; but she shook her head, and shook her hand. "No, it's all right . . . really, it just surprised me. Bad memories?"

He nodded, mouth tight.

She touched his shoulder, raised her fingers to his lips. "Kiss it, and make it well?" Gently he caught her hand, kissed it; she pressed against him. "It's very late. We should finish climbing the hill . . . ?"

"No." Hating himself, he set her back against the wall.

"No? But I thought—"

"I know you did. Your first space, I asked your name, you wanted me to; tradition says you lay the guy. But I'm a cyborg, Brandy. . . . It's always good for a laugh on the poor greenie, they've pulled it a hundred times."

"A cyborg?" The flickering gray eyes raked his body.

"It doesn't show with my clothes on."

"Oh . . ." Pale lashes were beating very hard across the eyes now. She took a breath, held it. "Do—you always let it get this far? I mean—"

"No. Hell, I don't know why I . . . I owe you another apology. Usually I never ask the name. If I slip, I tell them right away; nobody's ever held to it. I don't count." He smiled weakly.

"Well, why? You mean you can't—"

"I'm not all plastic." He frowned, numb fingers rapping stone. "God, I'm not. Sometimes I wish I was, but I'm not."

"No one? They never want to?"

"Branduin"—he faced the questioning eyes—"you'd better go back down. Get some sleep. Tomorrow laugh it off, and pick up some flashy Tail in the bar and have a good time. Come see me again in twenty-five years, when you're back from space, and tell me what you saw.'' Hesitating, he brushed her cheek with his true hand; instinctively she bent her head to the caress. ''Good-bye.'' He started up the hill.

''Maris—''

He stopped, trembling.

''Thank you for the brandy . . .'' She came up beside him and caught his belt. ''You'll probably have to tow me up the hill.''

He pulled her to him and began to kiss her, hands touching her body incredulously.

''It's getting—very, very late. Let's hurry.''

Maris woke, confused, to the sound of banging shutters. Raising his head he was struck by the colors of dawn, and the shadow of Brandy standing bright-edged at the window. He left the rumpled bed and crossed cold tiles to join her. ''What are you doing?'' he yawned.

''I wanted to watch the sun rise, I haven't seen anything but night for months. Look, the fog's lifting already: the sun burns it up, it's on fire, over the mountains—''

He smoothed her hair, pale gold under a corona of light. ''And embers in the canyon.''

She looked down across ends of gray mist slowly reddening; then back. ''Good morning.'' She began to laugh. ''I'm glad you don't have any neighbors down there!'' They were both naked.

He grinned, ''That's what I like about the place,'' and put his arms around her. She moved close in the circle of coolness and warmth.

They watched the sunrise from the bed.

In the evening she came into the bar with the crew of the *Kiss and Tell–736*. They waved to him, nodded to her and drifted into blue shadows; she perched smiling before him. It struck him suddenly that nine hours was a long time.

''That's the crew of my training ship. They want some white wine, please, any kind, in a bottle.''

He reached under the bar. "And one brandy, on the house?" He sent the tray off.

"Hi, Maris . . ."

"Hi, Brandy."

"To misty mornings." They drank together.

"By the way" —she glanced at him slyly— "I passed it around that people have been missing something. You."

"Thank you," meaning it. "But I doubt if it'll change any minds."

"Why not?"

"You read Ntaka—xenophobia; to most people in most cultures cyborgs are unnatural, the next thing up from a corpse. You'd have to be a necrophile—"

She frowned.

"—or extraordinary. You're the first extraordinary person I've met in a hundred years."

The smile formed, faded. "Maris—you're not exactly twenty-five, are you? How old are you?"

"More like a hundred and fifteen." He waited for the reaction.

She stared. "But, you look like twenty-five? You're real, don't you age?"

"I age. About five years for every hundred." He shrugged. "The prosthetics slow the body's aging. Perhaps it's because only half my body needs constant regeneration; or it may be an effect of the antirejection treatment. Nobody really understands it. It just happens sometimes."

"Oh." She looked embarrassed. "That's what you meant by 'come back and see me' . . . and they meant—Will you really live a thousand years?"

"Probably not. Something vital will break down in another three or four centuries, I guess. Even plastic doesn't last forever."

"Oh . . ."

"Live longer and enjoy it less. Except for today. What did you do today? Get any sleep?"

"No—" She shook away disconcertion. "A bunch of us went out and gorged. We stay on wake-ups when we're in port, so we don't miss a minute; you don't need to sleep. Really they're for emergencies, but everybody does it."

Quick laughter almost escaped him; he hoped she'd missed it. Serious, he said, "You want to be careful with those things. They can get to you."

"Oh, they're all right." She twiddled her glass, annoyed and suddenly awkward again, confronted by the Old Man.

*Hell, it can't matter*—He glanced toward the door.

"Brandy! There you are." And the crew came in. "Soldier, you must come sit with us later; but right now we're going to steal Brandy away from you."

He looked up with Brandy to the brown face, brown eyes, and salt-white hair of Harkané, Best Friend of the Mactav on the *Who Got Her–709*. Time had woven deep nets of understanding around her eyes; she was one of his oldest customers. Even the shape of her words sounded strange to him now: "Ah, Soldier, you make me feel young, always . . . Come, little sister, and join your family; share her, Soldier."

Brandy gulped brandy; her boots clattered as she dropped off the stool. "Thank you for the drink," and for half a second the smile was real. "Guess I'll be seeing you—Soldier." And she was leaving, ungracefully, gratefully.

Soldier polished the agate bar, ignoring the disappointed face it showed him. And later watched her leave, with a smug, black-eyed Tail in velvet knee pants.

Beyond the doorway yellow-green twilight seeped into the bay, the early crowds began to come together with the night. "H'lo, Maris . . . ?" Silver dulled to lead met him in a face gone hollow; thin hands trembled, clenched, trembled in the air.

"Brandy—"

"What've you got for an upset stomach?" She was expecting laughter.

"Got the shakes, huh?" He didn't laugh.

She nodded. "You were right about the pills, Maris. They make me sick. I got tired, I kept taking them . . ." Her hands rattled on the counter.

"And that was pretty dumb, wasn't it?" He poured her a glass of water, watched her trying to drink, pushed a button under the counter. "Listen, I just called you a ride—when it comes, I want you to go to my place and go to bed."

"But—"

"I won't be home for hours. Catch some sleep and then you'll be all right, right? This is my door lock." He printed large numbers on a napkin. "Don't lose this."

She nodded, drank, stuffed the napkin up her sleeve. Drank some more, spilling it. "My mouth is numb." An abrupt chirp of laughter escaped; she put up a shaky hand. "I—won't lose it."

Deep gold leaped beyond the doorway, sunlight on metal. "Your ride's here."

"Thank you, Maris." The smile was crooked but very fond. She tacked toward the doorway.


She was still there when he came home, snoring gently in the bedroom in a knot of unmade blankets. He went silently out of the room, afraid to touch her, and sank into a leather-slung chair. Filled with rare and uneasy peace he dozed, while the starlit mist of the Pleiades' nebulosity passed across the darkened sky toward morning.

"Maris, why didn't you wake me up? You didn't have to sleep in a *chair* all night." Brandy stood before him wrestling with a towel, eyes puffy with sleep and hair flopping in sodden plumb-bobs from the shower. Her feet made small puddles on the braided rug.

"I didn't mind. I don't need much sleep."

"That's what I told *you*."

"But I meant it. I never sleep more than three hours. You needed the rest, anyway."

"I know . . . damn—" She gave up and wrapped the towel around her head. "You're a fine guy, Maris."

"You're not so bad yourself."

She blushed. "Glad you approve. Ugh, your rug—I got it all wet." She disappeared into the bedroom.

Maris stretched unwillingly, stared up into ceiling beams bronzed with early sunlight. He sighed faintly. "You want some breakfast?"

"Sure, I'm starving! Oh, wait—" A wet head reappeared. "Let me make you breakfast? Wait for me."

He sat watching as the apparition in silver-blue flightsuit ransacked his cupboards. "You're kind of low on raw materials."

"I know." He brushed crumbs off the table. "I eat instant breakfasts and frozen dinners; I hate to cook."

She made a face.

"Yeah, it gets pretty old after half a century . . . they've only had them on Oro for half a century. They don't get any better, either."

She stuck something into the oven. "I'm sorry I was so stupid about it."

"About wlhat?"

"About . . . a hundred years. I guess it scared me. I acted like a bitch."

"No, you didn't."

"Yes, I did! I know I did." She frowned.

"Okay, you did . . . I forgive you. When do we eat?"

They ate, sitting side by side.

"Cooking seems like an odd spacer's hobby." Maris scraped his plate appreciatively. "When can you cook on a ship?"

"Never. It's all prepared and processed. So we can't overeat. That's why we love to eat and drink when we're in port. But I can't cook now either—no place. So it's not really a hobby, I guess, any more. I learned how from my father, he loved to cook . . ." She inhaled, eyes closed.

"Is your mother dead?"

"No—" She looked startled. "She just doesn't like to cook."

"She wouldn't have liked Glatte, either." He scratched his crooked nose.

"Calicho—that's my home, it's seven light years up the cube from this corner of the Quadrangle—it's . . . a pretty nice place. I guess Ntaka would call it 'healthy,' even . . . there's lots of room, like space; that helps. Cold and not very rich, but they get along. My mother and father always shared their work . . . they have a farm." She broke off more bread.

"What did they think about your becoming a spacer?"

"They never tried to stop me; but I don't think they wanted me to. I guess when you're so tied to the land it's hard to imagine wanting to be so free. . . . It made them sad to lose me—it made me sad to lose them; but, I had to go . . ."

Her mouth began to quiver suddenly. "You know, I'll never get to see them again, I'll never have time, our trips take so long, they'll grow old and die. . . ." Tears dripped onto her plate. "And I miss my h-home—" Words dissolved into sobs, she clung to him in terror.

He rubbed her back helplessly, wordlessly, left unequipped to deal with loneliness by a hundred years alone.

"M-Maris, can I come and see you always, will you always, always be here when I need you, and be my friend?"

"Always . . ." He rocked her gently. "Come when you want, stay as long as you want, cook dinner if you want, I'll always be here. . . ."

. . . Until the night, twenty-five years later, when they were suddenly clustered around him at the bar, hugging, badgering, laughing, the crew of the *Who Got Her–709*.

"Hi, Soldier!"

"Soldier, have we—"

"Look at this, Soldier—"

"What happened to—"

"Brandy?" he said stupidly. "Where's Brandy?"

"Honestly, Soldier, you really never do forget a face, do you?"

"Ah-ha, I bet it's not her face he remembers!"

"She was right with us." Harkané peered easily over the heads around her. "Maybe she stopped off somewhere."

"Maybe she's caught a Tail *already*?" Nilgiri was impressed.

"She could if anybody could, the little rascal." Wynmet rolled her eyes.

"Oh, just send us the usual, Soldier. She'll be along eventually. Come sit with us when she does." Harkané waved a rainbow-tipped hand. "Come, sisters, gossip is not tasteful before we've had a drink."

"That little rascal."

Soldier began to pour drinks with singleminded precision, until he noticed that he had the wrong bottle. Cursing, he drank them himself, one by one.

"Hi, Maris."

He pushed the tray away.

"*Hi*, Maris." Fingers appeared in front of his face; he started. "Hey."

"Brandy!"

Patrons along the bar turned to stare, turned away again.

"Brandy—"

"Well, sure; weren't you expecting me? Everybody else is already here."

"I know. I thought—I mean, they said . . . maybe you were out with somebody already," trying to keep it light, "and—"

"Well, really, Maris, what do you take me for?" She was insulted. "I just wanted to wait till everybody else got settled, so I could have you to myself. Did you think I'd forget you?

Unkind." She hefted a bright mottled sack onto the bar. "Look, I brought you a present!" Pulling it open, she dumped heaping confusion onto the counter. "Books, tapes, buttons, all kinds of things to look at. You said you'd read out the library five times; so I collected everywhere, some of them should be new . . . Don't you like them?"

"I . . ." he coughed, "I'm crazy about them! I'm—overwhelmed. Nobody ever brought me anything before. Thank you. Thanks very much. And welcome back to New Piraeus!"

"Glad to be back!" She stretched across the bar, hugged him, kissed his nose. She wore a new belt of metal inlaid with stones. "You're just like I remembered."

"You're more beautiful."

"Flatterer." She beamed. Ashen hair fell to her breasts; angles had deepened on her face. The quicksilver eyes took all things in now without amazement. "I'm twenty-one today, you know."

"No kidding? That calls for a celebration. Will you have brandy?"

"Do you still have some?" The eyes widened slightly. "Oh, yes! We should make it a tradition, as long as it lasts."

He smiled contentedly. They drank to birthdays, and to stars.

"Not very crowded tonight, is it?" Brandy glanced into the room, tying small knots in her hair. "Not like last time."

"It comes and it goes. I've always got some fisherfolk, they're heavy on tradition. . . . I gave up keeping track of ship schedules."

"We don't even believe our own; they never quite fit. We're a month late here."

"I know—happened to notice it. . . ." He closed a bent cover, laid the book flat. "So anyway, how did you like your first Quadrangle?"

"Beautiful—oh, Maris, if I start I'll never finish, the City in the Clouds on Patris, the Freeport on Sanalareta . . . and the Pleiades . . . and the depths of night, ice and fire." Her eyes burned through him toward infinity. "You can't imagine—"

"So they tell me."

She searched his face for bitterness, found none. He shook his head. "I'm a man and a cyborg; that's two League rules aginst me that I can't change—so why resent it? I enjoy the stories." His mouth twitched up.

"Do you like poetry?"

"Sometimes."

"Then—may I show you mine? I'm writing a cycle of poems about space, maybe someday I'll have a book. I haven't shown them to anybody else, but if you'd like—"

"I'd like it."

"I'll find them, then. Guess I should be joining the party, really, they'll think I'm antisocial"—she winced—"and they'll talk about me! It's like a small town, we're as bad as lubbers."

He laughed. "Don't—you'll disillusion me. See you later. Uh . . . listen, do you want arrangements like before? For sleeping."

"Use your place? Could I? I don't want to put you out."

"Hell, no. You're welcome to it."

"I'll cook for you—"

"I bought some eggs."

"It's a deal! Enjoy your books." She wove a path between the tables, nodding to sailor and spacer; he watched her laughing face merge and blur, caught occasional flashes of silver. Stuffing books into the sack, he set it against his shin behind the bar. And some time later, watched her go out with a Tail.

The morning of the thirteenth day he woke to find Brandy sleeping soundly in the pile of hairy cushions by the door. Curious, he glanced out into a water-gray field of fog. It was the first time she had come home before dawn. *Home?* Carefully he lifted her from the pillows; she sighed, arms found him, in her sleep she began to kiss his neck. He carried her to the bed and put her down softly, bent to . . . *No.* He turned away, left the room. He had slept with her only once. Twenty-five or three years ago, without words, she had told him they would not be lovers again. She kept the customs; a spacer never had the same man more than once.

In the kitchen he heated a frozen dinner, and ate alone.

"What's that?" Brandy appeared beside him, mummified in a blanket. She dropped down on the cushions where he sat barefoot, drinking wine and ignoring the TD.

"Three-dimensional propaganda: the Oro Morning Mine Report. You're up pretty early—it's hardly noon."

"I'm not sleepy." She took a sip of his wine.

"Got in pretty early, too. Anything wrong?"

"No . . . just—nothing happening, you know. Ran out of parties, everybody's pooped but me." She cocked her head. "What is this, anyway . . . an inquisition? 'Home awfully *early*, aren't you—?' " She glared at him and burst into laughter.

"You're crazy." He grinned.

"Whatever happened to your couch?" She prodded cushions.

"It fell apart. It's been twenty-five years, you know."

"Oh. That's too bad . . . Maris, may I read you my poems?" Suddenly serious, she produced a small, battered notebook from the folds of her blanket.

"Sure." He leaned back, watching subtle transformations occur in her face. And felt them begin to occur in himself, growing pride and a tender possessiveness.

> . . . Until, lost in darkness, we
> dance the silken star-song.

It was the final poem. "That's 'Genesis.' It's about the beginning of a fight . . . and a life." Her eyes found the world again, found dark eyes quietly regarding her.

"Attired with stars we shall forever sit, triumphing over Death, and Chance, and thee, O Time." He glanced away, pulling the tassel of a cushion. "No . . . Milton, not Maris—I could never do that." He looked back, in wonder. "They're beautiful, you are beautiful. Make a book. Gifts are meant for giving, and you are gifted."

Pleasure glowed in her cheeks. "You really think someone would want to read them?"

"Yes." He nodded, searching for the words to tell her. "Nobody's ever made me—see that way . . . as though I . . . go with you. Others would go, if they could. Home to the sky."

She turned with him to the window; they were silent. After a time she moved closer, smiling. "Do you know what I'd like to do?"

"What?" He let out a long breath.

"See your home." She set her notebook aside. "Let's go for a walk in New Piraeus. I've never really seen it by day—the real part of it. I want to see its beauty up close, before it's all gone. Can we go?"

He hesitated. "You sure you want to—?"

"Sure. Come on, lazy." She gestured him up.

And he wondered again why she had come home early.

So on the last afternoon he took her out through the stone-paved winding streets, where small whitewashed houses pressed for footholds. They climbed narrow steps, panting, tasted the sea wind, bought fruit from a leathery smiling woman with a basket.

"Mmm—" Brandy licked juice from the crimson pith. "Who was that woman? She called you 'Sojer,' but I couldn't understand the rest . . . I couldn't even understand you! Is the dialect that slurred?"

He wiped his chin. "It's getting worse all the time, with all the newcomers. But you get used to everything in the lower city. . . . An old acquaintance, I met her during the epidemic, she was sick."

"Epidemic? What epidemic?"

"Oro Mines was importing workers—they started before

your last visit, because of the bigger raw material demands. One of the new workers had some disease we didn't; it killed about a third of New Piraeus."

"Oh, my God—"

"That was about fifteen years ago . . . Oro's labs synthesized a vaccine, eventually, and they repopulated the city. But they still don't know what the disease was."

"It's like a trap, to live on a single world."

"Most of us have to . . . it has its compensations."

She finished her fruit, and changed the subject. "You helped take care of them, during the epidemic?"

He nodded. "I seemed to be immune, so—"

She patted his arm. "You are very good."

He laughed; glanced away. "Very plastic would be more like it."

"Don't you ever get sick?"

"Almost never. I can't even get very drunk. Someday I'll probably wake up entirely plastic."

"You'd still be very good." They began to walk again. "What did she say?"

"She said, 'Ah, Soldier, you've got a lady friend.' She seemed pleased."

"What did you say?"

"I said, 'That's right.' " Smiling, he didn't put his arm around her; fingers kneaded emptiness.

"Well, I'm glad she was pleased . . . I don't think most people have been."

"Don't look at them. Look out there." He showed her the sea, muted greens and blues below the ivory jumble of the flat-roofed town. To the north and south mountains like rumpled cloth reached down to the shore.

"Oh, the sea—I've always loved the sea; at home we were surrounded by it, on an island. Space is like the sea, boundless, constant, constantly changing . . ."

"—spacer!" Two giggling girls made a wide circle past them in the street, dark skirts brushing their calves.

Brandy blushed, frowned, sought the sea again. "I—think I'm getting tired. I guess I've seen enough."

"Not much on up there but the new, anyway." He took her hand and they started back down. "It's just that we're a rarity up this far." A heavy man in a heavy caftan pushed past them; in his cold eyes Maris saw an alien wanton and her overaged Tail.

"They either leer, or they censure." He felt her nails mark his flesh. "What's their problem?"

"Jealousy . . . mortality. You threaten them, you spacers. Don't you ever think about it? Free and beautiful immortals—"

"They know we aren't immortal; we hardly live longer than anybody else."

"They also know you come here from a voyage of twenty-five years looking hardly older than when you left. Maybe they don't recognize you, but they know. And they're twenty-five years older. . . . Why do you think they go around in sacks?"

"To look ugly. They must be dreadfully repressed." She tossed her head sullenly.

"They are; but that's not why. It's because they want to hide the changes. And in their way to mimic you, who always look the same. They've done it since I can remember; you're all they have to envy."

She sighed. "I've heard on Elder they paint patterns on their skin, to hide the change. Ntaka called them 'youth-fixing,' didn't he?" Anger faded, her eyes grew cool like the sea, gray-green. "Yes, I think about it . . . especially when we're laughing at the lubbers, and their narrow lives. And all the poor panting awestruck Tails, sometimes they think they're using us, but we're always using them. . . . Sometimes I think we're very cruel."

"Very like a god—Silver Lady of the Moon."

"You haven't called me that since—that night . . . all night." Her hand tightened painfully; he said nothing. "I guess they envy a cyborg for the same things. . . ."

"At least it's easier to rationalize—and harder to imitate."

He shrugged. "We leave each other alone, for the most part."

"And so we must wait for each other, we immortals. It's still a beautiful town; I don't care what they think."

He sat, fingers catching in the twisted metal of his thick bracelet, listening to her voice weave patterns through the hiss of running water. Washing away the dirty looks— Absently he reread the third paragraph on the page for the eighth time; and the singing stopped.

"Maris, do you have any—"

He looked up at her thin, shining body, naked in the doorway. "Brandy, God damn it! You're not between planets—you want to show it all to the whole damn street?"

"But I always—" Made awkward by sudden awareness, she fled.

He sat and stared at the sun-hazed windows, entirely aware that there was no one to see in. Slowly the fire died, his breathing eased.

She returned shyly, closing herself into quilted blue-silver, and sank onto the edge of a chair. "I just never think about it." Her voice was very small.

"It's all right." Ashamed, he looked past her. "Sorry I yelled at you . . . What did you want to ask me?"

"It doesn't matter." She pulled violently at her snarled hair. "Ow! Damn it!" Feeling him look at her, she forced a smile. "Uh, you know, I'm glad we picked up Mima on Treone; I'm not the little sister anymore. I was really getting pretty tired of being the greenie for so long. She's—"

"Brandy—"

"Hm?"

"Why don't they allow cyborgs on crews?"

Surprise caught her. "It's a regulation."

He shook his head. "Don't tell me 'It's a regulation,' tell me why."

"Well . . ." She smoothed wet hair-strands with her fingers.

" . . . They tried it, and it didn't work out. Like with men—they couldn't endure space, they broke down, their hormonal balance was wrong. With cyborgs, stresses between the real and the artificial in the body were too severe, they broke down too. . . . At the beginning they tried cyborganics, as a way to let men keep space, like they tried altering the hormone balance. Neither worked. Physically or psychologically, there was too much strain. So finally they just made it a regulation, no men on space crews.''

"But that was over a thousand years ago—cyborganics has improved. I'm healthier and live longer than any normal person. And stronger—'' He leaned forward, tight with agitation.

"And slower. We don't need strength, we have artificial means. And anyway, a man would still have to face more stress, it would be dangerous.''

"Are there any female cyborgs on crews?''

"No.''

"Have they ever even tried it again?''

"No—''

"You see? The League has a lock on space, they keep it with archaic laws. They don't want anyone else out there!'' Sudden resentment shook his voice.

"Maybe . . . we don't.'' Her fingers closed, opened, closed over the soft heavy arms of the chair; her eyes were the color of twisting smoke. "Do you really blame us? Spacing is our life, it's our strength. We have to close the others out, everything changes and changes around us, there's no continuity—we only have each other. That's why we have our regulations, that's why we dress alike, look alike, act alike; there's nothing else we *can* do, and stay sane. We have to live apart, always.'' She pulled her hair forward, tying nervous knots. "And—that's why we never take the same lover twice, too. We have needs we have to satisfy; but we can't afford to . . . form relationships, get involved, tied. It's a danger, it's an instability. . . . You do understand that, don't you, Maris; that it's why I don't—'' She broke off, eyes burning him with sorrow and, below it, fear.

He managed a smile. "Have you heard me complain?"

"Weren't you just . . .?" She lifted her head.

Slowly he nodded, felt pain start. "I suppose I was." *But I don't change.* He shut his eyes suddenly, before she read them. *But that's not the point, is it?*

"Maris, do you want me to stop staying here?"

"No— No . . . I understand, it's all right. I like the company." He stretched, shook his head. "Only, wear a towel, all right? I'm only human."

"I promise . . . that I will keep my eyes open, in the future."

He considered the future that would begin with dawn when her ship went up, and said nothing.

He stumbled cursing from the bedroom to the door, to find her waiting there, radiant and wholly unexpected. "Surprise!" She laughed and hugged him, dislodging his half-tied robe.

"My God—hey!" He dragged her inside and slammed the door. "You want to get me arrested for indecent exposure?" He turned his back, making adjustments, while she stood and giggled behind him.

He faced her again, fogged with sleep, struggling to believe. "You're early—almost two weeks?"

"I know. I couldn't wait till tonight to surprise you. And I did, didn't I?" She rolled her eyes. "I heard you coming to the door!"

She sat curled on his aging striped couch, squinting out the window as he fastened his sandals. "You used to have so much room. Houses haven't filled up your canyon, have they?" Her voice grew wistful.

"Not yet. If they ever do, I won't stay to see it . . . How was your trip this time?"

"Beautiful, again . . . I can't imagine it ever being anything else. You could see it all a hundred times over, and never see it all—

> Through your crystal eye,
> Mactav, I watch the midnight's
> star turn inside out. . . .

Oh, guess what! My poems—I finished the cycle during the voyage . . . and it's going to be published, on Treone. They said very nice things about it.''

He nodded smugly. ''They have good taste. They must have changed, too.''

'' 'A renaissance in progress'—meaning they've put on some *ver*-ry artsy airs, last decade; their Tails are really something else. . . .'' Remembering, she shook her head. ''It was one of them that told me about the publisher.''

''You showed him your poems?'' Trying not to—

''Good grief, no; he was telling me about his. So I thought, What have I got to lose?''

''When do I get a copy?''

''I don't know.'' Disappointment pulled at her mouth. ''Maybe I'll never even get one; after twenty-five years they'll be out of print. Art is long, and Time is fleeting . . . Longfellow had it backwards. But I made you some copies of the poems. And brought you some more books, too. There's one you should read, it replaced Ntaka years ago on the Inside. I thought it was inferior; but who are we . . . What are you laughing about?''

''What happened to that freckle-faced kid in pigtails?''

''*What*?'' Her nose wrinkled.

''How old are you now?''

''Twenty-four. Oh—'' She looked pleased.

''Madame Poet, do you want to go to dinner with me?''

''Oh, *food*, oh yes!'' She bounced, caught him grinning, froze. ''I would love to. Can we go to Good Eats?''

"It closed right after you left."

"Oh . . . the music was wild. Well, how about that seafood place, with the fish name—?"

He shook his head. "The owner died. It's been twenty-five years."

"Damn, we can never keep anything." She sighed. "Why don't I just make us a dinner—*I'm* still here. And I'd like that."

That night, and every other night, he stood at the bar and watched her go out, with a Tail or a laughing knot of partyers. Once she waved to him; the stem of a shatterproof glass snapped in his hand; he kicked it under the counter, confused and angry.

But three nights in the two weeks she came home early. This time, pointedly, he asked her no questions. Gratefully, she told him no lies, sleeping on his couch and sharing the afternoon . . .

They returned to the flyer, moving in step along the cool jade sand of the beach. Maris looked toward the sea's edge, where frothy fingers reached, withdrew, and reached again. "You leave tomorrow, huh?"

Brandy nodded. "Uh-huh."

He sighed.

"Maris, if—"

"What?"

"Oh—nothing." She brushed sand from her boot.

He watched the sea reach, and withdraw, and reach—

"Have you ever wanted to see a ship? Inside, I mean." She pulled open the flyer door, her body strangely intent.

He followed her. "Yes."

"Would you like to see mine—the *Who Got Her*?"

"I thought that was illegal?"

" 'No waking man shall set foot on a ship of the spaceways.' It is a League regulation . . . but it's based on a superstition that's at least a thousand years old—'Men on ships is bad luck.' Which is silly here. Your presence on board in port isn't going to bring us disaster."

He looked incredulous.

"I'd like you to see our life, Maris, like I see yours. There's nothing wrong with that. And besides"—she shrugged—"no one will know; because nobody's there right now."

He faced a wicked grin, and did his best to match it. "I will if you will."

They got in, the flyer drifted silently up from the cove. New Piraeus rose to meet them beyond the ridge; the late sun struck gold from hidden windows.

"I wish it wouldn't change—oh . . . there's another new one. It's a skyscraper!"

He glanced across the bay. "Just finished; maybe New Piraeus is growing up—thanks to Oro Mines. It hardly changed over a century; after all those years, it's a little scary."

"Even after three . . . or twenty-five?" She pointed. "Right down there, Maris—there's our airlock."

The flyer settled on the water below the looming, semitransparent hull of the *WGH–709*.

Maris gazed up and back. "It's a lot bigger than I ever realized."

"It masses twenty thousand tons, empty." Brandy caught hold of the hanging ladder. "I guess we'll have to go up this . . . okay?" She looked over at him.

"Sure. Slow, maybe, but sure."

They slipped in through the lock, moved soft-footed down hallways past dim cavernous storerooms.

"Is the whole ship transparent?" He touched a wall, plastic met plastic. "How do you get any privacy?"

"Why are you whispering?"

"I'm no—*I'm not*. Why are you?"

"*Shhh*! Because it's so *quiet*." She stopped, pride beginning to show on her face. "The whole ship can be almost transparent, like now; but usually it's not. All the walls and the hull are polarized; you can opaque them. These are just holds, anyway, they're most of the ship. The passenger stasis cubicles are up there. Here's the lift, we'll go up to the control room.''

"Brandy!" A girl in red with a clipboard turned on them, outraged, as they stepped from the lift. "Brandy, what the hell do you mean by— Oh. Is that you, Soldier? God, I thought she'd brought a man on board.''

Maris flinched. "Hi, Nilgiri.''

Brandy was very pale beside him. "We just came out to—uh, look in on Mactav, she's been kind of moody lately, you know. I thought we could read to her. . . . What are *you* doing here?'' And a whispered, "Bitch.''

"Just that—checking up on Mactav. Harkané sent me out.'' Nilgiri glanced at the panels behind her, back at Maris, suddenly awkward. "Uh—look, since I'm already here don't worry about it, okay? I'll go down and play some music for her. Why don't you—uh, show Soldier around the ship, or something . . .'' Her round face was reddening like an apple. "Bye?'' She slipped past them and into the lift, and disappeared.

"*Damn*, sometimes she's such an ass.''

"She didn't mean it.''

"Oh, I should have—''

"—done just what you did; she was sorry. And at least we're not trespassing.''

"God, Maris, how do you stand it? They must do it to you all the time. Don't you resent it?''

"Hell, yes, I resent it. Who wouldn't? I just got tired of getting mad. . . . And besides—'' he glanced at the closed doors—"besides, nobody needs a mean bartender. Come on, show me around the ship.''

Her knotted fingers uncurled, took his hand. "This way, please; straight ahead of you is our control room.'' She pulled him forward beneath the daybright dome. He saw a hand-printed sign above the center panel, NO-MAN'S LAND. "From here we program our computer; this area here is for the AAFAL drive, first devised by Ursula, an early spacer who—''

"What's awful about it?''

"What?"

"Every spacer I know calls the ship's drive 'awful'?"

"Oh— Not 'awful,' AAFAL: Almost As Fast As Light. Which it is. That's what we call it; there's a technical name too."

"Um." He looked vaguely disappointed. "Guess I'm used to—" Curiosity changed his face, as he watched her smiling with delight. "I—suppose it's different from antigravity?" Seventy years before she was born, he had taught himself the principles of starship technology.

"Very." She giggled suddenly. "The 'awfuls' and the 'aghs', *hmm* . . . We do use an AG unit to leave and enter solar systems; it operates like the ones in flyers, it throws us away from the planet, and finally the entire system, until we reach AAFAL ignition speeds. With the AG you can only get fractions of the speed of light, but it's enough to concentrate interstellar gases and dust. Our force nets feed them through the drive unit, where they're converted to energy, which increases our speed, which makes the unit more efficient . . . until we're moving almost as fast as light.

"We use the AG to protect us from acceleration forces, and after deceleration to guide us into port. The start and finish can take up most of our trip time; the farther out in space you are, the less AG feedback you get from the system's mass, and the less your velocity changes. It's a beautiful time, though—you can see the AG forces through the polarized hull, wrapping you in shifting rainbow . . .

"And you are isolate"—she leaned against a silent panel and punched buttons; the room began to grow dark— "in absolute night . . . and stars." And stars appeared, in the darkness of a planetarium show; fire-gnats lighting her face and shoulders and his own. "How do you like our stars?"

"Are we in here?"

Four streaks of blue joined lights in the air. "Here . . . in space by this corner of the Quadrangle. This is our navigation chart for the Quadrangle run; see the bowed leg and brightness, that's the Pleiades. Patris . . . Sanalareta . . . Treone . . . back to Oro. The other lines zigzag too, but it doesn't show. Now come with me . . . With a flare of energy, we open our AAFAL nets in space—''

He followed her voice into the night, where flickering tracery seined motes of interstellar gas; and impossible nothingness burned with infinite energy, potential transformed and transforming. With the wisdom of a thousand years a ship of the League fell through limitless seas, navigating the shifting currents of the void, beating into the sterile winds of space. Stars glittered like snow on the curving hull, spitting icy daggers of light that moved imperceptibly into spectral blues before him, reddened as he looked behind: imperceptibly time expanded, velocity increased and with it power. He saw the haze of silver on his right rise into their path, a wall of liquid shadow . . . the Pleiades, an endless bank of burning fog, kindled from within by shrouded islands of fire. Tendrils of shimmering mists curved outward across hundreds of billions of kilometers, the nets found bountiful harvest, drew close, hurled the ship into the edge of cloud.

Nebulosity wrapped him in clinging haloes of colored light, ringed him in brilliance, as the nets fell inward toward the ship, burgeoning with energy, shielding its fragile nucleus from the soundless fury of its passage. Acceleration increased by hundredfolds, around him the Doppler shifts deepened toward cerulean and crimson; slowly the clinging brightness wove into parabolas of shining smoke, whipping past until the entire flaming mass of cloud and stars seemed to sweep ahead, shriveling toward blue-whiteness, trailing embers.

And suddenly the ship burst once more into a void, a universe warped into a rubber bowl of brilliance stretching past him, drawing away and away before him toward a gleaming point in darkness. The shrunken nets seined near-vacuum and were filled; their speed approached $0.000c$ . . . held constant, as the conversion of matter to energy ceased within the ship . . . and in time, with a flicker of silver force, began once more to fall away. Slowly time unbowed, the universe cast off its alienness. One star grew steadily before them: the sun of Patris.

A sun rose in ruddy splendor above the City in the Clouds on Patris, nine months and seven light years from Oro. . . . And again, Patris fell away; and the brash gleaming Freeport of Sanalareta; they crept toward Treone through gasless waste, groping for current and mote across the barren ship-wakes of half a millennium. . . . And again—

Maris found himself among fire-gnat stars, on a ship in the bay of New Piraeus. And realized she had stopped speaking. His hand rubbed the copper snarl of his hair, his eyes bright as a child's. "You didn't tell me you were a witch in your spare time."

He heard her smile, "Thank you. Mactav makes the real magic, though; her special effects are fantastic. She can show you the whole inhabited section of the galaxy, with all the trade polyhedra, like a dew-flecked cobweb hanging in the air." Daylight returned to the panel. "Mactav—that's her bank, there—handles most of the navigation, life support, all that, too. Sometimes it seems like we're almost along for the ride! But of course we're along for Mactav."

"Who or what is Mactav?" Maris peered into a darkened screen, saw something amber glimmer in its depths, drew back.

"You've never met her, neither have we—but you were staring her right in the eye." Brandy stood beside him. "She must be listening to Giri down below. . . . Okay, okay!—a Mactavia unit is the brain, the nervous system of a ship, she monitors its vital signs, calculates, adjusts. We only have to ask—sometimes we don't even have to do that. The memory is a real spacer woman's, fed into the circuits . . . someone who died irrevocably, or had reached retirement, but wanted to stay on. A human system is wiser, more versatile—and lots cheaper—than anything all-machine that's ever been done."

"Then your Mactav is a kind of cyborg."

She smiled. "Well, I guess so; in a way—"

"But the Spacing League's regulations still won't allow cyborgs in crews."

She looked annoyed.

He shrugged. "Sorry. Dumb thing to say . . . What's that red down there?"

"Oh, that's our 'stomach': the AAFAL unit, where"—she grinned—"we digest stardust into energy. It's the only thing that's never transparent, the red is the shield."

"How does it work?"

"I don't really know. I can make it go, but I don't understand why—I'm only a five-and-a-half technician now. If I was a six I could tell you." She glanced at him sidelong. "Aha! I finally impressed you!"

He laughed. "Not so dumb as you look." He had qualified as a six half a century before, out of boredom.

"You'd better be kidding!"

"I am." He followed her back across the palely opalescing floor, looking down, and down. "Like walking on water . . . why transparent?"

She smiled through him at the sky. "Because it's so beautiful outside."

They dropped down through floors, to come out in a new hall. Music came faintly to him.

"This is where my cabin—"

Abruptly the music became an impossible agony of sound torn with screaming.

"God!" And Brandy was gone from beside him, down the hallway and through a flickering wall.

He found her inside the door, rigid with awe. Across the room the wall vomited blinding waves of color, above a screeching growth of crystal organ pipes. Nilgiri crouched on the floor, hands pressed against her stomach, shrieking hysterically. "Stop it, Mactav! Stop it! Stop it! Stop it!"

He touched Brandy's shoulder, she looked up and caught his arm; together they pulled Nilgiri, wailing, back from bedlam to the door.

"Nilgiri! Nilgiri, what happened!" Brandy screamed against her ear.

"Mactav, Mactav!"

"*Why?*"

"She put a . . . charge thrugh it, she's crazy-mad . . . sh-she thinks . . . Oh, *stop* it, Mactav!" Nilgiri clung, sobbing.

Maris started into the room, hands over his ears. "How do you turn it off!"

"Maris, wait!"

"*How*, Brandy?"

"It's electrified, don't touch it!"

"*How?*"

"On the left, on the left, three switches—Maris, *don't*—Stop it, Mactav, stop—"

He heard her screaming as he lowered his left hand, hesitated, battered with glaring sound; sparks crackled as he flicked switches on the organ panel, once, twice, again.

"—it-it-it-it!" Her voice echoed through silent halls. Nilgiri slid down the doorjamb and sat sobbing on the floor.

"Maris, are you all right?"

He heard her dimly through cotton. Dazed with relief, he backed away from the gleaming console, nodding, and started across the room.

"*Man*," the soft hollow voice echoed echoed echoed. "What are you doing in here?"

"Mactav?" Brandy was gazing uneasily to his left.

He turned; across the room was another artificial eye, burning amber.

"Branduin, you brought him onto the ship; how could you do this thing, it is forbidden!"

"Oh, God." Nilgiri began to wail again in horror. Brandy knelt and caught Nilgiri's blistered hands; he saw anger harden over her face. "Mactav, how could you!"

"Brandy." He shook his head; took a breath, frightened. "Mactav—I'm not a man. You're mistaken."

"Maris, no . . ."

He frowned. "I'm one hundred and forty-one years old . . . half my body is synthetic. I'm hardly human, any more than you are. Scan and see." He held up his hands.

"The part of you that matters is still a man."

A smile caught at his mouth. "Thanks."

"Men are evil, men destroyed . . ."

"Her, Maris," Brandy whispered. "They destroyed her."

The smile wavered. "Something more we have in common." His false arm pressed his side.

The golden eye regarded him. "Cyborg."

He sighed, went to the door. Brandy stood to meet him, Nilgiri huddled silently at her feet, staring up.

"Nilgiri." The voice was full of pain; they looked back. "How can I forgive myself for what I've done? I will never, never do such a thing again . . . never. Please, go to the infirmary; let me help you?"

Slowly, with Brandy's help, Nilgiri got to her feet. "All right. It's all right, Mactav. I'll go on down now."

"Giri, do you want us—?"

Nilgiri shook her head, hands curled in front of her. "No, Brandy, it's okay. She's all right now. Me too—I think." Her smile quivered. "Ouch . . ." She started down the corridor toward the lift.

"Branduin, Maris, I apologize also to you. I'm—not usually like this, you know. . . ." Amber faded from her eye.

"Is she gone?"

Brandy nodded.

"That's the first bigoted computer I ever met."

And she remembered: "Your *hand*?"

Smiling, he held it out to her. "No harm; see? It's a non-conductor."

She shivered. Hands cradled the hand that ached to feel. "Mactav really isn't like that, you know. But something's been wrong lately, she gets into moods; we'll have to have her looked at when we get to Sanalareta."

"Isn't it dangerous?"

"I don't think so—not really. It's just that she has special problems; she's in there because she didn't have any choice, a strife-based culture killed her ship. She was very young, but that was all that was left of her."

"A high technology." A grimace; memory moved in his eyes.

"They were terribly apologetic, they did their best."

"What happened to them?"

"We cut contact . . . that's regulation number one. We have to protect ourselves."

He nodded, looking away. "Will they ever go back?"

"I don't know. Maybe, someday." She leaned against the doorway. "But that's why Mactav hates men; men, and war—and combined with the old taboo . . . I guess her memory suppressors weren't enough."

Nilgiri reappeared beside them. "All better." Her hands were bright pink. "Ready for anything!"

"How's Mactav acting?"

"Super-solicitous. She's still pretty upset about it, I guess."

Light flickered at the curving junctures of the walls, ceiling, floor. Maris glanced up. "Hell, it's getting dark outside. I expect I'd better be leaving; nearly time to open up. One last night on the town?" Nilgiri grinned and nodded; he saw Brandy hesitate.

"Maybe I'd better stay with Mactav tonight, if she's still upset. She's got to be ready to go up tomorrow." Almost-guilt firmed resolution on her face.

"Well ... I could stay, if you think—" Nilgiri looked unhappy.

"No. It's my fault she's like this; I'll do it. Besides, I've been out having a fantastic day, I'd be too tired to do it right tonight. You go on in. Thank you, Maris! I wish it wasn't over so soon." She turned back to him, beginning to put her hair into braids; quicksilver shone.

"The pleasure was all mine." The tight sense of loss dissolved in warmth. "I can't remember a better one either ... or more exciting—" He grimaced.

She smiled and took his hands; Nilgiri glanced back and forth between them. "I'll see you to the lock."

Nilgiri climbed down through the glow to the waiting flyer. Maris braced back from the top rung to watch Brandy's face, bearing a strange expression, look down through whipping strands of loose hair. "Good-bye, Maris."

"Good-bye, Brandy."

"It was a short two weeks, you know?"

"I know."

"I like New Piraeus better than anywhere; I don't know why."

"I hope it won't be too different when you get back."

"Me too. . . . See you in three years?"

"Twenty-five."

"Oh, yeah. Time passes so quickly when you're having fun—" Almost true, almost not. A smile flowered.

"Write while you're away. Poems, that is." He began to climb down, slowly.

"I will ... Hay, my stuff is at—"

"I'll send it back with Nilgiri." He settled behind the controls, the flyer grew bright and began to rise. He waved; so did Nilgiri. He watched her wave back, watched her in his mirror until she became the vast and gleaming pearl that was the *Who Got Her–709*. And felt the gap that widened between their lives, more than distance, more than time.

"Well, now that you've seen it, what do you think?"

Late afternoon, first day, fourth visit, seventy-fifth year . . . mentally he tallied. Brandy stood looking into the kitchen. "It's—different."

"I know. It's still too new; I miss the old wood beams. They were rotting, but I miss them. Sometimes I wake up in the morning and don't know where I am. But I was losing my canyon."

She looked back at him, surprising him with her misery. "Oh . . . At least they won't reach you for a long time, out here."

"We can't walk home anymore, though."

"No." She turned away again. "All—all your furniture is built in?"

"*Um*. It's supposed to last as long as the house."

"What if you get tired of it?"

He laughed. "As long as it holds me up, I don't care what it looks like. One thing I like, though—" He pressed a plate on the wall, looking up. "The roof is polarized. Like your ship. At night you can watch the stars."

"Oh!" She looked up and back, he watched her mind pierce the high cloud-fog, pierce the day, to find stars. "How wonderful! I've never seen it anywhere else."

It had been his idea, thinking of her. He smiled.

"They must really be growing out here, to be doing things like this now." She tried the cushions of a molded chair. "Hmm . . ."

"They're up to two and a half already, they actually do a few things besides mining now. The Inside is catching up, if they can bring us this without a loss. I may even live to see the day when we'll be importing raw materials, instead of filling everyone else's mined-out guts. If there's anything left of Oro by then . . ."

"Would you stay to see that?"

"I don't know." He looked at her. "It depends. Anyway, tell me about this trip?" He stretched out on the chain-hung wall seat. "You know everything that's new with me already: one house." And waited for far glory to rise up in her eyes.

They flickered down, stayed the color of fog. "Well—some good news, and some bad news, I guess."

"Like how?" Feeling suddenly cold.

"Good news—" her smile warmed him—"I'll be staying nearly a month this time. We'll have more time to—do things, if you want to."

"How did you manage that?" He sat up.

"That's more good news. I have a chance to crew on a different ship, to get out of the Quadrangle and see things I've only dreamed of, new worlds—"

"And the bad news is how long you'll be gone."

"Yes."

"How many years?"

"It's an extended voyage, following up trade contracts; if we're lucky, we might be back in the stellar neighborhood in thirty-five years . . . thirty-five years tau—more than two hundred, here. If we're not so lucky, maybe we won't be back this way at all."

"I see." He stared unblinking at the floor, hands knotted between his knees. "It's—an incredible opportunity, all right . . . especially for your poetry. I envy you. But I'll miss you."

"I know." He saw her teeth catch her lip. "But we can spend time together, we'll have a lot of time before I go. And—well, I've brought you something, to remember me." She crossed the room to him.

It was a star, suspended burning coldly in scrolled silver by an artist who knew fire. Inside she showed him her face, laughing, full of joy.

"I found it on Treone . . . they really are in renaissance. And I liked that holo, I thought you might—"

Leaning across silver he found the silver of her hair, kissed her once on the mouth, felt her quiver as he pulled away. He lifted the woven chain, fixed it at his throat. "I have something for you, too."

He got up, returned with a slim book the color of red wine, put it in her hands.

"My poems!"

He nodded, his fingers feeling the star at his throat. "I managed to get hold of two copies—it wasn't easy. Because they're too well known now; the spacers carry them, they show them but they won't give them up. You must be known on more worlds than you could ever see."

"Oh, I hadn't even heard . . ." She laughed suddenly. "My fame preceded me. But next trip—" She looked away. "No. I won't be going that way anymore."

"But you'll be seeing new things, to make into new poems." He stood, trying to loosen the tightness in his voice.

"Yes . . . Oh, yes, I know . . ."

"A month is a long time."

A sudden sputter of noise made them look up. Fat dapples of rain were beginning to slide, smearing dust over the flat roof.

"Rain! not fog; the season's started." They stood and watched the sky fade overhead, darken, crack and shudder with electric light. The rain fell harder, the ceiling rippled and blurred; he led her to the window. Out across the smooth folded land a liquid curtain billowed, slaking the dust-dry throat of the canyons, renewing the earth and the spiny tight-leafed scrub. "I always wonder if it's ever going to happen. It always does." He looked at her, expecting quicksilver, and found slow tears. She wept silently, watching the rain.

For the next two weeks they shared the rain, and the chill bright air that followed. In the evenings she went out, while he stood behind the bar, because it was the last time she would have leave with the crew of the *Who Got Her*. But every morning he found her sleeping; and every afternoon she spent with him. Together they traced the serpentine alleyways of the shabby, metamorphosing lower city, or roamed the docks with the wind-burned fisherfolk. He took her to meet Makerrah, whom he had seen as a boy mending nets by hand, as a fishnet-clad Tail courting spacers at the Tin Soldier, as a sailor and fisherman, for almost forty years. Makerrah, now growing heavy and slow as his wood-hulled boat, showed it with pride to the sailor from the sky; they discussed nets, eating fish.

"This world is getting old . . ." Brandy had come with him to the bar as the evening started.

Maris smiled. "But the night is young." And felt pleasure stir with envy.

"True true—" Pale hair cascaded as her head bobbed. "But, you know, when . . . if I was gone another twenty-five years, I probably wouldn't recognize this *street*. The Tin Soldier really is the only thing that doesn't change." She sat at the agate counter, face propped in her hands, musing.

He stirred drinks. "It's good to have something constant in your life."

"I know. We appreciate that too, more than anybody." She glanced away, into the dark-raftered room. "They really always do come back here first, and spend more time in here . . . and knowing that they *can* means so much: that you'll be here, young and real and remembering them." A sudden hunger blurred her sight.

"It goes both ways." He looked up.

"I know that, too . . . You know, I always meant to ask: why did you call it the 'Tin Soldier'? I mean, I think I see . . . but why 'tin'?"

"Sort of a private joke, I guess. It was in a book of folk tales I read, *Andersen's Fairy Tales*"—he looked embarrassed—"I'd *read* everything else. It was a story about a toy shop, about a tin soldier with one leg, who was left on the shelf for years. . . . He fell in love with a toy ballerina who only loved dancing, never him. In the end, she fell into the fire, and he went after her—she burned to dust, heartless; he melted into a heart-shaped lump . . ." He laughed carefully, seeing her face. "A footnote said sometimes the story had a happy ending; I like to believe that."

She nodded, hopeful. "Me too— Where did your stone bar come from? It's beautiful; like the edge of the Pleiades, depths of mist."

"Why all the questions?"

"I'm appreciating. I've loved it all for years, and never said anything. Sometimes you love things without knowing it, you take them for granted. It's wrong to let that happen . . . so I wanted you to know." She smoothed the polished stone with her hand.

He joined her tracing opalescences. "It's petrified wood— some kind of plant life that was preserved in stone, minerals replaced its structure. I found it in the desert."

"Desert?"

"East of the mountains. I found a whole canyon full of them. It's an incredible place, the desert."

"I've never seen one. Only heard about them, barren and deadly; it frightened me."

"While you cross the most terrible desert of them all?— between the stars."

"But it's not barren."

"Neither is this one. It's winter here now, I can take you to see the trees, if you'd like it." He grinned. "If you dare."

Her eyebrows rose. "I dare! We could go tomorrow, I'll make us a lunch."

"We'd have to leave early, though. If you were wanting to do the town again tonight . . ."

"Oh, that's all right; I'll take a pill."

"Hey—"

She winced. "Oh, well . . . I found a kind I could take. I used them all the time at the other ports, like the rest."

"Then why—"

"Because I liked staying with you. I deceived you, now you know, true confessions. Are you mad?"

His face filled with astonished pleasure. "Hardly . . . I have to admit, I used to wonder what—"

"*Sol*-dier!" He looked away, someone gestured at him across the room. "More wine, please!" He raised a hand.

"Brandy, come on, there's a party—"

She waved. "Tomorrow morning, early?" Her eyes kept his face.

"Uh-huh. See you—"

"—later." She slipped down and was gone.

The flyer rose silently, pointing into the early sun. Brandy sat beside him, squinting down and back through the glare as New Piraeus grew narrow beside the glass-green bay. "Look, how it falls behind the hills, until all you can see are the land and the sea, and no sign of change. It's like that when the ship goes up, but it happens so fast you don't have time to savor it." She turned back to him, bright-eyed. "We go from world to world but we never see them; we're always looking up. It's good to look down, today."

They drifted higher, rising with the climbing hills, until the rumpled olive-red suede of the seacoast grew jagged, blotched green-black and gray and blinding white.

"Is that really snow?" She pulled at his arm, pointing.

He nodded. "We manage a little."

"I've only seen snow once since I left Calicho, once it was winter on Treone. We wrapped up in furs and capes even though we didn't have to, and threw snowballs with the Tails. . . . But it was cold most of the year on our island, on Calicho—we were pretty far north, we grew special kinds of crops . . . and us kids had hairy hornbeasts to plod around on. . . . '' Lost in memories, she rested against his shoulder; while he tried to remember a freehold on Glatte, and snowy walls became jumbled whiteness climbing a hill by the sea.

They had crossed the divide; the protruding batholith of the peaks degenerated into parched, crumbling slopes of gigantic rubble. Ahead of them the scarred yellow desolation stretched away like an infinite canvas, into mauve haze. "How far does it go?"

"It goes on forever. . . . Maybe not this desert, but this merges into others that merge into others—the whole planet is a desert, hot or cold. It's been desiccating for eons; the sun's been rising off the main sequence. The sea by New Piraeus is the only large body of free water left now, and that's dropped half an inch since I've been here. The coast is the only habitable area, and there aren't many towns there even now."

"Then Oro will never be able to change too much."

"Only enough to hurt. See the dust? Open-pit mining, for seventy kilometers north. And that's a little one."

He took them south, sliding over the eroded face of the land to twist through canyons of folded stone, sediments contorted by the palsied hands of tectonic force; or flashing across pitted flatlands lipping on pocket seas of ridged and shadowed blow-sand.

They settled at last under a steep out-curving wall of frescoed rock layered in red and green. The wide, rough bed of the sandy wash was pale in the chill glare of noon, scrunching underfoot as they began to walk. Pulling on his leather jacket, Maris showed her the kaleidoscope of ages left tumbled in stones over the hills they climbed, shouting against the lusty wind of the ridges. She cupped them in marveling hands, hair streaming like silken banners past her face; obligingly he put her chosen few into his pockets. "Aren't you cold?" He caught her hand.

"No, my suit takes care of me. How did you ever learn to know all these, Maris?"

Shaking his head, he began to lead her back down. "There's more here than I'll ever know. I just got a mining tape on geology at the library. But it made it mean more to come out here . . . where you can see eons of the planet laid open, one cycle settling on another. To know the time it took, the life history of an entire world: it helps my perspective, it makes me feel—young."

"We think we know worlds, but we don't, we only see people: change and pettiness. We forget the greater constancy, tied to the universe. It would humble our perspective, too—" Pebbles boiled and clattered; her hand held his strongly as his foot slipped. He looked back, chagrined, and she laughed. "You don't really have to lead me here, Maris. I was a mountain goat on Calicho, and I haven't forgotten it all."

Indignant, he dropped her hand. "You lead."

Still laughing, she led him to the bottom of the hill.

And he took her to see the trees. Working their way over the rocks up the windless branch wash, they rounded a bend and found them, tumbled in static glory. He heard her indrawn breath. "Oh, Maris—" Radiant with color and light she walked among them, while he wondered again at the passionless artistry of the earth. Amethyst and agate, crystal and mimicked wood-grain, hexagonal trunks split open to bare subtleties of mergence and secret nebulosities. She knelt among the broken bits of limb, choosing colors to hold up to the sun.

He sat on a trunk, picking agate pebbles. "They're sort of special friends of mine; we go down in time together, in strangely familiar bodies. . . ." He studied them with fond pride. "But they go with more grace."

She put her colored chunks on the ground. "No . . . I don't think so. They had no choice."

He looked down, tossing pebbles.

"Let's have our picnic here."

They cleared a space and spread a blanket, and picnicked with the trees. The sun warmed them in the windless hollow, and he made a pillow of his jacket; satiated, they lay back head by head, watching the cloudless green-blue sky.

"You pack a good lunch."

"Thank you. It was the least I could do"—her hand brushed his arm; quietly his fingers tightened on themselves—"to share your secrets; to learn that the desert isn't barren, that it's immense, timeless, full of—mysteries. But no life?"

"No —not anymore. There's no water, nothing can live. The only things left are in or by the sea, or they're things we've brought. Across our own lifeless desert-sea."

" 'Though inland far we be, our souls have sight of that immortal sea which brought us hither.' " Her hand stretched above him, to catch the sky.

"Wordsworth. That's the only thing by him I ever liked much."

They lay together in the warm silence. A piece of agate came loose, dropped to the ground with a clink; they started.

"Maris—"

"Hmm?"

"Do you realize we've known each other for three-quarters of a century?"

"Yes. . . ."

"I've almost caught up with you, I think. I'm twenty-seven. Soon I'm going to start passing you. But at least—now you'll never have to see it show." Her fingers touched the rusty curls of his hair.

"It would never show. You couldn't help but be beautiful."

"Maris . . . sweet Maris."

He felt her hand clench in the soft weave of his shirt, move in caresses down his body. Angrily he pulled away, sat up, half his face flushed. "Damn—!"

Stricken, she caught at his sleeve. "No, no—" Her eyes found his face, gray filled with grief. "No . . . Maris . . . I—

want you." She unsealed her suit, drew blue-silver from her shoulders, knelt before him. "I want you."

Her hair fell to her waist, the color of warm honey. She reached out and lifted his hand with tenderness; slowly he leaned forward, to bare her breasts and her beating heart, felt the softness set fire to his nerves. Pulling her close, he found her lips, kissed them long and longingly; held her against his own heart beating, lost in her silken hair. "Oh, God, Brandy . . ."

"I love you, Maris . . . I think I've always loved you." She clung to him, cold and shivering in the sunlit air. "And it's wrong to leave you and never let you know."

And he realized that fear made her tremble, fear bound to her love in ways he could not fully understand. Blind to the future, he drew her down beside him and stopped her trembling with his joy.

In the evening she sat across from him at the bar, blue-haloed with light, sipping brandy. Their faces were bright with wine and melancholy bliss.

"I finally got some more brandy, Brandy . . . a couple of years ago. So we wouldn't run out. If we don't get to it, you can take it with you." He set the dusty red-splintered bottle carefully on the bar.

"You could save it, in case I do come back, as old as your grandmaw, and in need of some warmth. . . ." Slowly she rotated her glass, watching red leap up the sides. "Do you suppose by then my poems will have reached Home? And maybe somewhere Inside, Ntaka will be reading *me*."

"The Outside will be the Inside by then. . . . Besides, Ntaka's probably already dead. Been dead for years."

"Oh. I guess." She pouted, her eyes growing dim and moist. "Damn, I wish . . . I wish."

"Branduin, you haven't joined us yet tonight. It is our last together." Harkané appeared beside her, lean dark face smiling in a cloud-mass of blued white hair. She sat down with her drink.

"I'll come soon." Clouded eyes glanced up, away.

"Ah, the sadness of parting keeps you apart? I know." Harkané nodded. "We've been together so long; it's hard, to lose another family." She regarded Maris. "And a good barten-der must share everyone's sorrows, yes, Soldier—? But bury his own. Oh—they would like some more drinks—"

Sensing dismissal, he moved aside; with long-practiced skill he became blind and deaf, pouring wine.

"Brandy, you are so unhappy—don't you want to go on this other voyage?"

"Yes, I do—! But . . ."

"But you don't. It is always so when there is choice. Some-times we make the right choice, and though we're afraid we go on with it anyway. And sometimes we make the wrong choice, and go on with it anyway because we're afraid not to. Have you changed your mind?"

"But I can't change—"

"Why not? We will leave them a message. They will go on and pick up their second compatible."

"Is it really that easy?"

"No . . . not quite. But we can do it, if you want to stay."

Silence stretched; Maris sent a tray away, began to wipe glasses, fumbled.

"But I should."

"Brandy. If you go only out of obligation, I will tell you something. I want to retire. I was going to resign this trip, at Sanalareta; but if I do that, Mactav will need a new Best Friend. She's getting old and cantankerous, just like me; these past few years her behavior has begun to show the strain she is under. She must have someone who can feel her needs. I was going to ask you, I think you understand her best; but I thought you wanted this other thing more. If not, I ask you now to become the new Best Friend of the *Who Got Her*."

"But Harkané, you're not old—"

"I am eighty-six. I'm too old for the sporting life anymore; I will become a Mactav; I've been lucky, I have an opportunity."

"Then . . . yes—I do want to stay! I accept the position."

In spite of himself Maris looked up, saw her face shining with joy and release. "Brandy—?"

"Maris, I'm not going!"

"I know!" He laughed, joined them.

"Soldier." He looked up, dark met dark, Harkané's eyes that saw more than surfaces. "This will be the last time that I see you; I am retiring, you know. You have been very good to me all these years, helping me be young; you are very kind to us all. . . . Now, to say good-bye, I do something in return." She took his hand, placed it firmly over Brandy's, shining with rings on the counter. "I give her back to you. Brandy—join us soon, we'll celebrate." She rose mildly and moved away into the crowded room.

Their hands twisted, clasped tight on the counter.

Brandy closed her eyes. "God, I'm so glad!"

"So am I."

"Only the poems . . ."

"Remember once you told me, 'you can see it all a hundred times, and never see it all'?"

A quicksilver smile. "And it's true . . . Oh, Maris, now this is my last night! And I have to spend it with them, to celebrate."

"I know. There's—no way I can have you forever, I suppose. But it's all right." He grinned. "Everything's all right. What's twenty-five years, compared to two hundred?"

"It'll seem like three."

"It'll seem like twenty-five. But I can stand it—"

He stood it, for twenty-four more years, looking up from the bar with sudden eagerness every time new voices and the sound of laughter spilled into the dim blue room.

"Soldier! Soldier, you're still—"

"We missed you like—"

"—two whole weeks of—"

"—want to buy a whole sack for my own—"

The crew of the *DOM–428* pressed around him, their fingers proving he was real; their lips brushed a cheek that couldn't feel and one that could, long loose hair rippling over the agate bar. He hugged four at a time. "Aralea! Vlasa! Elsah, what the hell have you done to your hair now—and Ling-shan! My God, you're pretty, like always. Cathe—" The memory bank never forgot a shining fresh-scrubbed face, even after thrirty-seven years. Their eyes were very bright as he welcomed them, and their hands left loving prints along the agate bar.

"—still have your stone bar; I'm so glad, don't ever sell it—"

"And what's new with *you*?" Elsah gasped, and ecstatic laughter burst over him.

He shook his head, hands up, laughing too. "—go prematurely *deaf*? First round on the house; only one at a time, huh?"

Elsah brushed strands of green-tinged waist-length hair back from her very green eyes. "Sorry, Soldier. We've just said it *all* to each other, over and over. And gee, we haven't seen you for four years!" Her belt tossed blue-green sparks against her green quilted flight-suit.

"Four years? Seems more like thirty-seven." And they laughed again, appreciating, because it was true. "Welcome back to the Tin Soldier. What's your pleasure?"

"Why you of course, me darlin'," said black-haired Brigit, and she winked.

His smile barely caught on a sharp edge; he winked back. "Just the drinks are on the house, lass." The smile widened and came unstuck.

More giggles.

"Ach, a pity!" Brigit pouted. She wore a filigree necklace, like a galaxy strung over her dark-suited breast. "Well, then, I guess a little olive beer, for old time's sake."

"Make it two."

"Anybody want a pitcher?"

"Sure, why not?"

"Come sit with us in a while, Soldier. Have we got things to tell you."

He jammed the clumsy pitcher under the spigot and pulled down as they drifted away, watching the amber splatter up its frosty sides.

"Alta, hi! Good timing! How are things at the *Extra Sexy Old–115?*"

"Oh, good enough; how's Chrysalis—has it changed much?"

The froth spilled out over his hand; he let the lever jerk up, licked his fingers and wiped them on his apron.

"It's gone wild this time, you should see what they're wearing for clothes. My God, you would not believe—"

He hoisted the slimy pitcher onto the bar and set octagonal mugs on a tray.

"Aralea, did you hear what happened on the—"

He lifted the pitcher again, up to the tray's edge.

"—*Who Got Her–709?*"

The pitcher teetered.

"Their Mactav had a nervous breakdown on landing at Sanalareta. Branduin died, the poet, the one who wrote—"

Splinters and froth exploded on the agate bar and slobbered over the edge, *tinkle, crash.*

Stunned blank faces turned to see Soldier, hands moving ineffectually in a puddle of red-flecked foam. He began to brush it off onto the floor, looking like a stricken adolescent. "Sorry . . . sorry about that."

"Ach, Soldier, you really blew it!"

"Got a mop? Here, we'll help you clean it up . . . hey, you're bleeding—?" Brigit and Ling-shan were piling chunks of pitcher onto the bar.

Soldier shook his head, fumbling a towel around the one wrist that bled. "No . . . no, thanks, leave it, huh? I'll get you another pitcher . . it doesn't matter. Go on!" They looked at him. "I'll send you a pitcher; thanks." He smiled.

They left, the smile stopped. *Fill the pitcher.* He filled a pitcher, his hand smarting. *Clean up, damn it.* He cleaned up, wiping off disaster while the floor absorbed and fangs of glass disappeared under the bar. As the agate bar-top dried he saw the white-edged shatter flower, tendrils of hairline crack shooting out a hand's-breadth on every side. He began to trace them with a rigid finger, counting softly . . . *She loved me, she loved me not, she loved me—*

"Two cepheids of wine, Soldier!"

"Soldier, come hear what we saw on Chrysalis if you're through!"

He nodded and poured, blinking hard. *God damn sweetsmoke in here . . . God damn everything!* Elsah was going out the door with a boy in tight green pants and a star-map-tattooed body. He stared them into fluorescent blur. And remembered Brandy going out the door too many times . . .

"Hey, *Sol*-dier, what are you doing?"

He blinked himself back.

"Come sit with us?"

He crossed the room to the nearest bulky table and the remaining crew of the *Dirty Old Man–428.*

"How's your hand?" Vlasa soothed it with a dark, ringed finger.

"It only hurts when I laugh."

"You really are screwed up!" Ling-shan's smile wrinkled. "Oh, Soldier, why look so glum?"

"I chipped my bar."

"Oh . . . nothing but bad news tonight. Make him laugh, somebody, we can't go on like this!"

"Tell him the joke you heard on Chrysalis—"

"—from the boy with a cat's-eye in his navel? Oh. Well, it seems there was . . . ."

His fingers moved reluctantly up the laces of his patchwork

shirt and began to untangle the thumb-sized star trapped near his throat. He set it free; his hand tightened across the stubby spines, feeling only dull pressure. Pain registered from somewhere else.

"—Oh, they fired the pickle slicer too!"

He looked up into laughter.

"It's a tech-one joke, Soldier," Ling-shan said helpfully.

"Oh . . . I see." He laughed, blindly.

"Soldier, we took pictures of our black hole!" Vlasa pulled at his arm. "From a respectable distance, but it was bizarre—"

"Holograms—" somebody interrupted.

"And you should see the effects!" Brigit said. "When you look into them you feel like your eyes are being—"

"Soldier, another round, please?"

"Excuse me." He pushed back his chair. "Later?" Thinking, *God won't this night ever end?*

His hand closed the lock on the pitted tavern door at last; his woven sandal skidded as he stepped into the street. Two slim figures, one all in sea-blue, passed him and red hair flamed; he recognized Marena, intent and content arm in arm with a gaudy, laughing Tail. Their hands were in each other's back pockets. They were going uphill; he turned down, treading carefully on the time- and fog-slicked cobbles. He limped slightly. Moist wraiths of sea fog twined the curving streets, turning the street lights into dark angels under fluorescing haloes. Bright droplets formed in his hair as he walked. His footsteps scratched to dim echoes; the laughter faded, leaving him alone with memory.

The presence of dawn took him by surprise, as a hand brushed his shoulder.

"Sojer, 'tis you?"

Soldier looked up fiercely into a gray-bristled face.

"Y'all right? What'ree doin' down here at dawn, lad?"

He recognized old Makerrah the fisherman, finally. Lately it amused the old man to call him "lad."

"Nothin'... nothin'." He pulled away from the brine-warped rail. The sun was rising beyond the mountains, the edge of fog caught the colors of fire and was burned away. It would be a hot day. "G'bye, ol' man." He began to walk.

"Y'sure y're all right?"

Alone again he sat with one foot hanging, feeling the suck and swell of water far below the pier. *All right...?* When had he ever been all right? And tried to remember into the time before he had known her, and could find no answer.

There had never been an answer for him on his own world, on Glatte; never even a place for him. Glatte, with a four-point-five technology, and a neo-feudal society, where the competition for that technology was a cultural rationale for war. All his life he had seen his people butchered and butchering, blindly, trapped by senseless superstition. And hated it, but could not escape the bitter ties that led him to his destruction. Fragments of that former life were all that remained now, after two centuries, still clinging to the fact of his alienness. He remembered the taste of fresh-fallen snow... remembered the taste of blood. And the memory filled him of how it felt to be nineteen, and hating war, and blown to pieces... to find yourself suddenly half-prosthetic, with the pieces that were gone still hurting in your mind; and your stepfather's voice, with something that was not pride, saying you were finally a real man.... Soldier held his breath unaware. His name was Maris, consecrated to war; and when at last he understood why, he left Glatte forever.

He paid all he had to the notorious space women; was carried in stasis between the stars, like so much baggage. He wakened to Oro, tech one-point-five, no wars and almost no people. And found out that now to the rest of humanity he was no longer quite human. But he had stayed on Oro for ninety-six years, aging only five, alone. Ninety-six years: a jumble of whiteness climbing a hill, constant New Piraeus; a jumble of faces in dim-blue lantern light, patterning a new life. A pattern endlessly repeated, his smile welcoming, welcoming with the patience of the damned, all the old/new faces that needed him but never wanted him, while he wanted and needed them all. And then she had come to Oro, and after ninety-six years the pattern was broken. Damned Tin Soldier fell in love, after too many years of knowing better, with a ballerina who danced between the stars.

He pressed his face abruptly against the rail, pain flickered. *God, still real; thought it all turned out to be plastic, damn, damn . . .* And shut out three times twenty-five more years of pattern, of everyone else's nights and cold, solitary mornings trying to find her face. Ninety-one hundred days to carry the ache of returned life, until she would come again, and—

"See? That's our ship. The third one in line."

Soldier listened, unwillingly. A spacer in lavender stood with her Tail where the dock angled to the right, pointing out across the bay.

"Can't we go see it?" Blue glass glittered in mesh across the boy's back as he draped himself over the rail.

"Certainly not. Men aren't allowed on ships; it's against regulations. And anyway—I'd rather stay here." She drew him into the corner; amethyst and opal wrapped her neck in light. They began to kiss, hands wandering.

Soldier got up slowly and left them, still entwined, to privacy. The sun was climbing toward noon; above him as he walked, the skyline of New Piraeus wavered in the hazed and heated air. His eyes moved up and back toward the forty-story skeleton of the Universal bank under construction, dropped to the warehouses, the docks, his atrophying ancient lower city. Insistent through the cry of sea birds he could hear the hungry whining of heavy machinery, the belly of a changing world. *And still I triumph over Death, and Chance, and thee, O Time—*

"But I can't stand it." His hands tightened on wood. "I stood it for ninety-six years; on the shelf." Dolefully the sea birds mocked him, creaking in the gray-green twilight, now, now— Wind probed the openings of his shirt like the cold fingers of sorrow. *Was dead, for ninety-six years before she came.*

For hours along the rail he had watched the ships in the bay; while he watched, a new ship had come slipping down, like the sun's tear. Now they grew bright as the day ended, setting a bracelet on the black water; stiffness made him lurch as he turned away, to artificial stars clustered on the wall of night.

Choking on the past, he climbed the worn streets, where the old patterns of a new night reached him only vaguely, and his eyes found nothing that he remembered anymore. Until he reached the time-eaten door, the thick, peeling mudbrick wall beneath the neon sign. His hand fondled the slippery lock, as it had for two hundred years. TIN SOLDIER . . . loved a ballerina. His hand slammed against the lock. *No—this bar is closed tonight.*

The door slid open at his touch; Soldier entered his quiet house. And stopped, hearing the hollow mutter of the empty night, and found himself alone for the rest of his life.

He moved through the rooms by starlight, touching nothing, until he came to the bedroom door. Opened it, the cold latch burning his hand. And saw her there, lying asleep under the silver robe of Pleiades. Slowly he closed the door, waited, opened it once more and filled the room with light.

She sat up, blinking, a fist against her eyes and hair falling ash-golden to her waist. She wore a long soft dress of muted flowers, blue and green and earth tones. "Maris? I didn't hear you, I guess I went to sleep."

He crossed the room, fell onto the bed beside her, caressing her, covering her face with kisses. "They said you were dead . . . all day I thought—"

"I am." Her voice was dull, her eyes dark-ringed with fatigue.

"No."

"I am. To them I am. I'm not a spacer anymore; space is closed to me forever. That's what it means to be 'dead.' To lose your life . . . Mactav—went crazy. I never thought we'd even get to port. I was hurt badly, in the accident.'' Fingers twined loops in her hair, pulled—

"But you're all right.''

She shook her head. "No.'' She held out her hand, upturned; he took it, curled its fingers into his own, flesh over flesh, warm and supple. "It's plastic, Maris.''

He turned the hand over, stroked it, folded the long limber fingers. "It can't be—''

"It's numb. I barely feel you at all. They tell me I may live for hundreds of years.'' Her hand tightened into a fist. "And I *am* a whole woman, but they forbid me to go into space again! I can't be crew, I can't be a Mactav, I can only be baggage. And—I can't even say it's unfair. . . .'' Hot tears burned her face. "I didn't know what to do, I didn't know— if I should come. If you'd want a . . . ballerina who'd been in fire.''

"You even wondered?'' He held her close again, rested her head on his shoulder, to hide his own face grown wet.

A noise of pain twisted in her throat, her arms tightened. "Oh, Maris. Help me . . . please, help me, help me. . . .''

He rocked her silently, gently, until her sobbing eased, as he had rocked a homesick teenager a hundred years before.

"How will I live . . . on one world for centuries, always remembering. How do you bear it?''

"By learning what really matters. . . . Worlds are not so small. We'll go to other worlds if you want—we could see Home. You'd be surprised how much credit you build up over two hundred years.'' He kissed her swollen eyes, her reddened cheeks, her lips. "And maybe in time the rules will change.''

She shook her head, bruised with loss. "Oh, my Maris, my wise love—love me, tie me to the earth.''

He took her prosthetic hand, kissed the soft palm and fingers. *And make it well . . .* And knowing that it would never be easy, reached to dim the lights.